LOVE WILL PREVAIL

The Sisters of Rosefield Book 5

EMMA EASTER

Love Will Prevail
by Emma Easter

Paperback Edition

CKN Christian Publishing
An Imprint of Wolfpack Publishing

6032 Wheat Penny Avenue
Las Vegas, NV 89122

Paperback ISBN: 978-1-64734-878-6
Ebook ISBN: 978-1-64119-884-4
Library of Congress Control Number: 2020935132

LOVE WILL PREVAIL

To my sweet baby boy, Joey

ONE

Audrey smiled when Trisha came into the living room with Ruby in her arms. She stood up from the sofa and quickly grabbed her niece. She hugged her and tickled her until the child began giggling and then laughing out loud. Finally, Audrey sat down, still holding her niece. She caressed Ruby's soft cheeks and said to Trisha, "Oh, I have missed her so, so much. It feels like I have been away from Rosefield for months instead of just three weeks."

Trisha beamed and asked, "When did you arrive?"

Audrey smoothed down Ruby's hair and answered, "Just yesterday. Ken had a case that dragged on forever. I didn't want to come to Rosefield without him, so I decided to wait until the case was over." She tickled Ruby again and laughed in pleasure as the little girl began to giggle once more.

"Lee me, Aunt Audee," Ruby chortled. She tried to wriggle away from Audrey's grasp, but Audrey held on to her.

Audrey laughed along with Ruby and then sobered as she remembered her recent argument with Ken. She looked up at Trisha and sighed, feeling suddenly weary.

"What's wrong?" Trisha asked.

Audrey thinned her lips and said, "It's just that it's been a while since Ken and I got married and I really want a baby now." She looked down at Ruby and hugged her tightly before looking up at Trisha again.

Trisha frowned and asked, "Why don't you just have a baby, then?"

"That's the problem. Ken doesn't want a child right now. He says we are too busy to have children." Audrey took a deep breath to keep her emotions in check and continued. "When we got married, he told me we would start having kids whenever I was ready. But when I told him I was ready to start a family, he totally refused to listen. He's the one keeping us from getting pregnant. I don't even know when he'll be ready to have a baby."

Trisha smiled sadly and said, "I remember you were the one who didn't want a baby right away. You told me you would not have one until years after you got married."

Audrey sighed loudly. "Now I want a baby. I really, really want to start having kids."

Trisha said, "Well, I guess you have to sit down and talk to Ken about it. Maybe he doesn't really understand how much you want a child. You need to let him know how important it is to you. I'm sure he'll understand once you speak to him about it."

Audrey shook her head. "I doubt he understands how much starting a family means to me. I think he just pretends he doesn't. I know we are very busy with our jobs, but I want to have a child so badly that I will quit my job if I have to. It's not like we need the money at all. We kept working after we received the inheritance because we both enjoy our jobs tremendously."

Trisha nodded. "I understand that. I could never give up the bookstore even though I don't need the money, and Frank loves his restaurants."

Ruby slipped out of Audrey's hands and went to her mother.

Trisha scooped her up into her lap and Audrey felt a sharp pain in her heart. In a way, she blamed herself for Ken's refusal to have a child. Before they got married and even after they did, she had told him repeatedly that they didn't need to start having babies until years into the future. But now, after about three years of marriage, Ken still wasn't ready to have a baby with her. She watched as Ruby wiggled out of her mother's hands again and pranced around the living room.

Trisha said, "I've never seen you like this, Audrey. You look so dejected. Just like I said, I think you should have a heart-to-heart with Ken. When he knows how much you really want a baby, he'll give in. He really loves you, you know."

"I don't think so," Audrey said. "The first time I brought up the topic, he did not even want to listen. He just stared at me as though I was insane and said, 'We are both flying back and forth from Miami to Rosefield and then to other cities in America because of our jobs. What time do we have to take care of a newborn?'" She pursed her lips. "The second time I brought it up, we had a fight about it. I don't like fighting with him, Trish. It gets my emotions all out of sync until we make up."

Trisha stood up and came to sit beside her. She put her hand around Audrey's shoulders and drew her closer. She said, "You can't hide your true emotions from him because you don't want to fight with him, Audrey. You have to let him know how you really feel." She sighed and said, "I feel kinda bad."

Audrey frowned as she looked at Trisha. "Why? What is it?"

"Remember I told you that I had big news to share with you when I called?"

Audrey nodded, still frowning.

Trisha looked down at the floor and then lifted

her eyes again. She started to shake her head and Audrey rolled her eyes. "Stop it, Trisha! What do you want to tell me?"

"Well..." Trisha didn't say anything for a minute, and then she gave Audrey a small nervous smile. "I'm pregnant, sis. That's my big news."

Audrey's jaw dropped. Trisha looked slightly guilty, as though she'd just told Audrey she'd done something really bad, when in actual fact this was really good news. Audrey finally shut her mouth as the news sank in. She screamed and hugged Trisha tightly as joy flooded her heart. "I'm so happy for you! Why would you want to hide this happy news from me?"

Trisha said, "I'm thrilled about it. Frank and I both are. But seeing you like this," she stared sadly at Audrey, "wanting to have a baby so much and yet not being able to because of your husband... makes me feel really bad about sharing news of my pregnancy with you."

"Well, stop feeling bad! I'm so happy for you. And what does your having a baby right now have to do with Ken's stubbornness? It's not your fault you can get pregnant, while I..." She bit her lip as bitterness suddenly gripped her so that she couldn't finish her sentence.

Trisha rubbed her back. "I'm sorry, Audrey."

"It's okay." She hugged Trisha again, grinned at her, and said, "You know you can smile. Don't hide your happiness from me just because I want a baby as well." She chucked Trisha under the chin and beamed. "Come on, Trish. Smile."

Trisha's mouth broke into a huge smile and Audrey nodded at her. Ruby came skipping back to Trisha and climbed onto her lap.

"So, when did you find out you were pregnant?" Audrey asked.

"Just a few days ago," Trisha answered. "I think Frank is the happiest father in the world. I am also the happiest…" Trisha suddenly blinked and then pressed her lips together. "I'm sorry."

Audrey rolled her eyes. "Here we go again! Stop apologizing or trying to hide your happiness because of me."

Trisha said, "It's just that I was going on about how Frank is so happy about having this baby," she put her hand on her belly, "when you just told me Ken doesn't want to have a child right now."

"Just like I told you," Audrey said, "It's not your fault or Frank's that Ken has refused to have a child with me." She pursed her lips and then said, "I knew he had a stubborn streak when I married him, but this…"

Trisha rubbed her back comfortingly. "And just like I told you, Audrey, you need to have a long, heartfelt conversation with Ken. I'm pretty sure he'll see things from your point of view once you explain everything to him."

Audrey looked down at the floor and then looked at Trisha again. "I don't know, Trish," she said. "You know how Ken is. He's just like me. Mostly left-brained. I understand exactly where he's coming from. We are both very busy at this time with our jobs. But if I found out I was pregnant today, I would gladly give up my job, even though I love it so much. I think he feels like having a baby now will make both of us resentful because we will have to cut back on work, or at least one of us will. And he thinks the person who does will end up resenting the other."

"Then when does he want to have a child?" Trisha asked.

Audrey shrugged. "I really don't know. We haven't had that conversation yet. Every time I bring up the topic, we always end up fighting. It's so tiring."

Trisha smiled sadly. "Well, the earlier you put away your fear of having a fight with him, the better. You both need to have a very serious conversation and decide jointly on what you need to do about having children. Ken can't put it off indefinitely."

Audrey nodded and changed the subject. They talked about Sienna and Bryan's baby. They had only seen him during video chats with Sienna. It wasn't the same as actually seeing him physically and getting to hold him.

Audrey said, "Ken and I have a joint leave coming up. We haven't yet decided on where to spend it, but I think we both want to take a holiday somewhere. Probably abroad. I was thinking about going to Peru to see Sienna, but I seriously doubt that Ken would agree to go."

Trisha said, "That is a really good idea. And you will get to brush up on your Spanish there as well."

"I partly live in Miami where there are many Spanish speaking people, remember." Audrey chuckled.

Trisha nodded. "I wish I could also go, but it isn't possible right now. So, it's probably another thing to talk to Ken about, though I actually think he will want to go as well. He likes Bryan and he hasn't seen him for some time. If you guys go, Ken will enjoy the time together with Bryan, I am sure."

Audrey thought about it for a short moment and nodded. "I will talk to him."

They changed the subject again and talked about random things while they played with Ruby and teased her. After a while, Ruby began to doze off where she sat and Audrey chuckled. Trisha got up and went to put Ruby to bed. She came back to the living room some minutes later and sat next to Audrey again.

Audrey tilted her head toward Trisha as her mind went to Faizan. She pushed down the sadness that welled up in her heart and said, "I know we all agreed not to talk about it or cry about it again, but I wish Faizan hadn't gone to Mali. I know that is really selfish of me to say since he went to rescue Zainah, but I miss him so much. It's been six months since he left and I haven't stopped missing him. I loved having him at the house whenever Ken and I came to Rosefield." She sighed wistfully. "I wish he was still here."

Trisha thinned her lips as her eyes grew watery. "I know," she said. "He used to visit me almost every day when he was here, and Ruby loved him. I've tried not to think about it anymore, but it's not so easy. At least, thanks to Ken, we know he's safe and that he married the love of his life. That's what is most important."

"I know," Audrey said. "But not being able to even video chat or call him is hard."

"That is the hardest part." Trisha shook her head. "Does Ken have any more info on when we will be able to call him again?"

"No," Audrey answered. "He just told me the same thing he said the last time I asked him about it. They don't want to risk giving away the location of the women's camp to anyone that might be trying to trace Faizan, so a call will not be possible right now."

"And he still can't come back here, even for a visit?" Trisha asked.

"He certainly can't. We're lucky the government isn't after him anymore, but one thing he cannot do is come back to the United States." Trisha wiped the tears that fell down her cheeks and Audrey said, "At least he sounded happy that one time we were able to speak with him and Zainah."

Trisha nodded and they changed the topic once more. They chatted about the new friends Audrey was making in Miami and laughed when Trisha told the story of the man who had hit on her at the park the day before, and then slowly backed away when he saw Ruby. "For some reason, it was just so funny to me," Trisha said, laughing. "One minute, he wouldn't take no for an answer even after I showed him my wedding ring, and the next, he was making a quick exit when Ruby ran up to me."

About half an hour later, the front door opened and Frank walked into the room. Trisha immediately stood up and went to hug him tightly. Audrey smiled as he kissed her as though he hadn't seen her in ages. For a minute, she forgot about her concerns as she watched them. She'd always known they would be great for each other, even when Trisha had continuously rebuffed Frank's advances.

He drew back from Trisha and turned to smile brightly at Audrey. "Hey, Audrey! When did you arrive in Rosefield?"

Audrey grinned at him. "Just yesterday."

"And did Ken come with you?" Frank asked.

"Yes, he did." Audrey answered. She asked him about his restaurants and he told her they were all doing well. She looked up at the clock on the wall and saw it was already eleven p.m. "I have to go now. Ken will be wondering if I plan to come back home today."

Just as she stood up, her phone rang. She looked at it and, as she'd guessed, it was Ken calling. She answered her phone. "Hey, Ken!"

"Audrey, it's getting a little late. Are you on your way back now?"

"I'm just about to leave Trisha's house. I'll be home in no time, babe." She clicked off her phone and smiled at Trisha and Frank. "I have to go. Ken is a little worried. I don't know why though, since he knows I'm at your house."

"He just misses you," Trisha said.

Audrey nodded. "I know. I guess I miss him, too." She murmured under her breath, "Though I don't miss the constant quarrels." Grabbing her purse from the coffee table, she brought out her car keys, kissed Trisha's cheeks and hugged Frank. "I'll see you guys tomorrow," she said. She went out the door, got into her car, and drove the short distance home. Minutes later, she stepped into the house.

Ken took her in his arms and kissed her passionately. When he drew back, she chuckled and said, "Okay... that was some kiss! I'm glad to see you too, but what's up?"

He shrugged. "I've just missed you. I've been at home alone all day and I wanted to see my wife again."

"Well, you should have come with me to Trisha's," Audrey said.

"No. You know I had to make some phone calls and do some work here. I would have been no good at Trisha's as I would constantly have been interrupting every conversation we had to answer numerous phone calls."

Audrey tried to bite back the words on the tip of her tongue, knowing it would do more harm than good, but she couldn't hold it in. She blurted out, "If we had a son or daughter, you might not have been so lonely."

Ken looked at her sternly and then backed away. He went to sit on the sofa and looked up at her. "We've talked about this again and again, Audrey," he said, narrowing his eyes. "You know we can't have a child right now."

Audrey came and sat beside him. She put her hand on his shoulder and said, "We really need to talk about this."

He turned away from her, but she refused to back down. "I've told you before that even if it means quitting my job, I'll do it if you agree for us to have a child," she said.

"Audrey, I can't..."

She cut him off. "Please, Ken, just listen! I know you said both of us will not have time right now to take care of a newborn, but just like I've said over and over again, I'm ready to quit my job if that's what it takes. Besides, we can afford to hire a nanny. You know that."

Ken stared intently at her for a long moment and

finally said, "I know you, Audrey. You love your job very much. Even when you got the large inheritance from your father and we all went on that vacation to Spain, you remember how much you missed your job. You couldn't wait to get back to work, even though you didn't have to work anymore. You are still very passionate about your job. And so am I. I don't think you'll be very happy if you quit your job. And I certainly won't quit my job. I know for sure that I would never dream of leaving you alone to take care of the baby while I am mostly away at work." He tucked a strand of her hair behind her ear and said softly, "When we are finally ready to have a baby, I want to be a hands-on dad, and I'm sure you want to be a hands-on mom as well."

Audrey shook her head slowly and said, "But when will that be, Ken? When exactly will we... no, you... be ready to have a baby?"

Ken shut his eyes briefly and opened them again. "I'm not sure. But I know we are not ready now."

Anger boiled in Audrey's stomach, and she got up from the sofa. She folded her arms and looked down at Ken. When he looked up at her, she said, "You know what, Ken? This is not just about you. You could try seeing things from my point of view. I'm getting older. In a few years, I will have very few viable eggs left. I want to have a baby right now." She narrowed her eyes as she stared at him. "And who are you to tell me how I will feel when I have a baby? Yes, I love my job. But that could never take the place of a child. Just say the truth, Ken. You don't want to have a baby for your own selfish reasons!"

Immediately as she uttered the words, she regretted them. Ken was anything but selfish. Still, his refusal to even try to see things from her point of view was annoying. Why he was so adamant about not having a baby right now was beyond her.

Ken stood up and faced her squarely. He looked

her in the eye and said, "How can you say that?"

She knew she should apologize, but she refused to. Instead, she said, "Then tell me why we can't have a baby now if it isn't for a selfish reason."

Ken replied, "I've already told you. You just want me to keep repeating myself over and over again."

Audrey's anger flared and she spat out, "Ken, you are a selfish man. You will deny me this one thing. Why?" She shook her head at him and marched out of the living room, her heart drumming with anger. She entered the bedroom, shed her clothes, and got into bed, still fuming.

After a while, she whispered to the Lord with tears in her eyes, "Why is he so stubborn? Why won't he give in? I don't want much. I just want a child, and so should he."

Tears slipped down her cheeks, soaking her pillow. She dashed them away angrily. She certainly didn't want Ken to see her crying. Taking in a deep breath, she looked at the door, expecting Ken to walk into their bedroom at any minute. But when he didn't after some minutes, she shut her eyes. She turned and put a pillow over her head as her anger simmered down. She didn't want to sleep, still angry with him, and so she kept waiting for him to come into the room so they could talk things through. But he didn't. Ten minutes passed, and then another ten, until she began to feel sleepy. After a while, she fell asleep.

TWO

Leila slowly sat up on the bed as someone opened her bedroom door. When she saw it was Dauda, she shut her eyes and grimaced in pain.

Dauda said to her, "The doctor is here to see you, Leila."

She pressed her lips together and opened her eyes. For a long minute, she stared at Dauda and then said in a small voice, "The doctor is here... again? But she came by yesterday."

"This is another doctor, Leila. We have to find the cause of this sickness. You've been ill for more than five months now and you still haven't recovered."

She sighed. "But doctors keep coming and they still haven't found out what is wrong with me, Dauda. I'm tired of seeing doctors almost every day. Their examinations last for so long and are a little invasive."

Dauda came and sat beside her on the bed. He put his hand on her shoulder and she shrank back. Since she'd arrived here almost six months ago, he thankfully hadn't touched her. That was thanks to her pretend illness. She'd had to feign being ill after the first few days of being here. Dauda had been busy with some business deals and had not had time to send for her at all.

She had felt great relief at that, until the day he told Rekiya, the senior wife, to tell her to prepare to perform her 'wifely duties' that night. She had become sick with worry and had begged off that night due to the illness. After that day, she knew she had to do something. And so she had pretended to be sick the next time he sent for her. And the next. Due to her constant "illness" he stopped insisting that she fulfill what he called her wifely duties. She was beyond thankful to the Lord for that. But she knew that the more doctors who came to see her, the higher the likelihood that her deception would be found out. She knew she couldn't continue to pretend for much longer, especially as none of the doctors had found out what was wrong with her.

Dauda sighed loudly and stood up. He looked down at her and said, "Since you are tired, you can rest for now. But the doctor will come back in a few hours' time. When she arrives, please try to describe in detail all the symptoms you have. Okay?"

Leila nodded slowly. When his eyes glittered as his gaze swept over her, she shuddered. He turned around, and she watched as he left the room and shut the door. When he was gone, she breathed a huge sigh of relief and stretched out on her bed again.

I cannot continue like this, she thought, looking up at the ceiling. Because she'd been pretending to be ill, she couldn't really leave her room the way she had been dying to. In fact, she had been lying almost continuously on this bed for months. The pretend illness had saved her from having to sleep with Dauda, which would have been a small death to her, but this was no way to live either.

She sat up again, leaned back against her pillow, and looked around the room. It was lavishly furnished, just like the other rooms in the house, but she found no pleasure from the wealth that surrounded her. Every day since she'd arrived here, her heart had ached continuously for Malik, and for Zainah. The only thing she held on to and that brought a measure of comfort was knowing Zainah was alive and was now probably married to her one true love, Faizan. If only she could experience that same happiness with Malik. But the Lord had not seen fit to answer her prayers.

She yearned with all her heart for a Bible to read, but there was none around. But that was another thing that this feigned sickness had saved her from. What would have happened to her if she were up and about and had to be forced to worship as a Muslim? By now, she would either have forcefully been converted to Islam—which she would never do—or met her demise.

She sat up to look out the window at the grounds of the mansion and sighed wearily. This house was like a fortress where there was no way of escape. She lay back down and soon fell asleep.

Sometime later, she felt someone tap her shoulder and she gradually awoke. Opening her eyes, she saw it was Rekiya.

"Leila," Rekiya said softly. "Dauda said you looked much better when he came to see you earlier today. He wants me to check and see if you are well enough to come to his room tonight."

Fear suddenly gripped Leila and her heart raced.

Rekiya smiled and touched her forehead. "What should I tell him?" she asked.

Leila looked at Rekiya and silently sighed in relief. The older woman had been kind to her since she'd moved into Dauda's house. She would tell Dauda whatever Leila told her to say to him.

"I feel feverish, Rekiya," Leila said, shutting her eyes. "I don't think I can go to Dauda today."

Rekiya nodded. "I will tell him," she said and then left the room.

Leila couldn't relax anymore, as she expected Dauda to come into her room any moment and call her bluff. After the first two days of pretending to be ill, he had come into her room, touched her forehead and said, "You don't have a temperature." He had frowned at her and said, "Are you pretending to be ill in order to avoid sleeping with me?"

She turned her face away from him and pretended to shiver, and he had backed away. After he left her room that day, she had sat up on her bed, knowing without a doubt in her heart that she had to keep pretending to be ill. She had no choice. There was no way she could bring herself to sleep with him.

Every day since then, she'd pretended to be ill. She stopped eating almost totally. That, more than anything else, convinced Dauda there might be something really wrong with her. When she started to waste away, he had called a doctor to examine her.

"I can't find anything wrong with her," the female doctor had said. "However, I will run some more tests and see if there's anything I can find."

The doctor had run her tests and found nothing. However, Leila had continued to shiver and even threw up the little food Rekiya had forced her to eat a few times a week. More doctors had come, but none could find what was wrong with her.

After a while, she knew she couldn't continue to eat only several times a week and had started to eat more frequently, albeit sparingly. She had probably added weight again. That would explain why Dauda had looked at her with interest today and told Rekiya she was looking much better. She had to cut down on her meals again.

She huffed as she remembered that another doctor would be coming later today to examine her. She was totally tired of lying on this bed and having Rekiya come to her room to help her do things she knew very well she could do for herself but could not afford to.

"I can't continue to do this anymore, dear Lord," she whispered. "You have to help me find a way out of here."

Her door opened and Rekiya walked in. She sat on the bed beside Leila and frowned in concern, as she usually did whenever she came into the room. "You do look a bit better today, Leila. But you're still too thin. Let me tell Nadiya to increase your food portion today."

Leila looked at her and felt sorry for her. Rekiya really did care for her. There was no reason why she should, but she did. If only she could share the gospel of Jesus Christ with the senior wife. Leila smiled sadly at Rekiya. With all her heart she wanted to, but she couldn't. It was too dangerous. She took a deep breath and said, "Okay, Rekiya, you can tell Nadiya to increase my portion today. But I cannot promise I will keep it down."

Rekiya smiled sadly at her. "The food the chef made today is delicious. I doubt you will throw it up. But, even if you throw some up, at least some of it will stay in you. You need as much nourishment as you can get."

Leila took her hand and smiled at her. "Thank you, Rekiya. You've been so kind to me since I came to live in Dauda's house as his wife."

Rekiya smiled back. "You remind me so much of myself when I first married Dauda. I loved him so much." A wistful expression appeared on her face. "I still do." She talked for a short while about how her life had been when she got married.

Leila tilted her head toward her and said, "I've always wondered how you felt when Dauda married a second wife and then a third… and then me."

Rekiya blinked rapidly, surprise etched on her face. For a minute, she didn't answer, and then she shrugged. "I always knew it was going to happen.

We were only married for a year when he decided to wed another girl. I took it in my stride. It's his right to have more than one wife."

For a second, her expression became wistful again, and then she sighed loudly. She put on a nonchalant look that didn't fool Leila and said, "As long as he takes care of all of us, I have no need to worry. Neither do you, Leila. We all have nothing to worry about."

Leila felt like throwing up.

Rekiya must have read her thoughts, because she said, "I know you don't like the idea of sharing your husband with other women, but at least Dauda is a good man. His brother, Jibril, however, is nothing like him. Jibril is a monster. Your friend was lucky to get the marriage dissolved."

Leila smiled again and nodded, even though she wanted to scream, "What about me?" She was happy for Zainah, but she wanted her own marriage dissolved as well so she could marry Malik.

Rekiya got up and looked down at Leila. She said, "It's a pity you're so ill. I will soon go to my yearly shopping vacation abroad. As usual, Dauda said I can pick any other wife to go with me. I would gladly have picked you, but unfortunately you are in no state to leave the country."

Leila's eyes widened in surprise and then panic. This might be the opportunity she'd been praying for since she'd come to Saudi Arabia. Rekiya began to leave the room and her panic increased. She had to act now.

Leila called back to Rekiya.

"Yes?" Rekiya turned around.

"What country are you going to?"

Rekiya came back and sat beside her. She touched Leila's hand and smiled. "I'm not yet sure where I want to go this time. I think it might be France or Italy. Why do you ask?"

Leila's heart began to race. She forced herself to

wear a detached look as she shrugged and asked, "Have you already selected another wife to go with you?"

"No, I haven't," Rekiya answered. "But I think Binta will do." She looked pointedly at Leila. "Like I said, I wish you were well enough to come with me instead."

"And is Dauda traveling with you?" Leila asked.

"No. But my brother will. Whenever Dauda cannot come with me, he does."

More eagerly than she wanted to, Leila asked, "What if I get better now? Can I come with you?"

Rekiya stared at Leila with an incredulous expression on her face. She said, "You've been sick for months. How will you suddenly just get better?"

Leila sighed. She had spoken much too eagerly. If she wasn't careful, Rekiya would suspect she wasn't really ill. Still, she couldn't let this opportunity pass her by. This might be her one and only chance to escape this place. She said to Rekiya, "I am already beginning to feel better. And you and Dauda said that I look better also. I think that by tomorrow, I will be myself again."

Rekiya chuckled and said, "I know how you feel, Leila. You're so eager to leave the house and go on holiday that you just want to pretend you aren't ill anymore. But even if you're getting better, you need to stay at home and try to fully recuperate. Traveling at this time will do you no good."

Leila put her palms together in a pleading gesture and looked up at the senior wife. "Please, Rekiya. Please. I am getting better. I feel so stir crazy. If I continue to stay in this room for much longer, I think I'll go mad."

Rekiya frowned. "I don't know, Leila. I will be travelling in a few days' time. Will you be well enough to travel by then?"

Leila nodded eagerly and then scolded herself silently for her over-eagerness. She forced herself to temper down her excitement. Rekiya would definitely suspect something if all of a sudden she went from being sick to being totally well. She injected pain into her voice as she sat up straight and said, "I already feel much better now. Once I start to eat regularly, I think I'll be good as new."

For a long moment, Rekiya studied her face and Leila was tempted to look away. But if she did, she would give away her guilt. She stared back unflinchingly, albeit with a pained look on her face. Finally, Rekiya smiled and relented. "Okay, if you start to eat regularly and walk around the house by this time tomorrow, I will tell Dauda that you are better and can travel with me."

Leila wanted to shout for joy, but she held herself back. She still had to plot her escape. Just traveling with Rekiya was not the end of her plan. She had to find a way to get money for her trip to Mali to find Malik. She also needed to get permission from Dauda to fly to Mali, which of course would never happen. That meant she had to find a way to change the settings on Dauda's Absher account somehow and grant herself permission to board a flight to Mali and escape this forced marriage forever. Rekiya had unwittingly told her all about it when they were talking about her many travels abroad one day.

But how will I get to Dauda's phone and change the settings on his Absher account? She didn't know how that was going to happen. Plus, she needed God's special grace to escape being caught before she got on the plane. It was a lot to think about and plan out, but it would be worth it if she succeeded. If not...

All she could do was depend on the Lord to help her escape. "Thank you, Rekiya," she said.

Rekiya nodded and stood up. "I will go and tell Nadiya to serve your meal now and this evening, I will tell the chef to prepare a sumptuous meal for you." She smiled at Leila. "Make sure you eat well. If you've not added weight by the time I am ready to leave, you won't be traveling with me. Okay?"

Leila smiled shyly and said, "I will."

After Rekiya left, Leila pondered on what the first wife had said to her. She'd always known that whenever she had the chance to escape this place, she would go back to Mali to find Malik. For a brief moment on the day she came here, she had not been sure. With everything that happened in Mali, with Karim Keita capturing her and Zainah, forcing them to marry his friends, being thrown into that awful shack for days and threatened with death, she had been momentarily unsure about the wisdom of going back. Instead, she had briefly considered going back to the women's camp.

But it had not taken long to realize she still wanted to be with Malik with all her heart, no matter the cost. She knew she would take whatever risk was needed in order to find him and be with him. Even if it meant facing Zainah's father again or being imprisoned by him. This time, though, she intended to be very careful. Most of all, she would depend on the Lord to help her and protect her.

"Oh, Lord Jesus, please help me," she prayed. "Help me to escape this time." This shopping trip with Rekiya was a chance from heaven and she couldn't afford to mess it up. She would find a way to escape, and she would find Malik, no matter how dangerous it was or how long it took. And then they would be together at last. For now, though, she had to concentrate on adding weight and making sure she went on that trip.

THREE

Lauren knocked on the front door of Trisha's house and waited. She and Trisha had grown even closer over the past few months and now she told Trisha almost everything she was up to. Today, she wanted to talk to Trisha about the new decision she was about to make. Every single day now felt like a struggle. Loneliness continuously consumed her. She wanted to be in a relationship again, but a loving relationship that was abuse-free this time. She smiled as the door opened and Trisha peered at her.

"Hey, Lauren!" Trisha said, smiling. "You didn't go to the welfare meeting today?"

Lauren shook her head, hugged Trisha briefly, and walked into the house. She sat down on the sofa and turned as Trisha sat beside her. Since Faizan had left, the welfare department hadn't really been the same. She said to Trisha, "We don't have as many activities or even ideas as we did when Faizan was the leader of the department." She sighed and then said more to herself than to Trisha, "I miss him."

She lifted her eyes and saw that Trisha was looking intently at her. She had shared more about her feelings than she'd meant to and she knew Trisha would think she was strange. Before Trisha could say anything, Lauren chirped, "I know, I know. I shouldn't be talking about Faizan like that anymore since he is a married man."

Trisha nodded. "Yes, you shouldn't. Though I understand how you feel. He leaves such a strong impression on anyone who meets him. I miss him, too."

Lauren smiled at Trisha, glad that she understood how she felt. It wasn't like she wanted Faizan for herself anymore. She knew he was married and belonged to someone else. He was just a guy who was easy to fall for and her loneliness these days made her think more about him than she should. What she wanted was a guy who was like him and not someone like her ex-husband, Richie. She took a deep breath and said, "Talking about marriage… it's why I actually came to talk to you today. I want to get married again and I think it's time I seriously started dating."

Trisha tilted her head and said, "I thought you had already started dating."

Lauren shook her head. "Not really. Actually, I haven't dated since I got a divorce. Except, of course, for that one date with Faizan." She chuckled. "I haven't met any guys that I like the way I liked him." Lauren sighed and went on, "I have decided to try online dating."

Trisha chuckled. She stared at Lauren's face and then sobered. "Please tell me you are just joking, Lauren! Online dating?"

"Yes," Lauren answered. "I want to use an online dating site to find dates."

Trisha stared at her with an incredulous look on her face and then frowned deeply. "Are you sure about that, Lauren? From what I have heard, there are so many creeps and scam artists on those online dating sites. You don't want to be catfished, do you?"

Lauren sighed loudly and looked into Trisha's eyes. She said, "I am so lonely, Trish. I need to find someone I can share my life with. I know my ex-husband was abusive, but he was also loving and romantic when he wanted to be. I miss that very much. I miss everything about having a significant other."

Trisha took her hand and searched her eyes. "I can't imagine how you feel right now, but please don't be too hasty to get into a relationship because you're lonely. You might get into trouble and the only thing you'd end up with is a broken heart... at best. You are a great girl, Lauren. I could look out for you and see if I can find someone I think is worthy of you."

Lauren pressed her lips together as she looked at Trisha. "I'm getting older as the days go by, Trish. I just want to get married and I want to have kids. Soon, I will not be able to have any."

Trisha squeezed her hand and said, "All right, Lauren. If you want to try online dating, then I won't stop you. But please be careful. You know what you're meant to do. Don't meet any guys you meet online in private. Make sure you only meet them in public places. Okay?"

Lauren laughed and gave her a mock salute. "Yes, ma'am!" She grew serious again and said, "I know all that, Trish. I will be careful." Trisha didn't look convinced, so Lauren changed the subject and asked the question that had been on her mind for some time now. "So, have you heard from Faizan lately? How is he doing?"

Trisha sighed heavily and said, "We haven't heard or spoken to him in a long time. But the last time we did speak to him, he was fine. In fact, he was ecstatic. He's happy with his Zainah and where they live now, and that's all that matters to us. Hopefully, we will be able to video chat with him soon. Since he's banned from entering the country, it's been hard, but I think Ken is working on that."

Lauren raised her brows. "I didn't know that. So, is he a fugitive now or something?" she asked, feeling a little sad that she would probably never see him again.

Trisha answered, "He has been pardoned by the government as long as he doesn't try to enter the United States."

"So, partly pardoned."

Trisha shrugged and said, "His handler, Jake, thankfully talked the high-ups out of hunting him down. As long as he doesn't try to come into this country again, he's fine. Nobody will trouble him where he is. The only problem is he wants to try to limit the contact he has with the outside world as much as possible so as not to compromise the place where he and Zainah are now. There are a lot of Christian refugees there, and making multiple calls might put them at risk if their location is found out." Trisha shook her head. "At least, that is what I am told. It's all so weird and confusing to me."

"Wow!" Lauren looked up thoughtfully. "Well, I am happy that he is happy... even though I wish I was the one with him."

Trisha laughed out loud. "Really, Lauren! You really think you could live a life of a semi- fugitive with Faizan?"

Lauren laughed along with her. "Maybe. I am so lonely right now that I could do anything."

Trisha grew sober again and she shook her head slowly. "Lauren, please be careful. You shouldn't say things like that. Remember, you don't have to be so lonely. I'm here, and you can always come and play with Ruby anytime you want. I know it's not the same as having a husband and a child of your own, but in the meantime, it could help stave off loneliness."

Lauren looked away, frustration growing in her heart. "Just like you said, it's not the same."

Trisha thinned her lips and took Lauren's hand. "Please, Lauren, don't be so desperate to be with someone that you lose yourself or do something stupid and let some guy take advantage of you. Remember to value yourself and know that on your own, you are enough."

Lauren sighed and nodded. She had heard all this before. But that didn't change the fact that she was lonely, very lonely. Nor did it change the fact that she was getting on in age and she had no children, even though she wanted that for herself with all her heart. She was already thirty-four. If she wanted children, she had to find her life partner now.

Trisha squeezed her hand again and said, "I remember when I was married to Stan. I was so blind to everything he did. I thought I was completely in love with him. I made excuses for all his bad behavior and let all the warnings from other people fly over my head. I should never have married him. Please, don't make the same mistake I did. If I had not married Frank, I would never have known what true love meant. I would never have known what it meant for a man to truly love me. I want you to wait for that kind of guy. For a man like Frank."

Lauren smiled sadly and said, "I do know what you mean, Trish. I was once married to someone like Stan as well. Just that he didn't cheat physically on me. But you know that he brutalized me."

"Then you know what I mean when I say you should wait for the man who will truly love you and respect you; that will treat you the way you should be treated."

Lauren nodded. "I will do that. But I have to date as many frogs as I can before I find my prince, don't I?"

"No. No, you don't," Trisha said, frowning. "Your prince might be near you, but you probably have never noticed him. Please, promise me you'll wait for a man that will love and treat you like a queen.

That is what God wants for you, and that is what you should want for yourself."

"I already told you I will, Trisha," Lauren said. She smiled widely at Trisha and then asked, "Talking about Frank, where is he today?"

"He went to put Ruby down for a nap when you came. He is probably preparing to go out now, but I think he will be down any moment now. He has to pick up his friend from the airport."

As if on cue, Frank walked into the living room and Lauren smiled at him. He smiled back at her and bent down to kiss her cheek. He straightened again and said, "I'm off to the airport. Nick has already arrived and he's waiting for me."

Trisha nodded and bade him goodbye.

After Frank left, Lauren turned to Trisha and asked curiously, "Who is Nick? Is he single?" Her ears always perked up in instances like this—a guy friend of a friend in town.

"Really, Lauren!" Trisha shook her head and laughed. "Nick is Frank's friend and business partner. He is single…" Lauren smiled and Trisha shook her head again. "Stop smiling at me like that, Lauren! The guy is a rogue, and he's not a believer. If you are thinking about dating Nick, stop right now. He is completely out of the question."

"Because he isn't a Christian?"

"Yes, and because he is a terrible womanizer. Don't even think about him and if you ever see him here in the house or outside, ignore him."

"Is he staying here with you and Frank?" Lauren asked, trying not to sound intrigued. She knew better than to be even slightly curious about this Nick, especially with what Trisha had just told her. But Trisha's description of him only made her even more curious about him. It was something in her she'd been trying to fight for a while. She was attracted to bad boys. That was why she'd broken up with Ken and married Richie. And she had also admitted to herself that it was why she was so attracted to Faizan. His past as a terrorist had intrigued her and drawn her to him, just as his handsome face had. Now, rather than repel her, which had been Trisha's intention, Trisha's words had unwittingly made her eager to meet this Nick.

Trisha frowned, her eyes studying Lauren. "He is supposed to stay at Hattie's Bed & Breakfast, but Frank wants to convince him to stay here with us." Suspicion clouded her features. "What does where he's staying have to do with anything, Lauren?"

"Well, you both are very exemplary Christians. You could convert him and then, if he's cute, maybe we can start dating and get married." Lauren roared with laughter at the look on Trisha's face. "I'm just joking, Trish. I know. It's wrong to want someone to change just so you can date that person. The guy is not a Christian and so he's out of bounds. I'm certainly not looking to date or marry another unbeliever like my ex-husband."

Trisha sighed loudly. "You can't exactly compare Nick to Richie, but he isn't any good, either."

Lauren chuckled and then her expression sobered again. She said, "But there is a very important question I need to ask, Trish."

Trisha stared quizzically at her. "What is it?"

"Is Nick cute?"

Lauren hid a smile as she watched confusion momentarily creep into Trisha's face. Trisha rolled her eyes and exclaimed, "Lauren! Be serious!"

Lauren threw her hands up and laughed again. "All right, Trish! I was just joking."

But are you?

She was glad when Trisha changed the subject and talked about her new pregnancy. Trisha had already told her she was pregnant on the phone yesterday and Lauren was very excited for her. But she was also slightly envious. Trisha was married to a good man she loved and who loved her.

Now she was pregnant again. She was expecting her second child while Lauren had no children at all. Worse, apart from Faizan, she hadn't met any godly man in a long time that she could fall in love, marry, and start a family with. She woke up alone every morning, ate breakfast alone, came back to an empty house, and went to bed alone. She was sick and tired of it. She didn't want to keep living her life alone anymore.

She listened to Trisha talk about her and Frank's plans for their new baby while trying to control her envy. And then they talked some more about their exes. Half an hour later, the sounds of Ruby's cries filled the air and Trisha smiled apologetically. "Let me go and check on her," she said.

Lauren stood up to leave. "I should go."

Trisha walked her to the door. Before she stepped out of the house, Trisha said, "Remember what I told you, Lauren. Wait for the right guy."

Lauren didn't say anything. She hugged Trisha briefly and walked out of the house.

*****

Nick leaned his back against a truck outside the small airport in Rosefield. He stared at his phone as he scrolled through the different profiles of women on the online dating site he'd joined a day ago. From time to time, he looked up to see if his friend, Frank, had arrived. Frank was supposed to have picked him up about ten minutes ago, but he was late. Nick glanced at his wristwatch again and then focused on his phone screen once more. He had set up the dating profile just ten minutes ago, immediately when he arrived in Rosefield. He had never had any problems meeting women and his dating life was rich, but he had decided to try something new now that he was in this small town.

He had joined the dating site because he was coming to Rosefield. Frank had told him a lot about the small town and the clean image it had. Maybe he could meet someone who lived here in Rosefield through the online site. He wanted something new. Not that he thought that an online dating site was the best place to meet girls, but he was here for work. Serious work. He probably wouldn't have time to go out and actually meet women. Usually, he met a lot of the women he'd dated or hooked up with at nightclubs and parties. But Frank had told him there weren't really any nightclubs in Rosefield. So, between work and a dearth of places to meet women, he knew he had to settle for online dating.

Or you could leave off dating or hooking up with anyone for now.

He frowned at the preposterous thought. He always needed female companionship. He wanted nothing serious, but he had to have a female to warm his bed at night. Surely, there was nothing wrong with wanting to have fun while working at the same time. And girls were a lot of fun.

He got tired of scrolling through numerous profiles when he didn't find anyone he wanted to message let alone go on a date with. Just as he logged out of the dating site, he saw Frank driving toward him in a black SUV. He lifted his hand and waved.

Frank stopped the car beside him and grinned up at him. "Look who's in Rosefield!"

"You're late," Nick said, returning the grin.

Frank exited his car and hugged him. He opened the trunk and hurled Nick's luggage in.

Nick got into the passenger seat just as Frank entered the driver's seat.

"How was your flight?" Frank asked.

"It was good. And how is your beautiful wife?" Nick asked as Frank started the car and pulled into the road.

Frank's face lit up at the mention of Trisha, and Nick shook his head. He punched Frank playfully on the arm. "Man, you're still so taken with your wife. Just look at how your eyes lit up when I mentioned her name just now. Maybe there is truly something to this marriage thing after all." He chuckled. "Maybe you could find me a beautiful wife like yours in Rosefield. That will be my challenge for you. Find me a gorgeous wife within these few months that I am here."

Frank laughed and answered, "I think I might know someone who would be perfect for you."

Nick shook his head slowly and said, "No, buddy! I was just joking. I'll find my own dates, thank you very much. And I'm definitely not looking for a wife."

Frank shrugged and said, "Well, suit yourself. The girl I have in mind is beautiful, but I guess you're not even her type."

Nick grinned. "I'm not her type? Well, I am sure she is not my type either. I certainly don't trust you to pick a girl for me. You'd probably pick a plain, mousy little Christian girl I have nothing in common with."

Frank chuckled and said, "Nick, tell me, is Trisha a plain, meek, Christian girl? She's a Christian all right, but she is anything but plain or mousy."

Nick laughed. "Okay. I definitely agree with you. Trisha is certainly not plain or mousy. But I still don't trust you to pick a date for me... not to talk of a wife. And just like I've told you before, I do not want a serious relationship right now."

"Of course you don't," Frank said. "You still want to play the field." He turned to look briefly at Nick and then turned back to the road. He said, "You really should give up your player image. I think you're too old to still play these games with women. Most of all, it's time you stopped running and gave your life to Christ."

"Ah! Preaching the gospel to me as usual, are you? Whatever happened to not beating people over the head with your Bible? I once heard you say that, but that is all you do anytime I see you." He pounded Frank's back good-naturedly.

Frank didn't say anything more. He only chuckled.

Nick studied his good friend and business partner. Frank now lived permanently in Rosefield because of his wife. He did come from time to time to visit the other restaurants, especially the one in Boise. Nick was here because of the new restaurant in Rosefield. Since it opened two months ago, he hadn't been here at all. He wanted to see the restaurant for himself. And he wanted to stay here for some time and make sure the financial aspect of the restaurant was being taken care of.

Frank was a great cook and a very nice guy. He would draw people to the restaurant with his warm personality. But whether the restaurant would make any profit in a year's time was questionable if only Frank was left to run it. That was why he had decided to come to Rosefield. And Frank had fully agreed with him. For a month he would be in Rosefield, planning and looking at different areas where they could maximize their profit, while Frank concentrated on cooking the food and also on the hospitality part. He was great at those two aspects of the business.

Frank was a stand-up guy; someone you could trust with your life. Nick knew that Frank's character had a lot to do with his faith, and Frank had always talked to him about his personal relationship with God. But he wasn't ready for that right now. And he didn't know when he would be. Just like he'd told Frank, he wasn't ready for a serious relationship, emotional or spiritual.

"So, Nick," Frank said. "Have you thought about what I asked you?"

Nick raised his brows and asked, "Asked me about what?"

"About staying with Trisha and I."

Nick groaned. "I already told you I wouldn't feel comfortable doing that, Frank. And you told me it's Trisha's house, didn't you?"

"We are a married couple. It's our home. Besides, what does it matter if it's her house? It's big enough for you to stay comfortably in." Frank grinned. "We won't get in your way or cramp your style, I promise."

Nick tilted his head toward Frank. "Really? So, you wouldn't mind if I brought a different girl back to the house every week?" He chuckled. "Because that is what I plan to do."

Frank sighed and shook his head. "Okay! That would be a problem. Well, I guess Hattie's Bed & Breakfast it will have to be."

"Yes," Nick simply said.

"You will like staying at Hattie's. I just wish you would change your plan about dating a different girl every week."

"Who said anything about dating?" Nick muttered, and then stared out the window, gazing at the small town. It was a beautiful town. He didn't expect it to be this beautiful. All he knew about Rosefield was from what Frank had told him. He'd always imagined it to be a small, old, sleepy town, with very few houses and nothing much to do. It was small, and a little sleepy, but it wasn't old and everyone he saw seemed to have a smile on their face. Still, just like Frank said, there didn't seem to be anything he would enjoy doing here except going to the park.

He turned to Frank and asked, "What do you even do for fun in this place?"

"Our church has a lot of activities and programs," Frank said. "When I'm in Rosefield, Trisha and I are always very busy with church. We rarely ever get enough time for other things. You can say our social life revolves around church and our friends. All our friends mostly attend our church as well."

"That sounds super boring," Nick said.

"Not for me or Trisha." Frank chuckled and said, "If you're thinking of nightclubs and places like that here in Rosefield, then forget about it. You will hardly find any here."

"Yeah! You've told me that before. I guess, then, that I will have to focus on finding pretty girls on-line."

Frank shook his head. "Oh, Nick, Nick, Nick. Just like I said before, it's time to change your ways."

"Not yet." Nick laughed at the look on Frank's face. "Maybe when I'm as old as you."

Frank howled with laughter. "Yeah. Since we are the same age, I guess it is time for you to change."

Nick stared out of the window again and then pressed his lips together. He was used to Frank constantly urging him to change his ways. But now that he was in this quaint town with nothing to do except spend time with Frank and his wife, he knew Frank would be on his case continuously. He groaned softly. Frank's incessant preaching was something he wasn't looking forward to.

*****

Lauren got to her house two hours later, having stopped at the grocery store after leaving Trisha's house. Her home was tiny compared to Trisha's. Going straight to her kitchen, she put away the groceries she had bought and then went to her bed-room. She flung her purse on the bed and went to stare out the window. It was a warm, sunny day, but she hardly noticed. Her heart felt cold. Trisha didn't really understand what it meant to be truly lone-ly. She had never really been alone for any length of time. She'd always had a man who loved her, fawned over her. Frank had always loved her. She was married to Stan for years before she divorced him. She wasn't long divorced from him before they got back together again, and then shortly after they broke up, she married Frank.

If only I had a guy like Frank who loved me. She sighed longingly and then walked away from the window. She sat on her bed for a while, allowing herself to wallow in self-pity. Saturdays weren't her favorite days. Since it was a work-free day, she had more time to think about how lonely she was. She hardly had friends, as Richie had isolated her when she lived with him. Here in Rosefield, she had Trish and Sally, but they were both married and she could only spend so much time with them before their kids and spouses required their full attention.

She finally stood up and went to the living room to watch some TV. She spent the day on the sofa, watching her favorite TV shows and then reading a novel. When it was some minutes past ten p.m., she retired to her bedroom. Tucking herself under the covers, she tried to fall asleep, but couldn't. She felt particularly lonely at night as she had to go to bed alone. Many nights, she wet her pillow with her tears. Tonight, she fought the tears.

After cuddling with her pillow for a couple of minutes, she got up from the bed. She got her laptop from the bedside table, sat on the bed again, and put the computer on her lap. Opening it up, she took a deep breath and then clicked on the dating website app that she had researched and then downloaded the day before.

The online dating site opened and the words LOVE FOREVER stared back at her in bold white letters on a scarlet background. She'd been trying to talk herself into setting up her profile for days now, but she had not been able to find the courage to do so. Somehow, like Trisha, she had always believed that online dating sites were full of creeps, scam artists, and the hopelessly desperate. Now, she was one of those desperate people. But there was nothing she could do. She had not met anyone she wanted to date. Not in church, not at work, not anywhere in Rosefield. This might be her only chance to find love.

She whispered a prayer asking the Lord for courage, and then immediately, so she wouldn't change her mind, began to fill out her profile on the dating website, her heart beating wildly. When she finished, she took another deep breath and logged out of the website. She closed her laptop, and then went to look at herself in the mirror.

Everyone said she was beautiful, but, unfortunately, her beauty had not helped her to find a man who truly loved her and who she could spend the rest of her life with. Hopefully, just like the dating website promised, she would find some perfect matches for her, and she could finally meet 'the one'.

She shut her eyes, trying to fight the voice in her mind telling her she was wasting her time. She asked the Lord again to help her meet the right guy because if she didn't meet him soon, she might never have her own children, as it would be too late for her. Worse of all, she would spend the rest of her life alone. That was not a future she was looking forward to.

FOUR

Sienna smiled at Bryan as he took baby Ethan from her and opened the car door. He put their precious son into the car seat, buckled him up, and shut the door. He went around to the other side of the car, opened the door, and got into the driver's seat. He smiled when Sienna got in beside him. She shut the car door and said to him, "It's good to finally be able to come out and get some fresh air. That prolonged bed rest was beginning to drive me mad."

Bryan laughed. "I can attest to that."

Sienna hit him playfully on his shoulder.

Bryan started the car and said to her, "The kids at the orphanage have missed you. They will be very happy to see you again."

"And I have missed them," Sienna said. "I can't wait to finally see the kids and the orphanage again."

Bryan nodded and pulled out of their driveway. As he drove to the orphanage, Sienna recalled the first time Bryan told her that Dr. Lincoln, his mentor and the senior chaplain at Beulah College, wanted them to run the orphanage for him. Dr. Lincoln and some of the leaders of his denomination had founded the orphanage and he had decided to put Bryan and her in charge of it.

At first, she had been unsure about her ability to run an orphanage. Not only did she not have any experience, there was also the language barrier. She didn't really speak the language. Audrey, on the other hand, spoke the language quite well, as she took Spanish throughout high school. She had also spoken Spanish with their father, who had picked up the language in the predominantly Spanish neighborhood he lived in with his mother when he was a child. It was Audrey and their father's "special thing".

Sienna understood some words and could speak simple sentences, but she couldn't communicate fluently. Bryan had urged her to learn the language with him when they first arrived and he had to take Spanish classes, but she had refused. When Bryan, because of the pressures placed on him by his pastoral and ministerial duties, fully handed the running of the orphanage to her, she had been totally shocked. She told him he needed to find someone else, especially since she was pregnant.

He agreed to do that, but told her she had to take up the running of the orphanage until he found someone who could take over from her. She had been forced to take daily Spanish lessons while taking over the reins of the orphanage and had gotten closer and closer to all the children. Consequently, her heart opened more and more to the needs of the orphanage. She soon became consumed with trying to find solutions to the many problems the orphanage faced, and soon she couldn't imagine not running it. She knew then that the Lord had actually called her to do just that—run the orphanage. That was why He had brought her here with Bryan—to take care of the precious orphans.

With all her heart, she loved finding homes for the kids. And when a child found adoptive parents, she felt overwhelmed with joy, seeing how excited the kids were to have real parents they could go home with. She grieved for some of the children who were almost growing out of the age where they could stay and were still not adopted. They would have to go into the world and fend for themselves unless a job position was found for them at the orphanage. Unfortunately, there weren't enough of those.

Sienna finally found a good purpose for the money she had inherited from her father. Since she' gotten her share of the inheritance, she and Bryan had hardly touched the money. Now, she pumped money into the orphanage, building a new hostel and renovating the dining hall for the children. She upgraded facilities, bought a new bus, and erected a small chapel where the children could go and be taught the word of God.

She had felt really fulfilled with the work she was doing, but after her difficult childbirth and being tired all the time, the doctor had told her to rest as much as possible. She hadn't been able to come out of the house much, not to talk of going to the orphanage and taking back the reins. Bryan had thankfully found someone to take over temporarily from her. Now, she could finally go back and continue running the orphanage that had totally captured her heart. She couldn't wait.

She turned when Bryan took her hand and kissed it. "A penny for your thoughts," he said.

"I was just thinking of how happy I am to finally go back to running the orphanage."

"I am glad about that," Bryan said. "However, because of the baby, I am not sure you will be able to give as much of your time and energy to running it as you did before."

Sienna frowned, knowing Bryan was right. Baby Ethan required a lot of her time and attention. She said, "Well, thankfully Mary is there to see to the daily running of the orphanage. Now that I am back, she will act as my assistant. Whatever I cannot do, she will have to do for me. And she's done a good job so far running the place."

Bryan sighed loudly and Sienna frowned. "What is it, Bryan?"

"I have been meaning to tell you, babe," Bryan said, his eyes focused on the road. "Mary will soon be leaving the orphanage. She's getting married and her husband-to-be doesn't live in Lima."

"Oh no!" Sienna exclaimed. "When exactly will that be?"

"She said in two weeks."

Sienna pressed her lips tightly together, feeling a little put out. Finally, she said, "Wow! That means we definitely need to find someone as soon as possible to assist me."

"I guess we do," Bryan said.

For the rest of the drive to orphanage, they both said nothing to each other. Sienna kept running through her mind what Bryan had said. Where would they find someone to assist her in such a short time?

They got to the orphanage, and Bryan parked in front of the hostel for the younger kids, a building which was painted a bright yellow. Sienna had personally picked this shade of yellow because she loved how bright it was. She knew the kids would love it. There were flowers and animals and boys and girls painted on the sides of the building. She unbuckled her seatbelt, opened the door, and got out of the car before Bryan could come around to open the door for her.

Bryan opened the backseat door, unbuckled Ethan's seatbelt, and carried him out of the car.

Sienna peered at Ethan over Bryan's shoulder and smiled. "Thank God he is still sleeping," she said to Bryan.

He nodded in understanding and smiled down

at their son. "He might not be asleep for too long, though," Bryan chuckled. "The boisterous kids here will probably wake him up with all their noise."

Sienna nodded. "I didn't even think of that. Thank God it's their naptime now." She chuckled again. "It will give me and Ethan a bit of time before the kids swoop down on us."

One of the children exited the building, and she said, "I spoke too soon." When the child saw her, he ran toward her.

"Here we go," she said in amusement. The child, a six-year-old boy named Roberto, reached her and wrapped his arms around her legs. He hugged her tightly and then looked up at her with a bright smile.

She ruffled his dark hair and said in Spanish, "How are you today, little man?"

He gave her a gap-toothed smile and nodded.

She chuckled. "I guess that means you're fine." She looked at her wristwatch and said to Roberto, "Isn't it still your naptime?"

Roberto shrugged and said with laughter in his voice, "No. Naptime is over."

She looked over at the hostel again, and her eyes widened as kids rushed out of the building, laughing and chattering. She braced herself. Any moment now, they would leap on her and surround her, giving her huge hugs and wet kisses. She looked at Bryan and was grateful that he held Ethan even more firmly. She wished they had brought the stroller.

Before she could plant her feet firmly on the ground, a seven-year-old girl named Esther pointed at her and raced toward her. Another child saw her and then others did, too.

She held the children tightly, trying not to drop them while also trying not to fall over. Soon, she was surrounded by the children. She hugged each of them tightly. They were about thirty of them.

She brought out the sweets and candies she had bought specifically for them from her purse and handed one to each child.

Esther, who she fondly called Queen Esther because of how beautiful, well behaved, and poised the child was, smiled widely at Bryan and pointed at Ethan. "Can I carry the baby?" Esther asked. She had a pleading look in her eyes as she looked at Bryan and then at Sienna. The other kids also began to beg to carry Ethan, especially the girls.

Sienna finally nodded and said, "Okay, children, you all can carry him as long as you first wash your hands and are seated. Let's go inside so you all can wash your hands and then you can carry him."

Sienna beamed at them as two of the children took her hands. She walked into the hostel with the children. They kept chattering and excitedly skipping and she couldn't help smiling at how impossible it was for kids to stay still for any length of time. Bryan followed behind, still holding Ethan. Esther was the first to wash her hands. She came and stood in front of Sienna, smiling.

"I've washed my hands now," she said. She had a bright smile on her face.

Sienna grinned at her. "Okay. Take a seat right here beside me."

Esther sat beside Sienna on the bunk bed, and Sienna carefully handed Ethan to her, placing the baby carefully on her lap. "Hold his head this way, Queen Esther," Sienna said, and then watched as Esther held up Ethan's head in her arm. "Good, now...." She didn't finish her sentence as the other children came bounding toward them.

Bryan made them all sit down so they could take turns carrying Ethan.

Sienna handed him carefully to each child while she sat beside each of the children to make sure Ethan was being held properly. After everyone had held Ethan, she carried him and smiled while the children ran out of the hostel to play outside. She looked up at Bryan, who was standing over her and Ethan, gently running a finger across Ethan's curly blond hair. "It is amazing how Ethan slept through all the noise," she said.

Bryan smiled. "It is. Thank God for that."

She heard the sound of shuffling feet and turned to her right. She raised her brows in surprise when she saw Esther standing in front of the next bunk, looking longingly at Ethan. She chuckled and said to the little girl, "I thought you had gone outside to play. Do you still want to play with the baby?"

Esther nodded vigorously and then grinned at Sienna.

Sienna told Esther to sit. She stood beside Esther, handed Ethan to her, and then watched as Esther stared fondly at the baby, smiling widely. She looked like she had been handed a box of precious jewels or, for a kid her age, a huge bag of candy.

"Let me go and talk to Mary," Bryan said.

Sienna nodded and told him she would join him later on. She watched as Bryan walked out of the hostel, and then she quickly turned back to Esther. She marveled at how well Esther held Ethan in her arms. It looked so natural. She couldn't help but smile and say to Esther, "You will make a great mother one day."

Esther's eyes widened and she looked up at Sienna with a look of astonishment on her face. "I will be a mother one day?"

Sienna nodded. "If you want to."

"I do," Esther said, her eyes shining.

"Then you will be," Sienna said to her.

Esther beamed and looked down at Ethan. She gently caressed his cheeks and kissed his tiny fingers. After a while, she said to Sienna with a mournful expression on her face, "When will I get a mommy and daddy like Rachel?"

Sienna blinked and looked intently at the child.

Her eyes were so sad that Sienna's heart began to hurt for her. Rachel had been Esther's very good friend at the orphanage. They had done everything together. But Rachel had been adopted last month by a couple who lived in Cusco. Bryan had told her that Esther had asked him a week ago when she would be adopted. Now, Esther was asking Sienna the same question.

Sienna's heart went out to the little girl. She couldn't imagine how much Esther was hurting right now. Getting a mommy and daddy was the dream of every child in the orphanage, and even though they were well taken care of here, she couldn't blame the children for wanting their own home and their own parents. She reached out and gently hugged Esther. If only she could adopt the precious girl. But right now, she just couldn't. There was baby Ethan to take care of, and she still wanted more kids of her own. She made a mental note to go home and pray for Esther—that the Lord would send her a mommy and a daddy.

Ten minutes later, when Ethan started to cry, Sienna took him from Esther and told the little girl to go outside and play with the other children. Esther left, and Sienna nursed Ethan. He sucked noisily and she kissed him from time to time until he had enough milk. She stood up with Ethan in her arms, left the hostel, and headed for the administrative building, partly to talk to Mary, and partly to look for Bryan.

She found Bryan talking with Mary and three other staff members of the orphanage in her old office.

Mary's eyes lit up when she saw Sienna with the baby. "Oh, thank God you are finally back. And you came with your precious baby boy." She hurried over to Sienna, gently hugged her, and then lifted Ethan from Sienna's arms. She rocked him in her arms, grinning at him. "He's so beautiful," she said.

"Just like his mom and dad."

The other women greeted Sienna and surrounded Mary, cooing at Ethan.

Ethan played with Mary's fingers and smiled at the other women, drinking in all the attention he was getting.

After a while, the other staff members left the office, and Sienna sat on the black leather couch near the door. Mary sat next to her, while Bryan took the chair in front of the desk. Sienna said, "Bryan told me you are leaving in two weeks to get married."

Mary nodded. "I am. I love this place very much, but my fiancé doesn't live around here." She smiled sadly at Sienna. "I'm so sorry. I thought I could stay for a bit longer after the wedding, but he insists that I move immediately after we get married. I wish I could stay, but I can't."

Sienna sighed and nodded. "I understand," she said. "I guess we'll have to find a replacement as soon as possible."

They began to talk about the running of the orphanage and the day-to-day needs of the children. Sienna and Bryan promised to stock up on food and other necessities. About an hour later, Sienna walked to the car with Bryan. After buckling Ethan into his car seat, they both got into the car.

As they drove home, an idea concerning finding a replacement for Mary came to Sienna. It wasn't a permanent idea, but it was one that made her excited, and which she found she was looking forward to. She turned to Bryan and told him what was on her mind. "Audrey told me when I called a few days ago that she and Ken are going on their annual work leave very soon. She said they wanted to spend their vacation abroad but were still considering which country to go to."

Bryan nodded. "Ken told me."

Sienna said, "I am going to ask Audrey to come

and spend the vacation with us, here in Lima. It will be lovely to have her and Ken here. And Audrey can help me run the orphanage. It will be such fun. Audrey speaks Spanish quite well and she is so knowledgeable about a lot of things. I think she will do well running the orphanage with me until we are able to find someone else."

Bryan chuckled and said, "Audrey and Ken will be taking a short work leave, not leaving their jobs forever. And even if they were, I doubt they would choose to come here to run the orphanage with you."

Sienna shook her head and tapped Bryan on the shoulder. "Don't be silly, Bryan," she said. "I know Audrey and Ken are only taking a short vacation. But just like Audrey told me yesterday, they're taking at least a month off work. They could spend it here and Audrey can help me run the orphanage while we look for someone else to replace Mary."

Bryan nodded. "Well, I guess it's a good idea if Ken agrees. He might think coming to Peru to spend his leave would not be a very good vacation idea."

Sienna said, "I'll call Audrey immediately when we get home. Hopefully, she can convince Ken to come here with her."

Bryan turned to look briefly at Sienna before turning back to the road. "And how do you know Audrey will want to come here for her vacation?"

"I think she will," Sienna said. "Besides, she's been yearning to see baby Ethan for some time now. I don't think it'll be hard to convince her to come. However, convincing Ken to come here will be another matter. I just hope he agrees."

Brian smiled at her and then focused on the road again.

Ethan began to coo and babble, and Sienna turned around to smile at him. "Are you okay, buddy?" she bent her head to ask him, and then chuckled when he covered his face with his pudgy hand.

She turned around again and looked out the window. Excitement bubbled up in her as she thought about Audrey coming to spend a whole month with her and Bryan here in Peru and helping out with the orphanage. After Faizan left the United States, they had all been terribly worried about him. A sense of gloom had settled over all of them. But after Ken found a way to contact him outside the women's camp and they spoke to him, a measure of peace had finally settled in their hearts. They knew he was not just okay, but was very happy because he had married Zainah at last. They still missed him terribly, but they were very happy for him and Zainah. Sienna hoped with all her heart that one day, they would all be reunited again.

"I can't wait for Audrey to come," she said excitedly to Bryan.

Bryan chuckled and said, "You're getting ahead of yourself, baby. You don't yet know if they will agree to come. Even if Audrey wants to come, Ken might not want to. I know if Ken doesn't agree to come here, Audrey won't either."

"I just hope they do," Sienna sighed. "I know that we'll have so much fun together, and Audrey will finally get to see her nephew. Maybe seeing Ethan will convince Audrey that it's finally time that she and Ken had a baby."

"Are you sure she doesn't want one now?" Bryan asked.

"I don't think so," Sienna answered. "When Audrey got married, she told me it would be years before she and Ken would have a child. But I can't wait for her to have one." Sienna chuckled. "A baby will soften Audrey. She can be so brusque sometimes."

Bryan smiled but said nothing.

All the way home, Sienna prayed that Audrey would want to come to Peru to spend her vacation, and that Ken would also agree to come. It would be good for both of them. Sienna somehow knew they needed the trip. She could feel it in her heart.

*****

Malik threw his hoe and cutlass on the ground and stretched. He had been working for hours now. He shielded his eyes from the sun and wiped the sweat off his forehead with his sleeve. Looking around him, he noted that he had nearly finished weeding the half-acre of land he had started about two days ago. In another hour or two, he would be through.

A sliver of excitement went through him as he thought about seeing his daughter, Fanta, in a few days' time. Every time he was here, he missed her terribly. But he knew he could not afford to stay in Nira with her as he had to work in order to provide sufficiently for her. He also couldn't bring her here as this place was hardly appropriate for a little girl. He hated leaving her in his father's house, even though she stayed in his mother's care most of the time. Karim Keita was a wicked man.

He bent down and started to cut the grass again. As he did, his stomach boiled in anger as he recalled what his father had told him when he'd come back to Nira months ago. He had found out from his father and from Khadija that Leila and Zainah had returned to Nira and had been promptly married off to his father's friends. But not only that, he had also found out that Zainah had been shot. Thankfully, she was alive and well now. However, what he feared the most had happened. Leila had not been as lucky as Zainah in the sense that she had not been rescued. She was still married and had left with her husband to Saudi Arabia. He had mourned for weeks about that.

After she and Zainah were rescued by Zainah's

now-husband's men the first time they came to
Nira, he had fully believed they would be together
soon. He hadn't known they'd married his father's
friends before they were rescued. But even after
he knew that, he still held on to a sliver of hope in
his heart. He didn't know why, but he still believed
that, somehow, he would get to see Leila again, that
her marriage to Dauda would be dissolved, and that
they would finally be together. But she had returned
to Nira and been held ransom by his father until
she moved into her husband's house. Now, she had
left the country with Dauda. He would probably
never see her again.

He straightened and groaned as the pain of constantly missing her tore at his heart. In the little
time he had known Leila, he had fallen deeply in
love with her. No matter how hard he had tried
since he found out she was married to rid his heart
of her, he could not forget about her. She was in his
thoughts every day and in his dreams every night.

Why do you torture yourself so? he chided himself. With everything that was in him, he pressed
away Leila's image from his heart and focused on
his daughter. As much as he was looking forward
to going to Nira to see her, he was not looking forward to seeing his father. The man was a monster.

He remembered months ago when some men
had arrived at the farm. Without warning, they had
bundled him up and thrown him into a hut some
distance away from his own small house. They had
tied him to a chair and then taken a photograph of
him. After that, they'd released him again without
a word.

He had railed and ranted, and had cursed them
bitterly. After he was tired of ranting, he had asked
why they had done all that to him, but they did not
answer. Instead, they went away and left the farm
that same day.

It was only when he went back to Nira that

Khadija told him exactly why he had been tied up and his picture taken. She told him how their father had used the picture to threaten Leila and Zainah. That was how their father had gotten Zainah to come back to Nira and marry his friend. Because of him, Zainah had been shot and Leila had been married off and shipped to another country.

Malik had been enraged and had confronted his father. But the man seemed different. Rather than the boisterous, abusive man he knew, or the angry defiance he had expected, his father had apologized and told him he would never do such a thing again. Malik had been taken aback, and because of that, he had not fought with his father the way he had wanted to. But he was still angry at the man. He was angry at him for putting Zainah's life at risk, for marrying Leila off to his friend; in fact, for everything.

Abu, the man his father had put in charge of gathering the harvest, walked up to him and said, "We need more hands on the farm. When you go back to Nira in a few days' time, can you tell your father about it?"

Malik looked at him and nodded. As usual, his father would look for youths in the village who had nothing much to do, talk them into coming to this awful place, and pay them a pittance to work for him on the farm.

Abu went away and Malik bent down again and continued to cut the grass. He worked fast, but his mind was already in Nira; already with his daughter and the fact that in a few days' time, he would see her again. He could also feel a terrible ache in his heart. The ache that he always felt every time he was in Nira. Whenever he went there, for some reason, he thought about Leila more than he did here. Maybe it was because he was consumed with work in this place and didn't have time to think about much else. He thought about what could have been between him and Leila and how happy they would have been together if not for his father.

After a long time of torturing himself with thoughts of what could have been with Leila, with all the willpower he could muster up in him, he pushed her image from his mind. He focused once more on his daughter and told himself to completely stop thinking about the woman who he loved but who was now married. There was no point continuously holding her image close to his heart when he knew he would never see her again. And even if he did, she belonged to someone else now. He had to let her go, and forever too.

FIVE

Leila checked her bedroom door once again to make sure it was locked and then opened her closet. She rifled through the exotic dresses that hung there, bought for her by Dauda on one of his many trips abroad. She had not worn a single one of the flamboyant outfits at all, as she lived mostly in this room and in her abayas.

She finally found what she was searching for and brought out the outfit—an elegant, black, sequined boubou with deep pockets. Sticking her hand into one of the pockets, she brought out a bundle of cash and counted the money once again.

The money was almost ten thousand riyals, enough for her to make her escape once she got to France with Rekiya. That is, if they succeeded in convincing Dauda that she was strong enough to travel for the shopping trip. She had been saving the money since she came here. Dauda gave each wife a monthly allowance to do with as they pleased. Since she'd hardly left the house, she hadn't spent hers at all.

She still had some things to do in order to perfect her escape plan. The most important thing she had to do and the one she was not looking forward to was to try to get access to Dauda's phone in order to change the settings on his Absher account. If she played her cards wrongly, her efforts could end up in an outcome that she had been trying to prevent ever since she came to this country. She would be forced to be intimate with Dauda. She would rather die than do that.

She shuddered at the thought. That couldn't happen. She had to be careful with her plans and make sure everything went well.

A knock sounded at the door, and Leila jumped. Quickly, she put the money back into the pocket of the boubou, shut the closet door, and stepped back. She quickly glanced at herself in the mirror and noted that she had put on some weight. But only a little. She sighed, cursing her over-efficient metabolism. Hopefully the little she had added would be enough to convince Rekiya that she was almost fully recovered and could accompany her to the shopping trip in France. She hastily opened the door and let Rekiya into the room.

Rekiya smiled at her and looked her over. "Well Leila, you look much better than the last time we talked. And you have added a bit of weight. That's good."

"I told you I was feeling better, Rekiya. Right now I feel great. Will you tell Dauda that I can travel with you to Paris?"

Rekiya's eyes searched hers, and Leila's heart raced. There was something in the senior wife's eyes; something that made Leila afraid that Rekiya suspected she was being deceived. Leila held her breath, hoping that she was wrong and that Rekiya didn't suspect a thing. Because if she did, she would definitely tell Dauda and that would be the end of Leila's plan to escape. And, who knew what Dauda would do to her if he found out she was planning to run away.

Rekiya said, "So, you have to come with me to our husband's room. I will first tell him that I want you to travel with me for the shopping trip. When he asks how you can do that since you've not been feeling well, you will come into the room and show him that you are much better now."

Leila nodded as her heart drummed. Hopefully Dauda would decide that she looked well enough to travel with Rekiya to Paris and give his permission.

There was more she hoped for than just for him to see she was well enough to travel. And that was the dangerous part of her plan. She hoped he would not only find her looking healthy, but he would find her desirable and well able to perform her 'wifely duties', as he would say. If he did, he might ask her to spend the night with him. That way, she could gain access to his phone and change his Absher account, giving herself permission to travel to Mali. She wasn't planning to sleep with him, as that was the very reason she had pretended to be sick since she came here. However, she had to spend the night in his room in order to get access to his phone when he was asleep. How exactly she would do that without him touching her in any way was not yet clear to her. But she was determined to find a way.

"So, when are we going?" she asked Rekiya. She had already set aside the outfit she would wear to Dauda's room when it was time to talk to him about the trip to France. It was a glittering, turquoise dress, casual enough to wear at home without raising any eyebrows, but still dressy enough and seductive enough to catch his attention and arrest it fully.

Rekiya frowned and said, "We are going right now. That's why I came here." She waved her hand. "Come on now, Leila. Let's go talk to Dauda."

Leila's eyes widened in panic. She had just woken up and was still in her rumpled pajamas. Her hair was in a mess, and she had no makeup on.

Before she could protest, Rekiya took her hand and literally dragged her out of the room.

They went down the long hallway together, Leila praying incessantly that the Lord would help her and, like Queen Esther, give her favor before Dauda.

If only Rekiya had given her some time so she could change into the outfit she had prepared to wear to Dauda's room. Right now, she wasn't sure that Dauda would want her. Apart from her messy appearance, she'd just started eating well again. She hadn't yet gone back to her normal weight. She still looked slightly gaunt. The beautiful turquoise dress was meant to hide her gauntness. With the way she looked right now, he would probably have no interest in her. How would she be able to carry out her plan if he didn't find her desirable enough to want her?

They finally reached Dauda's ornate bedroom door and stopped. Rekiya knocked on the door and gave Leila a big smile.

"Come in!" Dauda's deep voice called out from the other side of the door.

Rekiya opened the door and stepped into the room. Leila stood at the door, waiting, just like Rekiya had told her to do. She watched as Rekiya approached Dauda, who was on the bed reading the newspaper... or maybe a magazine. She wasn't sure.

"So, I have chosen another wife to go with me to the shopping trip in Paris," Rekiya said cheerfully to him. Leila noted how Rekiya's eyes sparkled as she looked at him. The woman was still in love with him, while he gave her something that looked like a fond, fatherly smile. Leila felt sorry for Rekiya. She had to share the man she loved with other women, and the man didn't even care how she felt about it.

Dauda put down the newspaper and said to Rekiya, "Okay, who did you choose?"

Rekiya turned and beckoned for Leila to come into the room.

Leila stepped in, said another quick prayer, and

walked up to the bed. Dauda's eyes were firmly planted on hers. He stared at her curiously and her heart raced.

Dauda frowned and looked her up and down. He turned away from her and looked at Rekiya. "You want Leila to go to France with you? But she hasn't been feeling well." He turned to Leila and said, "I am surprised you are out of your bed. How are you feeling today?"

Leila mustered up a bright smile for him and said, "I feel great, actually. Two days ago, I realized I didn't feel so sick anymore. Today, I feel totally well."

Dauda sat up and swung his left leg out of the bed and then his right. He planted his feet on the floor and gazed at up Leila. His eyes carefully scrutinized her face, and then moved down to her body, and then up to her face again.

Leila held a breath while he inspected her closely. She felt a mix of conflicting emotions raging in her mind. As he studied her, she felt anger, anxiety, dread, and hope, all rolled into one.

Lord, please, let him agree to allow me to travel with Rekiya, she prayed in her heart. She wanted to also ask the Lord to cause Dauda to find her desirable, but she couldn't bring herself to do that. She had turned into a player; into a person who scammed, plotted and lied. But she had no choice. She had to find a way to escape this place and her situation.

Anxiety continued to course through her as she waited for him to say something. If he said 'no,' she would not be able to change his mind. No one, not even Rekiya, would. He was the king of the house. Once he made up his mind about something, he stuck to it and there was no changing his mind.

At last, he said, "You do look better than the last time I came to your room to see you." He smiled at her and said, "But I'm not yet sure that you're totally well enough to travel at this time."

Leila's heart sank to her feet. She felt her heart aching as all her plans for the past few days disappeared before her eyes.

Rekiya said, "I think she is well enough. I mean, she has not been able to really stand up on her own for months, not to talk of walking all the way here and standing for this long. And she has been eating well, which she has not been able to do for some time now. Leaving the house and travelling to some other place will be beneficial for her health, Dauda. I think she actually needs this trip. It will do her good, I'm sure."

Dauda looked up thoughtfully and then looked at Leila. He said, "Are you sure you feel well enough to travel out of the country? You don't feel sick at all?"

She nodded. "I feel really well. And just as Rekiya said, I think leaving the house and even traveling will do me good."

Dauda didn't say anything for long moment, and Leila kept sending silent prayers to God, asking the Lord to touch Dauda's heart so he would agree to give her permission to travel to Paris with Rekiya.

Finally, Dauda sighed and said, "Okay, you can go with Rekiya to France."

Leila's heart soared again. She smiled widely and said to Dauda, "Thank you so much." And then she bit her lip as she remembered there was still one very important thing that needed to happen in order for her plan to be complete. Unfortunately, this part depended solely on Dauda. She shifted her feet as she waited for Dauda to say something else.

I could have looked better and had a better chance to impress him if I had been given sufficient time to prepare, she thought bitterly. But she had not. Rekiya had dragged her here looking very messy, and in these pajamas, Dauda would also see how thin she looked.

She suddenly felt self-conscious as Dauda's eyes swept over her body again. Without a doubt, he was dismissing her in his mind right now. He had several wives. He had no need for her.

Oh Lord, please help me. She needed the Lord's intervention right now.

Rekiya tapped her on the shoulder and said, "Let's go, Leila."

Leila felt embarrassed. She had been standing there for a while, unknowingly staring at Dauda. Rekiya took her hand, and they began to walk out of the room together.

As they left the room, Leila's shoulders sagged. As she had guessed, he had not found her desirable enough to want to spend time alone with her now. How would she gain access to his phone when he wasn't looking and get enough time to do what she wanted on it? He was never without his phone. It was virtually impossible. There was no chance of escape now. She would have to wait for another trip, and who knew when that would be or if he would even agree for her to travel. If she didn't leave now, then she would have to keep pretending to be sick, and for how long would she be able to pull that off?

She walked down the hallway with Rekiya, still hoping that somehow he would call her back. But she reached her room and entered and he did not call for her.

She opened her closet and looked at the dress she had planned to wear to his room and then she sighed. She could put on the dress now and hope he would come to her room for some reason. But it was unlikely. And she couldn't just go to his room, either.

And then she blinked. Why can't I anyway? She could just go to his room without him sending for her, but she had to wait until it was nighttime. If not, her intentions would be known by everyone in the house, and she would be shamed.

She stepped back from the closet and took a deep breath. That was what she would do. She would wait until it was midnight before going to his room dressed in this turquoise dress. She would fix her hair and apply makeup as well.

With a lighter heart than she'd had since she came to Saudi Arabia, she left her bedroom and went to the kitchen to find the chef.

She found the chef as usual, cooking up a storm for the large household.

Leila smiled at the chef, a plump, pleasant-looking woman, and said, "I would like to eat now. Just something simple."

The chef smiled back at Leila and said, "I'm glad you feel better. You look better."

"Thank you,"

"What would you like to eat?" the chef asked.

Leila said, "You can surprise me. Just something simple but nourishing."

The chef nodded and said, "I know just the thing."

Leila went back to her room, showered, and changed into a simple kaftan. She picked up a book Khadija had given her to read in Mali. For a long moment, she stared at the book, too distracted to read, and then she got up once again. She left the room and went out of the house. She started to stroll about the grounds, admiring the tall imposing trees that surrounded the house and then the beautiful garden at the back.

Everything here was so different from the women's camp she had lived in for years. While the grounds teemed with brightly colored flowers and plants, the grounds surrounding the camp were dry desert sand. She had lived in a tent at the women's camp, while she lived in a mansion here. Food was rationed at the camp, while people in this household had sumptuous meals for breakfast, lunch, and dinner. And the differences went on and on. Yet, if she had the opportunity to return to the women's camp right now, she immediately would, and never look back.

She sat on one of the chaise lounges and breathed in the fresh air. She had not been able to do this since she arrived here. The morning sun shone on her face and she shaded her eyes with her hand.

Binta, the second wife, came out of the house in her abaya. She had a shopping basket in her hand and she headed toward the white Mercedes parked alongside a red car. That was another thing that was different here. There were at least seven cars parked around the grounds of the house that Leila could see. At the camp, they only saw a vehicle once a month, when someone came to collect the rugs made by the women, and the driver took Miriam to town.

Binta's driver opened the door for her and she entered. A boy of about thirteen years, who Leila guessed was Binta's son, came out of the house and entered the car, and then the car drove out of the gate.

Leila watched with detached curiosity. Since she had never stepped out of the gates since she'd arrived here, she wondered what it would be like to leave the house now and explore the city. She knew she would not be allowed out of the house alone. She quickly put that out of her mind. She had one goal now and one goal only. She had to get out of this house and out of this country as soon as possible so she could go find Malik. That was all she cared about now.

One of the maids, a woman named Nadiya, soon brought her food to her, a mafruka, a watermelon milkshake, and a pistachio cake for her sweet tooth. It was far from the simple meal she had requested, but she ate with relish. She had not eaten this much for so long and she enjoyed every bite. When she finished, she dropped her plate on the floor. Soon, another maid came and carried the plate away.

She remained in the garden for what seemed like hours, enjoying the fresh air and the sun on her face. From time to time, she watched the guards that watched the gates and those that patrolled the house, and then she turned away to look up at the sky. After a while, she studied the flowers while she thought about how she would make her escape. She kept trying to figure out how she could stay in Dauda's room for the night without letting him touch her, but still, she could not come up with any plan that seemed plausible.

I guess I will have to wing it when I get to his room, she thought. But that seemed dangerous. Just winging it. She needed to come up with a concrete plan before she went to his room tonight.

After a while of thinking and coming up with nothing, she stood up and entered the house again. She went back to her room and sat on the bed. She stood up again, feeling restless. To pass the time, she began to pack for the trip. She made sure to leave many of her personal items behind so that when she made her escape, no one would actually suspect that she was gone for good until it was too late to get her back.

After she had packed all her things, she went back to reading, and soon fell asleep.

SIX

Leila woke up with a start and glanced at the clock on the wall, afraid that it was the morning of the next day and she had missed her opportunity. She breathed a sigh of relief when she saw it was almost noon. Why had she even thought she had slept for hours when she'd only been asleep for a short time?

She climbed out of her bed, went through the house once more, and then came back to her room again. It was easy to walk around the house without talking to anyone. The children mostly stayed in the upper wing, while the wives and Dauda stayed in the lower. The other wives did not speak to her, but that was just fine by her. The fewer personal attachments she made in this place, the easier it would be for her to leave with no regrets whatsoever.

In the afternoon, she had another heavy meal, and just like her breakfast, she relished it. It might not be possible for her to add the amount of weight she wanted to before she went to Dauda's room tonight, but she would do her best.

She stretched out on her bed again and forced herself to go back to sleep. She would need to be wide awake and alert for tonight. She quickly fell asleep again.

When she awoke, her room was dark. She climbed out of bed and switched on the light. Glancing at the clock on the wall, she saw that it was already nine p.m. She still had three more hours to wait before Dauda was in his room and on his bed. Also, by then, the other wives would have retired to their rooms as well.

She went to the kitchen and this time she didn't ask the chef to prepare something for her or get Nadiya to serve her food. She got herself something to eat and then went back to her room. After eating and dropping her plate in the kitchen, she went back to her room and entered the bathroom to take a slow, luxurious bath. After the bath, she put on some simple makeup, unbraided her raven-black hair and began to gently brush it until it shone and flowed down her back.

Finally, she put on the turquoise dress and glanced at herself in the mirror. She smiled with satisfaction. She looked good. A little thin, but still good.

Once again, she glanced at the clock on the wall and saw it was now five minutes to midnight. She glanced at herself once more in the mirror and then stepped out of the room. She walked down the hallway in her bare feet, her heart pounding in her chest. She reached Dauda's room in a short time and paused briefly in front of it, doubts assailing her mind.

What if her plan didn't work? Or worse, what if it went horribly wrong? There were two things that could happen that she prayed wouldn't. She had come to Dauda's room of her own accord. He could insist she did what she'd come to do and force her if she refused. Or he could catch her trying to take his phone or in the middle of changing the settings on his Absher account.

She took another deep breath to try to let go of

her doubts. This was not the time to worry about all these things. The Lord would help her and make her plan successful.

She gathered herself together and turned the doorknob slowly. And then she breathed a sigh of relief when the door opened. Thank God it isn't locked.

"Lord, please help me," she whispered, and then slowly and soundlessly shut the door behind her.

The room was dark and she could hear the faint sound of Dauda's snoring. She took another deep breath as her hands grew clammy and her heart raced with nervousness. And then she switched the lights on. The room flooded with light, but Dauda still did not open his eyes or even move. She was surprised, as she had thought he'd only just gone to bed.

She saw his phone lying on the table beside the bed and blinked. Maybe she could get it and do what she wanted to do right now without having to stay here with him. Maybe she would not have to think up ways to prevent him from touching her while she tried to find a way to get to his phone.

She took a deep breath and tiptoed to the table where his phone was, knowing full well that Rekiya had told her Dauda was a light sleeper. It was the reason she had not considered simply sneaking into his room while he was asleep and changing his Absher account setting.

When she reached the table, she glanced at him to make sure he was still sleeping and then reached out her hand to take the phone, her heart thudding. Just before she picked it up, from the corner of her eye, she noticed him turn around. She turned her eyes to him and froze in fear as he slowly opened his eyes.

He stared at her as though she were an apparition, and then sat up on his bed, still gazing curiously at her. "What are you doing here?" he finally asked in a voice that rang with curiosity.

Leila quickly collected herself, and then forced herself to smile widely at him. She stepped forward to the bed and said to him, "I just thought I would perform my wifely duties tonight."

He stared at her, the expression on his face incredulous. "Really?" he asked.

She nodded. "I feel completely well now."

He grinned at her and patted the space beside him on the bed. "Come and sit next to me," he said.

Dread gripped her and her heart drummed as she went to sit next to him. Oh Lord, please help me. I can't do this.

She wasn't sure what to do now, but there was no way she was going to sleep with him. She had to find a way to stop this from going any further. But how?

Immediately, an idea came to her and she turned to him. "Can I use your bathroom?" She turned away, afraid he would see the truth in her eyes—that she was lying to him and had no intention of spending the night with him. Her plan was to go to the bathroom and pretend to throw up. It wasn't a very good plan and it might backfire, but it was all she could come up with. If it went wrong, at best, he could send her away, insisting that she was too sick. At worst, he would ignore her pretend sickness and insist that she carry out her wifely duties.

He smiled again and then nodded. "Of course you can."

She stood up and started to head toward the bathroom, silently praying as she did. Just as she got to the bathroom door, he said, "Leila, I know why you're really here."

Her eyes widened in horror and she could not move. If he really knew why she was here, then she was in deep trouble. At best, she would remain a prisoner in this house and sleeping with Dauda might be the least of her worries.

She turned around slowly and stared at him with dread as she immediately knew that he wasn't bluffing. He really knew why she was here.

Slowly, she made her way to the bed and stood before him. She said in a small, shaky voice, "How did you know?"

He smiled wanly at her and said, "I've known you would try to run away almost immediately when we left for Saudi Arabia. First, there was that commotion you caused at the airport. It clearly told me you wanted absolutely nothing to do with me. I was a fool to think that would change." He looked up with a thoughtful expression and continued, "And then, when you immediately fell ill after we arrived here," his eyes searched hers, "or clearly pretended to be, I knew it would not be long before you began to plot your escape."

Leila stared at him, unable to breathe or speak. Finally, she took a deep breath and found her voice. She said as bravely as she could, "If you knew I was pretending to be sick all this time, why didn't you say anything?"

He chuckled and said, "I felt sorry for you, Leila. Besides, I really do not want to be with a woman who doesn't want me. It's not my way. It was actually my brother, Jibril, who convinced me to marry you. When he saw Zainah the first time she came back to Nira, he wanted her for himself. He saw you as well and decided that I would marry you while he married Zainah. Since Karim, Zainah's father, owed us money, it wasn't difficult to convince him to give us your hands in marriage."

Leila could not breathe again. All this while she'd been pretending to be sick, and smug in her belief that she had successfully deceived this man, he had known she wasn't. And he'd done absolutely nothing about it. He had neither threatened nor tried to make her look like a fool. He had not called her bluff.

She marveled as she said to him, "Why did you call all those doctors to examine me knowing I wasn't really ill?"

"When you stopped eating, I grew concerned for you. I felt that you would fall really ill, and it would be my fault. I wanted to make sure they were monitoring your health at least." He stared into her eyes and said, "You were planning to change my Absher account setting, were you not?"

She nodded, knowing he already knew everything.

"And you were not interested in being with me tonight, were you?"

"No," she said simply. She sat next to him, looked into his eyes and then looked away. "I'm sorry," she said. "I was just desperate. But it's not right to be forced into a marriage you don't want to be in." She did not look at him, afraid of what his reply would be. When he touched her, her muscles tensed up. Would he now insist that she do what she had pretended to come here for? Lord, give me strength, she cried out in her heart.

He gently turned her around to face him and said, "Just like I said before, I don't believe in being with a woman who doesn't want to be with me. If you are so desperate to leave that you would come here pretending to want to be with me when I know fully well how afraid you are to spend any time with me, then I think we shouldn't be married anymore."

Her eyes widened in shock as she stared at him. "Are you serious?"

He nodded and said, "I am." Smiling wistfully, he lifted her hands to his lips and kissed first the back of her right hand, and then her left. "It's a pity, because you're so beautiful," he said to her. "However, I'll do what you want. I'll let you travel out of the country, back to Mali or wherever it is you want to go. Once I'm able to go back to Mali, we can have the marriage dissolved."

She felt a mix of emotions waging war in her heart. Joy, relief, sadness, and guilt all fought for her attention. But the most prominent emotions were relief and joy. "Thank you," she said, and nearly hugged him. She held back at the last minute, instinctively knowing it would not be a good idea. "Thank you," she said again.

He stood up from the bed and went and got his phone from the table. She watched him typing away on his phone. About a minute later, he came back and sat beside her again. "You have permission to travel anywhere you want to. I'll also give you five thousand dollars when you leave so you can go wherever you want to and at least have something to start a new life with."

Her jaw dropped and she gazed at him for a long moment, feeling too overwhelmed to speak. She clearly knew that this was the Lord intervening on her behalf. However, she had not expected this amount of generosity from the man who was beside her. She finally found her voice and said to him, "You are a good man, Dauda." She wanted to tell him that the other wives, except of course for Rekiya, might be like her, and might not exactly want to be second and third wives either. However, she stopped herself. That would be pushing her luck.

She got up, smiled at him, and began to head toward the door. His voice stopped her before she left the room. She turned around again to face him.

"I will transfer the money into your account tomorrow," he said to her. "You can leave anytime you want to."

She nodded, thanked him again, and then walked out of the room. Closing the door behind her, she literally skipped down the hallway, even though it was the middle of the night, and went to her room.

She fell to her knees immediately after she got into her room and then lifted her voice in thanksgiving to the Lord. When she had come here months ago, she'd thought her life was over. Now she knew it was just beginning. The Lord had done a great miracle for her. Now, she could leave this country and never look back. And, she had enough money to search for Malik and also live on for some time until she could find a job for herself. "Thank you, Lord," she said again.

Finally, she could not contain her joy anymore and got to her feet. She danced around her room and lifted up her voice in songs of praise to the Lord who had delivered her. She didn't really care if anyone in the house heard her singing. The Lord had answered her prayers, and she would give Him thanks for all He had done.

SEVEN

Audrey got out of her car and locked the door. She walked up to the house, unlocked it and stepped in. She collapsed on the sofa and sighed wearily. She had spent all day at the mayor's office, discussing new and different ideas on how to improve security in Rosefield. Not that Rosefield really needed it. But after that terrorist scare at her and Ken's wedding, the mayor had been spooked and had asked her as police chief to beef up security in town.

She sat up. Talking about Ken, the door was locked when she came in. That meant he still wasn't back from the station. He spent a lot of time there whenever they were in Rosefield. She sighed loudly as she thought about him and the state of their relationship. For the past two days, they had barely spoken to each other. She hated that they were always fighting now. It was wrong to go for days without really speaking to each other. She just wanted the fights to end, but it didn't seem like it was going to end anytime soon. She couldn't give up the idea of having a baby right now while he couldn't stomach it. It was her dream to start a family, and she needed to make Ken see that she was getting older and the earlier they tried to get pregnant, the better.

She stood up once again and lifted up her backpack with her. Just as she started to make her way to the bedroom, the front door opened and Ken walked into the house. Their eyes immediately met and Ken gave her a small smile.

It was all she needed. She walked up to him and put her arms around him. Hugging him tightly, she whispered, "I love you, Ken."

He kissed the top of her head and said, "I love you too, Audrey." He held her slightly away from him, looked into her eyes and then kissed her forehead. He said, "I've missed you."

"I've missed you too," she smiled and hugged him again.

She looked up at him and he brushed his nose against hers. "I hate this," he said. "We shouldn't keep fighting. It's so tiring."

She nodded and then took his hand. They both sat on the couch and for the first time in almost a week, they held each other tightly, chatting and laughing, simply enjoying each other's company. After a while, Ken said, "I'm thirsty. I need a drink of water. Do you want me to get you some water or lemonade, Audrey?"

She smiled and nodded. "Water. Thanks."

He stood up and left the living room and fearful thoughts immediately raced through Audrey's mind. Without a doubt, she knew this happy time with him was just a short reprieve. Soon, they would be fighting again, because of the same thing—her desire to have a baby now.

He came back to the living room carrying two glasses of water and handed her one. Settling down on the couch beside her, he drew her close once more.

She burrowed her head in his chest and sighed. If only this time didn't have to end. However, this was the best time to talk to him. She had to bring up the matter that had been causing them to fight all the time. As much as she wanted to avoid conflict, this was too important to sweep under the carpet. He would be angry again, for sure. But they had to talk about it… now. Time was running out for her.

She finally drew back from him, and then smiled slightly. She wove her fingers through his and then said softly, "Ken, we need to talk."

He frowned. "About what?"

She pressed her lips together and then said, "About having a baby…"

"Audrey, please… not now!"

"I understand everything you said about not wanting a baby right away, but try to see things from my point of view," she said. "I am in my mid-thirties now, Ken. According to the doctor, my eggs are aging rapidly. Soon, I won't have any good ones left."

He scowled at her.

She smiled to try to lighten the mood, but he didn't smile back. "Please, just consider what I am asking, Ken. We need to start trying to have a child now."

Ken sighed loudly and then looked away from her. She squeezed his hand and he turned to look at her again. "I understand what you're saying, Audrey," he said tightly. "But how about we leave off talking about having a baby for now… for about a year or two."

She snatched her hand from his and groaned. She wanted to scream at him. He wasn't even listening to everything she was saying about time running out on her. Anger boiled in her stomach and she glared at him. She took a deep breath and pushed it down. Getting angry right now would do no good.

She studied him. He had an unyielding expression on his face. Why couldn't he just understand that as a woman she knew when her body was ready to conceive, and it was now? She was ready to have a baby now.

Ken put his hand on her shoulder, but she shrugged it off.

He moaned and then stood up from the couch. "I'm going to the bedroom," he said.

She covered her face with her hands and said a silent prayer, asking the Lord to touch Ken's heart and help him fully understand where she was coming from. "Lord," she prayed, "I hate that we're always fighting these days, but I just can't give up on the idea of having a child right now. Please, help Ken see how important this is to me." She remembered what Trisha told her about not giving up on talking to Ken and trying to get him to see how she felt. She stood up and went into their bedroom. She found Ken standing in front of the closet, putting on an old white T-shirt.

He looked at her as she entered and then quickly looked away again. He said without looking at her, "If you are here to try to get me to change my mind, then I suggest you save it."

"Ken!" Audrey said exasperatedly. "Why won't you just understand? Why don't you get it?"

Ken looked at her and shook his head. "I do get it, Audrey. The thing is, you tend to make rash decisions a lot of the time without thinking it through. I don't want this to be another one of your rash decisions. As you have said, it's a very important decision and it should not be made hastily."

Audrey's mouth dropped open and she stared at him. She finally said, "How can you say that, Ken? How can you say I tend to make rash decisions? That is untrue and just mean."

"But it's true," Ken said. "You might think you want a baby now until we actually have one. And then you will see how constricting having a child is and come to regret your decision."

He sat down on the bed and the angry expression

on his face changed to one of weariness. He said, "I am just tired of all this, Audrey. You told me to consider what you said about having a child, and I'm asking you right now to also consider what I just said. Think about it for some time and see if this is really what you want. I, for one, know that I am not yet ready to take on the responsibilities of having a newborn. And no, don't say again that we will have a nanny. Even if we do, I still want to be a hands-on father. That has always been my dream. But right now, things are really hectic at work. And it's the same for you. Plus, we are continuously traveling back and forth. I don't see myself being the kind of father I would like to be right now, especially to a newborn baby. I am really sorry."

She kept staring at him with her mouth open and then she finally nodded. She said, "Do you think I would have brought this up if I had not thought about it for some time? You don't get to tell me what I am ready to do or not. I told you that I am ready to have a child now, and yet you insist that I'm not. And on top of that, you're accusing me of making rash decisions without properly thinking about it. That is unfair and totally wrong."

Ken sighed loudly and shut his eyes, as though he couldn't bear to look at her any longer. He opened them again and turned to her. "Audrey, I am sick and tired of fighting with you. How about we stop discussing this topic for now... at least until after we get back from vacation. Let's talk about something else that we can agree on."

She folded her arms and huffed. "Right now, I don't think we can agree on anything!"

"Why don't we talk about where we will spend our vacation?"

For a long moment, Audrey stared at him, refusing to oblige. Why should she put aside a topic that was extremely important to her, and also to him if he were being honest with himself, in order to talk about where they would spend their vacation? She searched his eyes for a few seconds and saw the pain in them. She knew all the arguing they were doing was hurting him much more than she thought. She was terribly hurt by it all, but she had not known how much he hurt because of it as well. Even though she did not understand why he wouldn't give in to what she wanted, she decided that they did need a break from all the arguing. They needed to discuss something they would at least both agree on.

She finally relented and sat on the bed beside him. "Okay, Ken, so what do you have in mind? Since we can thankfully afford to go anywhere we want to, where would you like us to spend our vacation?"

Ken didn't say anything for a minute. He finally ran his fingers through his hair and said, "I'm not really sure where I want to go now, but I was thinking we might go to Boise and spend it with my parents."

Audrey groaned and said, "As much as I like your parents, Ken, spending our work leave with them isn't exactly my idea of the perfect vacation." She leaned forward and looked into his eyes. "Come on, Ken. We can do better."

"Okay then," he murmured. "Where do you suggest we go?"

She shrugged. "Right now, I'm not exactly sure, but maybe somewhere in Europe." She thought about telling him she would love to go to Peru to see Sienna and especially the baby, but she changed her mind. He would never agree to spend their vacation there.

"Okay, I like that. But we have to decide where exactly in Europe we want to go. Maybe we could take a cruise?"

She considered what he'd just said. It sounded like a good idea, but she still wasn't sure. She opened her mouth to tell him what she was thinking, and then looked away from him when her phone rang. She picked it up from the bed and stared at it. "It's Sienna," she said to Ken before answering the phone. "Hi, little sis! How are you doing?"

"Audrey, I'm good." She chuckled. "Apart from the fact that I've not slept for several months now, I guess I am fine."

Audrey laughed and said, "So, baby Ethan is keeping you up at night... or is it your other baby?"

Sienna didn't say anything for a few seconds and Audrey giggled while she waited for Sienna to get it. Finally, Sienna howled and said, "You are crazy, Audrey! No, Bryan isn't keeping me up at night. It's just Ethan. He sleeps all day and then stays awake at night."

"Well, I guess you can also sleep when Ethan is asleep during the day."

Sienna sighed. "Except for the fact that I would actually like to work during the day, and sleep at night like normal people do." There was a short pause and then she said, "Audrey, have you and Ken decided where you would like to spend your vacation?"

Audrey glanced at Ken, who was looking inquisitively at her, and then said, "Ken and I were just discussing it now. We still haven't really decided yet but we are both thinking of Europe. Maybe a trip around the continent."

Sienna said, "That sounds really nice. Umm, I was just thinking that you both might want to come to Peru . . . maybe? We would have so much fun together. And I know Ken and Bryan get along really well."

Audrey sighed. She had just been thinking about Peru before Sienna called. She had wanted to see Sienna since she and Bryan had moved to Peru, and especially after Sienna gave birth to her baby boy. But she knew Ken would not agree to go. She said to Sienna, "I would love to come, especially to see the baby. Just as you said, I know we would have so much fun together, but I don't think Ken will want to spend his vacation in Peru." Audrey glanced at Ken and then said, "I'll have to talk to him about it."

Sienna said, "When is your leave starting?"

"In a few days' time," Audrey answered.

"Okay, talk to Ken about it and please let Bryan and I know as soon as you have come to a decision. I would really love to have both of you. And you can also help me with Ethan if you come."

Audrey laughed. "So, Sienna, that's why you want me to come to Peru. You just want a free babysitter."

Sienna chuckled and said, "Maybe. And I know you'll be a great babysitter."

Audrey smiled. "I am. Seriously, though, I know we would have loads of fun together and I really miss you. But it all depends on if Ken agrees."

Ken put his hand on her back and she turned to look at him. He was still staring quizzically at her. She held up her hand to indicate that he should wait and then spoke into the phone again, "Okay, Sienna. I'll get back to you as soon as possible. Let me talk to Ken right now. He's been staring quizzically at me since you called. He is bursting with questions." Audrey laughed at the look on Ken's face and then ended the call with Sienna.

"What was that all about?" Ken asked.

Audrey sighed as she looked him in the eye. With all the fighting that had been going on for some time now, they weren't exactly seeing eye to eye on a number of things. She hoped Ken would not refuse Sienna's invitation for them to go to Peru. It would be a great way to spend their vacation.

She took his hand and said, "Sienna wants us to go to Peru to spend our vacation with her and Bryan. I personally love the idea. What do you think?" She held her breath as she looked at him, praying he would agree but not holding out much hope. Unfortunately, she had just refused a request by him to spend their vacation with his parents. Would he refuse her request to spend the vacation with her family since she told him she didn't want to spend it with his?

He looked up with a thoughtful expression on his face and then focused on her again. "Peru," he said. "Umm, okay. I think it will be an interesting place to visit. And Bryan is a hoot. Okay, Audrey. We will spend the vacation with Bryan and Sienna in Peru."

Audrey's eyes widened in surprise. Ken had just agreed without any argument. She whooped and then stood up to do a little jig around the room.

Ken laughed and shook his head at her. After a while, she came to sit beside him again. She hollered, "Peru, here we come!" Then she hugged him tightly and kissed his cheeks.

She started to pull away, but he held her to himself and kissed her tenderly on the lips. When he started to draw back, she held on to him and she sighed in contentment as she wrapped her arms tightly around him. If only things could always be like this between them, instead of the constant fights they had every single day now. But in order for total peace to reign, it would mean someone had to compromise and give in to the other's desire. And that she could not do. She could not give up on her desire to have a baby now. Which meant they would have more fights in the future. That would not be good for their marriage at all. She wasn't looking forward to any of that.

She thought about Sienna's invitation again. She was looking forward to seeing her sister and spending time with her nephew, but she knew that seeing Ethan and taking care of him would probably make her yearning for a baby worse. Still, she couldn't wait to go to Peru. Hopefully spending time there would give her and Ken a well-needed break from the fights, at least for a month. And then it would start all over again. And there was nothing she could do about that, as she wasn't going to give up her dream.

She sighed again and whispered to herself, "If only Ken would let us have a baby."

Ken rubbed her back and said, "What did you say, Audrey?"

"Nothing, Ken," she replied. "I said nothing."

*****

After Dauda's driver had lugged her suitcase into the trunk of Dauda's silver jeep, Leila hugged Rekiya tightly and said, "Thank you so much for everything you have done for me." Tears swam in her eyes as she looked at the senior wife's face.

Rekiya held Leila's hands and said, "Can't you still go with me to Paris instead of leaving immediately? Surely, you can postpone your trip back to Mali and travel with me."

Leila smiled sadly and shook her head. "I would have loved to go with you, Rekiya, but I need to go back to Mali as soon as possible."

Rekiya searched Leila's eyes and said, "And you won't tell me what is so urgent that you have to leave so quickly." She squeezed Leila's hands. "However, I already know why you don't want to go with me."

Leila raised her eyebrows and stared at Rekiya, surprised. She asked, "You do?"

"Yes, I do. You are in love with someone. I can see it in your eyes. Actually, I have guessed that that was the case for some time. Now, I am sure about it."

Leila smiled sadly and then nodded. "You are right, Rekiya. I am in love with someone. I have to get to him now. We would have been together if I had not married Dauda."

"I understand," Rekiya said.

Leila nodded. "I know you do. You love Dauda

even after all these years of..." She pressed her lips together, pushing back the words that had nearly slipped through her lips. It would not be right at this time to question Rekiya for loving a man who seemed to care nothing about her feelings.

Rekiya sighed sadly, but she didn't seem angry or put off by Leila's words. She drew Leila close and hugged her tightly again. And then she let her go.

Leila opened the car door and got in. She shut the door and stuck her head out the window. Waving at Rekiya, she mouthed, "Thank you so much. I'll never forget you, Rekiya."

Rekiya waved back.

The driver began to drive away from the house and Leila kept waving at Rekiya until the man drove out of the gate and Rekiya's figure disappeared. Leila turned around and settled on her seat. She wasn't surprised that none of the other wives had come to see her off. Actually, she wasn't even sure any of them knew she was leaving. However, she had thought Dauda would say goodbye today before she left. But he had not. Instead, he had stayed in his room and had not come out at all. But she guessed that was for the best.

She looked back one more time at the mansion and kept looking at it as it grew smaller and smaller. At last, she turned around again and sighed in relief. Waves of excitement flooded her body as she thought about finally leaving this country. Soon, she would see Malik again. She had been dreaming of seeing him for such a long time. Her dream would finally come true.

Her excitement suddenly turned to nervous anticipation, and then uncertainty and dread overwhelmed her. What if the same thing that happened last time happened again? Even if Karim Keita did not have another husband to marry her off to, if he saw her in Nira, who knew what he would do to her? Besides, if she got to Nira and Malik was not there, how would she find out where he was and how to get there?

She looked out of the car window and sighed. She had to put all these fears and concerns out of her mind and focus on the fact that she was now free; free to see the love of her life again and even marry him one day, when her marriage to Dauda was dissolved.

But you can't marry him until he becomes a Christian, a voice in her mind said.

That was true. There was no way she could marry Malik until he became a Christian. No matter how much she loved him, the word of God still held sway over her and the decisions she made. And the word said she could not be unequally yoked to an unbeliever.

Worry began to envelope her and she shut her eyes. I can't think about all that right now, she thought to herself. She had to be positive. The Lord had miraculously delivered her and now she was leaving this country and going back to look for Malik. Surely He would not do all this for her if He did not want her and Malik to be together. She had to believe Malik would become a Christian soon. She would take everything one step at a time. For now, she would find Malik no matter what, and then they would have a happy reunion. She couldn't wait to hold him and kiss him.

The meddlesome voice in her head screamed again, You can't kiss him when you are still married to someone else.

She sighed wearily. Well, she couldn't wait to at least hold and hug him. Soon, by God's grace, she would be able to do much more than that. Soon, she would be his wife.

*****

After a long day's work, Malik went back to his house near the farm—a tiny one-bedroom unpainted building. Around the farm were huts where the other workers stayed. Because his father owned the farm, Malik acted as the overseer here in Dogon and lived in the only home that wasn't a hut.

He went into the kitchen to get the loaf of bread he had bought this morning. Unlike his house in Nira, the kitchen here was just a tiny space with a single kerosene stove. He never cooked anything here anyway. Usually, he bought food from the sole canteen near the small market or ate bread. He got the small loaf from the wooden shelf, took a tin of milk, and went to his small living room. He sat down on the old couch and ate his food. After that, he went to get water from the well outside with a metal bucket and then went in to bathe quickly with the water.

He felt more relaxed after his bath, went to his room, and stretched out on his narrow bed. Once again, excitement ran through him as he thought about seeing his daughter, Fanta, tomorrow. He could hardly wait. As usual, he would be staying in Nira for only a few days, thanks to his heartless father, but he tried as much as possible to enjoy the time he spent with Fanta.

It was getting more and more difficult to be away from her, but it wasn't as if there were any jobs in Nira. Most of the people who were employed had their jobs because of his father and worked on this farm. He was glad his mother and stepmother took good care of Fanta, but he was still perturbed by the fact that he couldn't do so himself. He needed to be there for her but he never was. Plus, he hated the fact that she stayed in his father's house. If only he were married, his wife would watch over her while he was away.

His mind immediately went to Leila at the thought of being married and he groaned. Would he ever be able to forget her? He sighed loudly and then turned his face to the wall. He shut his eyes and tried to go to sleep, but Leila's face appeared in his mind and refused to leave. He needed to wake up early tomorrow for his trip to Nira, but he couldn't sleep. He tossed and turned, until finally, he thankfully drifted off.

From inside his dream, he heard someone wailing and then jerked up as someone banged loudly on his door. He could hear loud voices outside his small house and he wondered what all the commotion was about. Quickly, he climbed out of bed, put on a T-shirt over his pajama pants, and opened the door.

Abu, the caretaker, barged into his room, sweating profusely. "Malik, there's a fire!"

Malik's mouth fell open and he shook his head. "What do you mean there's a fire?" he asked Abu, scowling at the diminutive man.

Abu put his hands on his head, his eyes red. He shouted, "You need to come now. The farm is on fire... Come outside. It's burning away all the crops... the harvest."

Malik's eyes widened in alarm and he raced past the caretaker and ran out of the house. He skidded to a stop as he reached the farm. The sight before him was unlike anything he had seen. Fire and smoke rose high. The fire had consumed the farm and was spreading fast to the huts near it. Many of the men who worked on the farm were running helter-skelter, fetching buckets of water from the nearby well, carrying them to the farm, and pouring water continuously on the fire, trying to put it out. The flames began to spread to some of the huts where the farm workers lived.

For a moment, Malik stared at the scene in front of him with his mouth open, his feet refusing to move, and then he took off running. He found an empty bucket near one of the huts, grabbed it, and raced to the well to fetch water.

For what seemed like an eternity, he and the other workers on the farm when to and fro, from the well back to the site of the fire, pouring water on the flames.

Finally, the flames began to lessen until they died out completely. However, billows of smoke rose high in the sky, causing the farmers, including Malik, to cough violently.

Malik gazed all around him. The farm was burnt to the ground. All the crops were gone, burnt to ashes. He put his hands on his head and stared at the ruin, feeling completely devastated. Everyone had worked so hard to make sure the abundant crops the farm had produced this year were harvested. Half of the crops had been harvested already, but had not yet been stored in the barn. All of the crops—those harvested and those yet to be—were gone, burnt to ashes. He felt like crying as he looked around him. Some of the huts near the farm had also been burnt to the ground.

For a long time, he couldn't speak. Some of the men whose huts had been burned down stood where their huts had been, lamenting over their personal property and items that had been destroyed. Malik did not know what to do or say to them.

Abu the caretaker came and put his hand on Malik's shoulder.

"Do you know how this fire started?" Malik asked the caretaker.

"I don't," the man answered.

"We have to find out what really happened."

"It's all been destroyed!" Abu exclaimed as though he did not hear what Malik had said.

Malik sighed and said slowly, "Not all of it. There is still some part of the farm that the fire didn't touch. We have to start planting as soon as possible." As much as he felt an overwhelming sadness, he knew not to give into his feelings. There was no use doing that. Instead, they would have to start all over again, planting crops. Thankfully, there were a variety of seedlings in the barn.

He sighed. This meant he couldn't go back to Nira now and he didn't know when he would be able to. If there were no crops to be harvested, the men who had been working and laboring for weeks would not be paid. They were already very poor. Their plight would be much worse if they were not paid.

His heart sank to his feet as he realized he would not be able to see his daughter for a long time.

She's in good hands, he told himself. But he didn't like the fact that she was in the same house as the man who called himself his father. That man was wicked.

Once again he thought about marrying a wife; someone who he could trust to take care of his daughter. At least his daughter would be able to stay in his house and not have to live in the same house as his father. Like before, Leila's face appeared in his mind. This time, he refused to let it stay and forcefully pushed it away. This was not the time to think about Leila. She would never be his. She now belonged to someone else.

For now, he had to stay focused on planting the corn and millet, and helping the men who had lost their personal items with some of their basic needs. Once he was able to get back to Nira, he would have to start searching for a wife. Obviously, it would not be a love match the way he and Leila were . . . or had been. But that didn't really matter. All he wanted was a mother for his daughter, not a lover. His late wife had not been a love match either, but they had lived in peace with each other. Their marriage had been arranged by both their families.

He moved toward the men who had lost their property and houses, and put away thoughts of finding a wife and mother for his daughter so he could concentrate on the matter at hand.

EIGHT

Nick settled back on the couch, opened the dating app on his phone, and went to his profile. He slowly scrolled down the screen, reading the messages he had received and looking at the profiles of the different girls he had been chatting with. After about half an hour, he sighed and logged out of the dating site. He was tired of swiping. He had been chatting with a few girls for some time now, but he hadn't found any one he actually wanted to meet up with.

He felt slightly lonely and bored in Rosefield. He'd been here for about a week now, but apart from Frank and his wife, Trisha, he knew no one. He had gone to work early every day, including Saturday, and always came home late. Sundays were his only free days. He'd hardly had any time to socialize here. The only socializing he had done was on the online dating site. Since today was a Sunday and the restaurant was closed, he had decided to come to Frank's house and spend the day with him and Trisha rather than stay in his room at the Bed & Breakfast alone. He looked up when Frank walked into the living room.

Frank came and sat beside him on the couch and

asked, "Were you on that dating site again?"

For some reason, he felt defensive. "What if I was?" he said. Frank raised his eyebrows and Nick sighed. "I'm sorry." He gave Frank an apologetic smile and focused his gaze on Frank's face. "It's just that I'm used to having company. Lots of company. I know I have only been here for a week, but I am bored and kinda lonely."

Frank gave him a small smile. "By company, you mean girls, right? You are used to having girls always flocking around you, isn't that so?"

Nick rolled his eyes. "Frank, stop looking at me like that," he said. He opened his mouth to tell his friend that he was actually ready to start dating seriously when Trisha walked into the living room. He stood up and briefly hugged her before sitting down again. She sat on the sofa facing him and smiled at him. When Frank got up and went to sit next to Trisha on the single sofa, Nick hid an amused smile. There was more than enough space on the couch, but Frank chose to squeeze in beside his wife.

"So, how have you been enjoying Rosefield so far?" Trisha asked.

"I can't say I am really enjoying it," Nick answered. "I mean, it's a beautiful place. But like I was telling Frank just now, it's a bit boring, and I'm lonely because I haven't had time to make any friends yet."

Frank smirked and said to Trisha, "Nick was on a dating app just before I came into the living room."

Trisha raised an eyebrow and said with a tease in her voice, "So, you've been busy swiping left and right, have you? And have you found anyone yet, Nick?"

Nick ignored Frank's smirk and Trisha's incredulous expression and said, "Not yet. But actually, I think I want to start dating seriously now. Maybe in a few years, I might even consider getting married like Frank." He smiled at Trisha. "That is if I find a smart and beautiful woman like you."

Trisha leaned slightly forward and gave him a look that melted the smile off his face. He frowned slightly. The look on her face was one of disbelief, as though the very thought of him settling down was completely laughable.

Frank said, "I told Nick I might know someone who would be perfect for him, Trisha."

This time, Trisha raised both eyebrows. "And who might that be?" she asked.

"A certain divorced friend of yours," Frank said.

Guys, I am still here, Nick thought, slightly amused. He opened his mouth to tell them that, but was taken aback when Trisha's features hardened. She said tersely, "I don't think she and Nick would be a very good match, Frank."

Nick felt slightly angry at Trisha's words and the look on her face. It was a look that clearly said whoever that friend of hers was, she was too good for him. He sighed and let go of his anger. Why would he blame Trisha? She knew he had a reputation as a player. But nobody really understood him. It wasn't as if he enjoyed tagging girls along. It was just that he was afraid of commitment.

And isn't it time you put away that fear? a voice in his head said.

He pressed away the voice and said defensively, "I guess you're right, Trisha. I'm probably not ready for anything serious now. It's why I am on a dating app. I'm just looking for someone to hook up with."

Trisha seemed to bristle, but Frank chuckled. "You know what, Nick? I actually think you are ready for something serious now."

Nick stared at Frank inquisitively and then said, "No, Frank, I am not. Just as I said, I am only looking for something physical."

Frank did not back away. Instead, he said again,

"No, Nick. I know you are ready for a serious relationship right now."

Nick scowled at him. "I just told you I wasn't."

Frank smiled and said again, "I know you are ready to give your heart to Christ and start a relationship with him now."

Nick shook his head slowly and said, "Frank, that is so corny! Be serious!"

Frank put his hand on his chest and said, "I am being very serious. You are the one that isn't serious, Nick. There's only one relationship you actually need right now, and that is a relationship with Jesus."

Nick groaned and then glowered at Frank. "Will you please give it up, Frank? I am not ready to turn religious like you."

Frank said, "It's not religion, it's…."

"Yeah, yeah! I know. It's a relationship with Jesus." Nick leaned forward and stared at Frank. "Well, I am not ready for a relationship with Jesus or anyone else for that matter. All I want right now is to find someone to be with while I am in Rosefield so I don't feel so lonely."

Trisha said, "I hope you don't find anyone, Nick. Rosefield is not that sort of place."

Nick said, partly incredulous and partly teasing, "So there are no lonely people in Rosefield?"

"You know what I mean," Trisha huffed.

"Yes, I do know what you mean, Trisha," Nick replied and sighed wearily. He was tired of this conversation. He needed a short break from it. He stood up and asked to use the restroom. When Frank told him how to find it, he thanked him and left the living room.

After he finished using the restroom, he began to make his way back to the living room, and then he stopped abruptly in the hallway, overhearing Trisha and Frank's conversation. They were talking about him.

"Why would you even tell Nick about her? You know she's lonely right now and a bit vulnerable. I certainly don't want them to meet. I want her to find a good man and not someone like your friend. I don't want her heart played with. She's a great girl and she deserves the best."

Frank apologized and whispered something to Trisha that Nick could not make out.

Trisha sighed loudly and said, "I know he is involved with several charities and is a generous person, but that doesn't change the fact that he isn't very good with romantic relationships."

For a long moment, Nick stood in the hallway without moving. He knew he had quite a reputation with women amongst his friends, but he did not know it was so bad that Frank's wife would talk about him as though he had some contagious disease he could spread to her friends.

Well, he certainly didn't want to meet that friend or have anything to do with her either. He was handsome and never had any trouble meeting women. He would get his own dates and maybe, just to spite Trisha, he would find a good girl to date, at least while he was in Rosefield. He might even be able to commit to her. But he doubted it. He just wasn't ready for a very serious relationship right now.

He walked out to the living room again, smiled at Trisha and Frank as though he had heard nothing, and said, "I think I have to go now." He turned to Frank and said, "I'll see you at the restaurant tomorrow." Again, he smiled brightly at Trisha and walked hastily to the door before the couple could say anything. Opening it, he went out quickly. Rather than take a taxi, which was how he had come to Frank and Trisha's house, he walked briskly to the bed and breakfast. Twenty minutes later, he got there, climbed up the stairs, and went to his room.

He sat on the bed and turned on the television to watch a football game. But he couldn't concentrate on it. He turned the TV off again and his mind went around and around on what Trisha had said to Frank.

He remembered what Frank had said to him and muttered, "Maybe it is time to give up my player image." It was probably time to find a woman who he could spend the rest of his life with. He wasn't getting any younger. However, he doubted he would find her in Rosefield. At least not in person. But maybe he could find her online. Since he had already checked the dating site and hadn't found anyone he would consider going out on a date with, he would leave off until tomorrow. Then, he would check again and maybe he would be lucky. If not, he would have to settle for someone to share some intimate time with. That was the best he could do right now. He got up from the bed and went to fix himself lunch.

*****

Lauren lifted Ruby into her lap and kissed the little girl's cheeks. She tickled Ruby and chuckled when the toddler howled with laughter.

"How are you, darling?" Lauren asked, smiling at her.

Ruby laughed as though Lauren had asked her the funniest question she had ever heard. She wiggled around and then slipped out of Lauren's lap.

Lauren watched her with amusement as she toddled round the living room like a drunken person. Lauren turned to Trisha, who was seated beside her, and laughed. "Maybe Ruby is drunk on milk. I think we should stage an intervention for her."

Trisha chuckled and then the expression on her face suddenly turned sober. She said to Lauren, "Are you still considering doing that online dating thing?"

Lauren sighed and looked away. She felt even lonelier now than she had when she first told Trisha she wanted to find a date online. She had opened an online dating account and set up her profile. But she had not yet checked to see if she had a match. For some reason, she felt terribly nervous about doing so, but if she wanted to start dating seriously again, she had to muster up courage and check the site. It was the only way she would know if there was a match for her and the only way left for her to find someone right now.

Turning to Trisha again, she said, "I have set up my dating profile, but I haven't checked to see if I have a match since I did. I will probably check the site this evening or tomorrow morning before work. I mean, I haven't been asked out by anyone I would ever consider dating in a very long time. I have to do something right now or I might be single for the rest of my life."

Trisha looked at her with disbelief written on her face and said, "No one in church has asked you out?"

Lauren sighed. "You know that most of the good men there are already taken."

"There are some eligible bachelors," Trisha said.

"Not many. And I think part of the problem is that I am divorced… I don't know. I only had one guy at church ask me out some time ago, but he isn't someone I could ever consider dating." Trisha frowned and Lauren shook her head. "Don't look at me like that. I can't just date anyone because I am single, and you know that."

"Well, what is wrong with the guy from church who asked you out?"

Lauren sighed again. "He is staid and boring. Not my type."

Trisha shook her head. "By boring and staid, you mean he is not a bad boy. You could consider dating someone different this time, Lauren. Why not give him a chance?"

"Are you kidding me, Tricia?" Lauren stared at her friend incredulously. "I know I sound kinda desperate, but I still have standards. Do you want me to drop my standards just so I can date some-one?"

"I am not saying you should drop your standards, Lauren. I am only saying you should try something new. Remember the definition of insanity?"

"When you say something new..."

"I mean someone who isn't the typical bad-boy type you usually go for." Trisha leaned forward. "And don't look at me like that. I know that is the kind of guy you gravitate toward, but that needs to change. Give that guy at church a chance."

Lauren's mouth fell open and then she shut it again. A slice of shame ran through her and she looked away. She said defensively, "It's not just the fact that the guy is boring. I want something dif-ferent for myself, something better... and that guy isn't it. What is wrong with having standards?" She turned once more to look at Trisha.

Trisha thinned her lips, and then said, "I'm sorry, Lauren. Of course you shouldn't lower your stan-dards as long as they are reasonable standards. I would never ask you to do that. I'm just really wor-ried about the online dating thing. I don't think I know anyone who has met their spouse through an online dating site."

"Do you know anyone in Rosefield at all who is on an online dating site?" Lauren asked her.

Trisha did not say anything for some time, and then she shrugged. "Okay, I admit I don't know anyone who is using an online dating site at this time to find a spouse, Lauren." She frowned, and said again, "I do know someone I guess, but he isn't looking for anything serious."

"And who is he?" Lauren asked curiously.

Trisha waved her hand dismissively, and said,

"Just a friend of my husband's."

"Is he the one Frank went to pick up the other day?"

"Yes. Just as I said, he's not looking for anything serious. Anyway, just be careful if you're truly determined to do the online dating thing. I've heard so many stories about scammers catfishing people online. All those stories have made me question the safety and validity of finding someone through an online dating site."

"You've told me all this before," Lauren said.

Trisha nodded. "Yes, I know I have. But I am repeating myself again because I want you to be really careful."

Lauren gave Trisha a small smile and said, "Just like I told you before, I will be careful." She turned to look at Ruby, who was still prancing around the living room, and sighed wistfully. She pointed at Ruby and said to Trisha, "This is why I want to try online dating. When will I have my own little daughter if I don't start seriously dating now?"

Trisha pursed her lips and said nothing for a few seconds, and then nodded. "I guess I understand. Or at least, I can see why you want to go down the route of dating online to find someone. I guess you just have to pray and believe that the Lord will send you a good man that way. I mean, there's nothing impossible for Him."

Lauren smiled. "Yes, there isn't." She decided to change the subject and asked Trisha about how she was doing with her pregnancy. Trisha was glowing, either from the pregnancy, or from being deeply in love with her husband, Lauren wasn't sure.

"I haven't yet had any real morning sickness, thank God," Trisha said. "I was quite sick when I was pregnant with Ruby."

Soon, they began to chat about church, and then about Trisha's sisters, Sienna and Audrey. When the conversation shifted to their exes, Lauren said,

"It's so strange, but I still miss Richie sometimes."

Trisha said, "That's understandable, since you were married to him for years. However, when you find someone who truly loves you, you will soon stop missing him. That is the way it was with me."

Lauren smiled sadly and said to Trisha, "You aren't helping my loneliness problem, Trish. Talking about how much Frank loves you only makes me sadder and more despondent about not yet finding the right guy."

"I am sorry," Trisha said.

Lauren laughed. "I was just joking, Trish." But she really wasn't.

The conversation shifted to random stuff and they continued to chat for another hour. Lauren didn't want to leave and go back to her lonely apartment. But she had no choice. Frank would soon be back from his men's meeting at church. Frank and Trisha were shameless with their PDA. Lauren didn't want to be here when Frank came back. It would only make her yearning for a spouse worse.

She stood up and said, "I have to go, Trish. It's getting late."

Trisha glanced at the clock on the wall. "It is just seven o'clock."

"I have to get up early for work."

Trisha nodded and followed Lauren to the door.

Lauren hugged Trisha, smiled at Ruby, who was playing with her toys at the far end of the living room, and then went out of the house.

She got home some minutes later, went into her room, sat on the bed, and set her laptop on her lap. Opening it, she took a deep breath and, with grim determination, went to the online dating website she had joined but had never had the nerve to check. She nervously opened her own profile, and then took another deep breath before she looked at it.

Her jaw dropped at what she saw. She had thought

she would be matched with one or, at most, two people; but there were several guys—good looking, interesting guys, judging from their profiles—who were suggested as potential matches for her.

Nervous but excited, she quickly began to check each of their profiles. Three of them had already sent her messages, telling her they were interested in knowing more about her and meeting up for a date soon.

She carefully read their profiles again, and then read the profiles of the guys that had not yet sent her any messages. And then she decided to reply to those that had sent her messages. But before she could start typing out the first message, her eyes went back to the profile of one particular guy.

When she started going through all the profiles, his face had immediately struck her. And it wasn't just because he was handsome, though he was very good-looking, but there was something about the way he looked that appealed to her. From his profile, she discovered that he was an outgoing guy, but sensitive too. He loved the same movies that she did. Most of all, he was into charitable causes, just like she was. That was why she had joined the welfare department in church. The one thing his profile did not say about him, though, was whether he had a strong faith. It said he believed in God, but nothing more than that. Even though he had not yet sent her a message, she decided to send him one.

What on Earth are you doing, Lauren? She asked herself as she began to type out a message to him. Why was she so drawn to him, anyway?

She told him he looked like someone should would enjoy getting to know and that they had some things in common, things that were important to her. She finally finished typing the message. Before she could overthink it, she sent the message to him, and then shut her eyes as embarrassment settled over her.

Oh my god! Did I just do that? What was it with her being especially forward with guys these days? Since she'd divorced Richie, this was the second time she was asking a guy out. Something she would never have dreamt of doing before. The first guy she'd asked out was Faizan.

Thinking about Faizan brought a mild ache to her heart. She had really liked him and had thought there would be a future with him, especially the day he'd asked her out. She had finally reconciled herself to the fact that he was now married to someone he loved dearly and that she was not meant for him and vice versa. Still, sometimes she thought about him and what it would have been like if he was the one he'd loved and married. Every time she had that thought, she felt guilty and asked the Lord for forgiveness. He was married now. Thinking about him in that way was totally wrong.

She looked again at her online profile, staring at it intently as though by doing that, she could make the guy she had sent the message to message her back immediately. She finally chided herself after a long moment of staring at the screen.

Give him some time to answer, she said to herself. She logged off the website and shut her laptop. She had to give it some time. She would check back tomorrow evening, after work, to see if he had answered. Hopefully, by then, he would have replied to her message with good news—that he was also interested in her and wanted to get to know her better.

The thought sent a shiver of excitement and dread through her. Soon, she would start to date again. Apart from the one date she'd had with Faizan, she hadn't dated in years. If only she could bypass all of that and just find her spouse and get married right now. Unfortunately, things did not work that way. One would think that in this fast-paced era, relationships would progress quicker, but sadly, things were even slower than ever.

Panic suddenly gripped her and she felt like retrieving the message she had sent to the stranger. What if this online thing wasn't God's will for her? What if she was going ahead of God? Maybe Trisha was right. She should wait on the Lord and not try to make things happen for herself.

She covered her eyes with her hand and said, "Lord, was I wrong to set up this dating profile?" It was too late anyway to take back the message she had sent to that guy. The only thing she could do now was delete her profile from the dating site. She opened her laptop again and went to the site. She stared at her profile for a long time, varying emotions warring in her heart as she wondered whether to delete her profile or not.

Finally, she logged off again, clicked off her computer, and put her laptop aside. She stood up and went out of her bedroom quickly.

In the living room, she prayed again, asking the Lord to accomplish His will, and only His will in her life. "If it's not your will for me to find my spouse through an online dating site, then please help me to know and I will delete my profile. I just want to do your will."

She took a deep breath and stretched out on her couch. Just a year or two ago, she would not have cared what God's will was for her. But now, it was what she cared about the most. She wanted to please the Lord, but with all that was in her, she also wanted to get married. She hoped that was the Lord's will for her, too. But if it wasn't, she would have no choice but to submit to His will, and even though it would be very painful, she would stay single for the rest of her life if that was what the Lord wanted of her.

The thought was unsettling and tears swam in her eyes as she thought about staying single for the rest of her life. Her heart ached, but if that was God's will, then it was what you would do, no matter how hard it would be.

NINE

Audrey took Ken's hand as they got off the plane at Jorge Chávez International Airport in Lima. They both walked into the airport while Audrey's heart raced with excitement. She couldn't wait to see Sienna and the baby.

After they had both gone through customs, they strolled through the airport until they saw Sienna and Bryan. Audrey ran straight to Sienna, her arms wide open. They fell into each other's arms and Audrey hugged her sister tightly.

"It's so good to see you, Sienna," Audrey said. She drew back slightly from her sister and looked her over. "You look beautiful as usual."

Sienna smiled and caressed Audrey's cheeks. "You look great as well, Audrey."

Ken and Bryan shook hands and then hugged each other. Audrey was happy that both men genuinely liked each other. She hugged Bryan while Sienna hugged Ken. They left the airport together and got into Bryan's car after they had put their luggage into the trunk.

All the way to Bryan and Sienna's house, Audrey eagerly asked about baby Ethan, how he was doing, and how Sienna was coping as a new mom.

Sienna regaled her with stories about the baby's unique personality, which had already started to show. "He's usually a quiet baby and he hardly cries," Sienna said. "But when he does cry, it is as though the world is about to end. He bawls for such a long time. At first, whenever he started to cry, I was appalled and really fearful, but after some time, I began to understand from the different ways he cried what exactly he wanted."

Audrey beamed at Sienna. She looked and sounded like such a proud mom. And then, suddenly, without warning, her heart began to ache. She wanted what Sienna had: to be a proud mom of a beautiful baby. She glanced at Ken sitting in the passenger seat next to Bryan, and then focused once more on Sienna. Ken and Bryan were having a quiet conversation, and they weren't paying much attention to their wives.

Audrey forcefully pushed away the envy that had entered her heart and focused totally on what Sienna was saying to her. She genuinely laughed as Sienna told her about the unique way Ethan scrunched his whole face whenever he pooed. "I can't wait to see and hold him," Audrey said to Sienna.

"He is with our nanny, Veronica, now," Sienna said. "She's great."

Audrey glanced once more at Ken. If only he was listening and could hear the pride in Sienna's voice as she spoke about her son, and then see that even busy people could have babies and be hands-on parents as well. Just like Sienna and Bryan, they would have to hire a nanny, but a trustworthy one.

Bryan finally pulled up to a beautiful duplex, smaller than her and Ken's house in Rosefield, but definitely bigger than their apartment in Miami. The house was surrounded by a vast land covered with bright flowers of varying hues that made Audrey gasp in delight and brightened her slightly sad heart. She got down from the car and looked around her with wide eyes. "I love this place, Sienna. It's beautiful."

Sienna smiled and Bryan said, "Sienna also loved the plants more than anything else about this house. That was the main reason she wanted us to move in here when we were looking for a new house after the baby was born. I love it as well."

Ken's eyes went around the vast compound and he said, "It's such a lovely place, and the house is simple but beautiful."

Bryan brought out their luggage from the trunk of the car. He hefted Audrey's suitcase while Ken lifted his. The men carried both suitcases into the house while Audrey held Sienna's arm and grinned at her as they both entered the house together. The living room was furnished simply with tan and cream furnishings, but was brightened by multiple potted plants placed all around the space. Because of the plants, it was almost as bright as the outside of the house. It had a very homey and pleasing effect about it. "I love it, Sienna," Audrey said.

Sienna beamed and then said to Audrey and Ken, "Let's show you guys to your room." She put her arm around Audrey's waist and led the way, while Ken and Bryan followed behind with their luggage.

They climbed the stairs and stopped at the first door to the left. Sienna opened the door, and they all stepped into the room as Sienna said, "This is the room you and Ken will stay in for the duration of your stay here." She squealed, and said again, "I am so glad you guys are here! We will have so much fun together!"

Audrey looked around her. The room was bright and very airy. It was simply furnished with cream drapes and light brown wardrobes. An ornate mirror and dresser gave it a slightly more expensive look. But, again, what she loved most were the bright potted plants in the room. Just like the living room, the plants were everywhere.

"Okay, it's time to meet Ethan," Sienna said.

"Yay!" Audrey lifted her hands and smiled.

Sienna led them down the hallway and stopped at another door. Opening the door, she stepped into a brightly painted room with blue and white furnishings. She smiled at a woman who Audrey guessed was Veronica and then walked to the cot at the far end.

Audrey followed her.

Bending down, Sienna lifted the baby out of the cot and showed him to Audrey, her face beaming with pride.

Audrey eagerly held out her hands and took him. He was wide awake, and just as Sienna said, he made no sound except for small gurgling ones.

"Oh my goodness, he is gorgeous!" Audrey exclaimed. He was dressed in a light blue onesie, and he had chubby cheeks and platinum blond hair like his mom and dad. She took his tiny hand and kissed his fingers. Turning around, she showed him to Ken. "Isn't he absolutely beautiful?" she said to Ken. If only this beautiful baby boy would get him to reconsider his stubborn stance.

Ken beamed at the baby and ran his fingers through his hair. His eyes studied Ethan's face and then he looked at Bryan and said, "He has your nose, Bryan."

"But he looks more like Sienna," Bryan said. "Thank God for that."

Audrey chuckled and said, "Come on, Bryan! You know you're a pretty boy. Your son inheriting your features is a good thing."

Bryan laughed out loud and said, "Pretty boy? I don't know if I like that."

"It's a compliment," Audrey said, smiling.

Bryan nodded. "All right, then. I'll take it."

They stayed in the baby's room for some time, simply cooing at the tiny little boy and talking nonstop about him. After some time, they finally left the room, Audrey still holding him in her arms. She loved the feel and scent of him. He was so soft and cuddly, and he smelled heavenly. She kissed his chubby cheeks and said to Sienna, "I just can't stop smiling at him."

In the living room, she and Sienna sat closely together on the couch, while Bryan sat on the love-seat. Audrey caught Ken's eyes as he sat on the sofa facing her and Sienna, and smiled at him.

He smiled back, and she hoped he understood everything her smile said—that she loved him very much and couldn't wait to have a baby, like the one she was holding now, with him.

They all continued chatting, mostly about random things and then how they planned to spend the next month.

"Are you up to going to the orphanage with me now or do you want to rest and go tomorrow?" Sienna asked Audrey.

Audrey nodded eagerly. "Yeah. I slept a lot on the plane so I don't need to rest. I can't wait to see the orphanage."

Sienna looked at Ken and Bryan, and Bryan said, "Ken, will you go with them?"

Ken shook his head. "Unlike Audrey, I didn't sleep much on the plane. I will rest today, and then we all can go again tomorrow."

Audrey was reluctant to hand the baby over to Veronica. She just wanted to hold him forever, but that was impossible. When Veronica took Ethan away, Audrey grabbed her purse from the coffee table, kissed Ken on his cheek, and went out of the house with Sienna.

Getting into the car beside her sister, she buckled her seatbelt as Sienna drove away from the house and said, "Ethan is so precious." She sighed wistfully and looked out the window.

Sienna turned briefly to her and said, "Ken still

doesn't want to have a child now?" Her voice rang with sympathy.

"No," Audrey said in a voice choked with emotion. She did not turn around to look at Sienna. Her eyes had grown watery and she didn't want Sienna to see her crying. She watched the city through her tears as they sped down the road.

"Maybe this vacation will help convince Ken that you guys can take care of a baby," Sienna said. "I'll keep praying for you, Audrey. I hope Ken comes around soon."

Audrey sighed softly. "I hope he comes around soon, too. But I just can't keep waiting for when he does."

Sienna said, "But you don't really have a choice, do you?"

"No, I guess I don't," Audrey said, trying not to break down. She wiped the tears from her eyes and turned to look at Sienna. "At the rate we are going now, he might never come around, or it would be too late for me to have a child by the time he does. I remember what he said before we got married. He told me he would be ready to have a baby whenever I was. Now, he is reneging on what he said."

Sienna briefly faced her and touched her arm, and then focused on the road again. "I'm so sorry, Audrey. I didn't know it was so painful for you. Maybe I should get Bryan to talk to him?"

"I doubt it will do any good," Audrey said, sighing again.

Sienna didn't say anything more and they drove in silence the rest of the way.

Sienna finally pulled up in front of a building painted a bright yellow and Audrey got out of the car. She walked alongside Sienna as they made their way to another single-story building that Audrey guessed was the administrative block.

Sienna said to her, "I just want to see Mary, my assistant, briefly, and then we will go and see the children." She glanced at her wristwatch and said, "By this time, they will still be napping. But in about fifteen minutes, their siesta time will be over."

"Siesta time?" Audrey smiled. "I think after we leave this place it will be time for mine also."

Sienna chuckled. "I thought you said you slept a lot on the plane. You still need to take an afternoon nap?"

"Yes," Audrey replied. "Yes, I think I do."

They walked into the administrative block and went straight into an office where a petite woman with long dark curly hair stood looking at a shelf filled with books. She turned around as they came in and smiled brightly.

"Sienna! You are here!" The woman Audrey guessed was Mary exclaimed in Spanish. She looked at Audrey quizzically, and then turned to Sienna.

Sienna said in surprisingly good Spanish, with a tinge of an American accent, "This is my sister, Audrey. Audrey, this is Mary."

Audrey smiled and greeted the woman warmly.

Sienna sat on the sofa beside the desk. Audrey sat next to her and Mary sat behind her desk.

"Thank you so much for the recent donation you made to the orphanage, Sienna. It will go a long way in helping get more school supplies for the kids."

Sienna shook her head. "It's not exactly a donation, Mary. It's more like a responsibility; my responsibility. Remember, this orphanage was handed over to Bryan and me. I have just not had the time to be present as much as I want to." Sienna turned to Audrey and smiled, and then turned back to Mary. "Mary, my sister will be in Peru for a month before she has to go back to the United States. She'll take over the full running of the orphanage from you once you go."

Audrey's mouth dropped open and she stared at her sister. Sienna had never mentioned that to her.

All she had said was that Audrey would help out with the orphanage. This thing about running it was something she hadn't mentioned, and it made Audrey really nervous.

Audrey took Sienna's hand and whispered in English, "You never told me you wanted me to run the orphanage for you. I would have told you I couldn't if you had."

Sienna smiled and said, "It's just temporarily, Audrey. Until you go back to America."

"Even if it's temporary, I cannot run an orphanage. I have no experience running one and I think I don't have the ability, either."

Sienna smiled but said nothing.

Audrey whispered again, "We will talk about this once we get back to the house."

Sienna and Mary talked about the ins and outs of the day-to-day running of the orphanage while Audrey wondered what had gotten into Sienna to make her want to hand over the reins to her. Or maybe Sienna was just joking about her running the orphanage. There was no way she could do that. She looked at Sienna as she spoke with her assistant.

I think she was joking, Audrey told herself.

Through the window, Audrey saw more than two dozen kids pour out of the bright yellow building like waves of the ocean splashing onto the shore. She smiled as she watched them. They hopped, skipped, and chased each other around, laughing and playing like only kids can.

Sienna stood up and said, "The kids are out." She looked down at Audrey and said, "Well, Audrey, let's go and say hi to the kids now."

Audrey stood up and followed Sienna out of the office and out of the administrative building. Her heart beat faster and faster as they approached the children. She frowned. Maybe this wasn't such a good idea, coming to an orphanage. She was at odds with herself and with Ken about having children. Coming to a place full of kids was probably not the best idea for her. She nearly laughed harshly. And Sienna wanted her to run this place. Impossible.

Also, the fact that these children had no parents tore at her heart. She sighed and then struggled to put away her concerns and worries. It would do no good to go to the children looking like she had the care of the whole world on her shoulders. She put on a bright smile as they neared the kids.

Some of the children turned in her and Sienna's direction, and then raced toward them. Audrey's eyes widened, and then a huge genuine smile broke out on her face as the children hugged Sienna fiercely.

More of the children rushed toward Sienna and struggled to get their turns to hug her.

Audrey smiled at how well-loved Sienna was by the kids. She wasn't surprised, though. Sienna captured hearts wherever she went. She was such a sweetheart. That difficult time when she was consumed with that anxiety and panic attacks that had nearly cost her her life was one brief, dark blotch in her sunny life. Thankfully, the Lord had delivered her fully from it. As far as Audrey knew, she'd had no other episodes since the Lord had rescued her from it.

Audrey watched the children hop away and then she gasped and her heart almost stopped as a beautiful little girl with dark hair and eyes, who looked about six or seven, put her arms around her and hugged her after giving Sienna a huge hug.

Sienna bent down to the girl's level and smiled. She patted the girl's head as the little girl drew back from Audrey. "Audrey," Sienna said, "This is our Queen Esther. Esther, this is my oldest sister, Audrey."

Audrey bent down as well and beamed at the girl. "You are such a lovely girl, Esther. How old are you?"

Esther said with a smile, "I am seven." Audrey's eyes widened in surprise when she took her hand and said, "You are very pretty."

"She really likes you, Audrey," Sienna said. "She is usually shy around strangers, but she has immediately taken to you." She smiled at the girl. "Haven't you, Esther?"

Esther grinned but didn't reply.

Audrey straightened with her heart beating even faster. The little girl was so precious. Audrey's mouth dropped open in astonishment when Esther wove her little fingers through hers and said, "Will you be my mommy?"

TEN

For a long moment, Audrey couldn't speak. From the corner of her eye, she could see Sienna watching her with a smile. The little girl was looking at her expectantly, as though she had just asked Audrey to give her a piece of candy instead of something that had literally grabbed her heart. At last, she put on a smile and squeezed Esther's hand.

Esther stayed with Audrey for the rest of the time they were at the orphanage. She did not leave Audrey's side while Audrey and Sienna played with the other children, and even as they discussed the running of the orphanage and the cost of managing such a place.

Audrey avoided talking to Sienna about what Sienna had said to her concerning taking the reins of the orphanage. She didn't want to talk about it here because Esther was with them, her pretty brown eyes fixed solely on Audrey. Her hand was in Audrey's as they walked around the compound and into the buildings. Audrey was fascinated as they toured the hostels, the dining hall, and the auditorium where Sienna told her different events like the children's Christmas plays and shows took place. "We also have staff meetings here sometimes," Sienna said.

The last building they visited was the chapel. Sienna told her she'd had it built with her own money only recently.

Audrey was impressed with how dedicated Sienna was to the place and how much she had put into it. But throughout the tour, Audrey's heart had been partly on the little girl whose hand was in hers. Esther had said nothing throughout the time they toured the orphanage. From time to time, Audrey had glanced at the little girl and smiled at her, and her heart had flooded with joy as Esther smiled back.

Finally, about two hours after Audrey and Sienna arrived at the orphanage, they walked back to Sienna's car. Esther's hand was still in Audrey's, and the little girl skipped happily as they walked.

Sienna got into the driver's seat and then Audrey went around to the door of the passenger's seat. Audrey let go of the little girl's hand so she could enter the car. She looked down at Esther and smiled once again at her. This time, Esther did not smile back. Esther looked at the car, and then looked up at Audrey with sadness in her eyes.

Audrey stooped down to Esther's level. She felt like crying as she saw the tears in Esther's eyes. Audrey said, "I have to go now, Esther. But I promise I will come back tomorrow."

Esther cried, "Please, don't go!"

Her words tore at Audrey's heart. She reached out and pulled the little girl in a tight hug. She drew back again and in spite of the ache in her heart, beamed at Esther. She said again, "I promise you, Esther, I will be back tomorrow morning. You won't even notice that I left." She knew the words she'd just said weren't exactly the right thing to say, but she had no other words to console the girl with.

"Will you be my mommy, then?" Esther asked again, looking straight into Audrey's eyes.

Feeling like the girl was looking into her soul, Audrey shut her eyes as sadness overwhelmed her. The poor girl was desperate to have a mother. And for some reason, she wanted Audrey to be her mom.

Audrey opened her eyes to look at Esther again and her heart flooded with an unexplained aching affection for the girl. Suddenly, Audrey's heart began to tug at her as she looked at Esther. And then she knew without a doubt that she felt the same way the girl did. As impossible and strange as it was, since they had only met for the first time and she had not been planning to do anything like adopt a child, she too wanted to be Esther's mother. It was a feeling so strong she felt it in her soul. She felt love for the little girl overwhelming her. She hugged Esther again and promised once more that she would be back the next day.

She entered the car, shut the door, and then waved at the beautiful little girl.

Esther waved back eagerly.

Audrey kept waving to Esther until the girl disappeared from sight. She turned to Sienna as they drove down the road and said, "Wow! That was really strange!"

Sienna kept her eyes on the road and said, "What is it?"

Audrey pressed her lips together for a few seconds, trying to process what she had just felt. Was it the Lord that had put such a strong affection for Esther in her heart? She said softly, "As crazy as it sounds, I think I want to adopt Esther."

Sienna turned briefly to her and frowned, and then turned back to the road again. She chuckled. "You're joking, right? Is it because Esther said she wants you to be her mommy? From what I saw just now, I know Esther particularly likes you, but come on, Audrey..." Sienna did not finish her sentence and Audrey wondered what she wasn't saying. After a long moment, Sienna said again, "Are you really serious about what you just said, Audrey?"

Audrey looked out of the window and said, "I am extremely serious."

"But you were just talking about having a baby yesterday. Now you want to adopt a seven-year-old. I doubt Ken would agree to that. He's not open to having a baby with you. He would be even less open to adopting a seven-year-old girl. I want Esther to have a mom and dad, and you, I know, will be a great mother. But Ken will probably flip out if you tell him about this. And besides, are you sure it's what you want?"

Audrey sighed loudly. "Why does everyone doubt I can handle motherhood?"

"I have no doubt that you can handle it. I just said now that I know you will be a great mother. It's just that adoption is not a small matter. You have been thinking of having your own baby. How come you've changed your mind all of a sudden?"

Audrey looked at Sienna and said, "I haven't changed my mind about having a baby. And it's not so much about adopting a child as it is about adopting Esther. I don't know why, but I have simply fallen in love with that little girl."

Once again, Sienna said nothing for a long time. Audrey turned to look out the window again, her heart beating. Sienna was right. Ken wasn't open to having a baby with her; he would probably shut down any talk of adopting a child. But that would not stop her from bringing it up with him. Maybe when he came to the orphanage tomorrow and met Esther, he would feel the same way about her that she did. And if he didn't, she would not give up until he began to.

Sienna finally said, "You know what, Audrey? I think you should go ahead and follow your heart. I actually think it would be wonderful if you adopted Esther. I was just worried that you were making a hasty decision. But I think you are a very logical person — much more logical than I am — and you think things through. Granted, you haven't had the time to think this over, but when you do and you still decide you want to adopt Esther, I'll support you completely."

Audrey's eyes filled with tears of appreciation and she leaned in to kiss Sienna on the cheek. "Thank you, sis. I really appreciate that. At least someone believes in me and in my ability to be a good mother right now."

"Awww, you will be a great mother. And I think Ken also believes in your ability to be a great mother too; it's just that he doesn't think both of you are ready to be parents right now. Just as I told you earlier, I can ask Bryan to speak to him and let him see that you are really ready now."

Audrey thought about it for only a second and then said, "I don't think it will help any. And also, with my new desire to adopt Esther, I think it will be best if I spoke to him myself." She sighed loudly again and said, "I am not looking forward to speaking to him at all. Every time I have brought up the idea of starting a family now, it's always ended up with us fighting. I am afraid of what he'll say and what will happen when I bring up my desire to adopt a seven-year-old child. I hate our fights. Apart from the fight about Lauren before we got married, we have not had any fights at all until this whole thing about having a child. It's so exhausting."

"I'm really sorry," Sienna said. "That must really hurt. I know how I would feel if Bryan had said he didn't want a child with me when I wanted to start trying. But, please remember that Ken loves you. Maybe there's a good reason why he doesn't want to have a child now that goes beyond his concerns that both of you will not be able to dedicate enough time to the child."

Audrey couldn't imagine what reason Ken could

possibly have and shrugged. "Maybe there is," she said.

They changed the subject and talked about Rosefield. "I miss Rosefield so much," Sienna said.

"I understand that. I miss it too when Ken and I are in Miami."

"I hope I don't decide to go back with you when you and Ken are ready to leave Peru." She sighed. "That day will be difficult for me."

Audrey chuckled. "We have only just arrived, Sienna, and you are already thinking about the day we leave. Let's just live in the moment and enjoy the time we have."

Sienna smiled. "You are right."

When they got to Sienna and Bryan's, Audrey went into the house feeling nervous.

I wonder what tonight will be like, she wondered to herself. Would Ken end up sleeping on Sienna and Bryan's couch after they had a huge fight, or would they be wrapped up in each other's arms in bed, unable to wait until the next day so they would see Esther and start the process of adopting her? Audrey knew it was a tall order to actually expect Ken to immediately agree to the adoption. It was more likely that the former would be the case for them.

Ken walked up to her and kissed her immediately when she stepped into the living room. Sienna and Bryan went out of the living room, hand in hand. Audrey could hear the faint sound of the baby crying. Her heart raced as she looked into Ken's eyes. She had to tell him now or she would lose her courage.

He smiled curiously at her and said, "Why are you looking at me like that? What's on your mind, Audrey?"

"I have something very important to talk to you about."

Ken sighed deeply and, with weariness in his

voice, said, "Please don't tell me it's about having a baby again. I thought we promised not to talk about it for this month that we are on our vacation."

Audrey said, "It's not really about that."

Ken stared quizzically at her, but said nothing.

Audrey took his hand and said, "I think it would be best to talk about it in the privacy of the bedroom."

Ken lifted his brows and stared incredulously at her. "You are expecting a fight, then. That means this discussion is serious and will not end very well." He groaned. "Must we talk about it right now? Can't we wait until our vacation is over to talk about whatever it is?"

Audrey shook her head and wove her fingers through his. She led him to the guest bedroom where they would be staying for the month. She sat down on the bed and smiled nervously at him as he sat beside her.

He looked her straight in the eye and asked, "So, what do you want us to talk about, Audrey?"

Audrey took a deep breath, and then went ahead without wasting any more time. "When Sienna and I went to the orphanage today, a little girl called Esther ran up to us with the other children. But immediately when I saw her, I knew there was something special about her. When Esther threaded her fingers through mine and told me she wanted me to be her mommy, there was something that took hold of my heart."

Audrey looked up as the memory of that moment flooded her mind. She looked at Ken again. He had an astonished look on his face. "It wasn't just her words or the look in her eyes that got to me. It was something deep inside of me. I just knew in my heart that I loved this girl."

Audrey paused for a second to gather her thoughts and then went on. "When we were leaving, she looked so sad and begged me not to go. I knew then that I didn't want to leave her and I wanted her to be mine." Audrey took a deep breath again and looked into Ken's eyes. She said, "I knew with my whole heart that I wanted to be her mother." She smiled softly. "I want to adopt Esther, Ken... No, I want us to adopt Esther."

Ken's eyes bulged and there was a throbbing vein in his neck. He shot up from the bed as though his body were on fire. "You cannot be serious, Audrey!" he exclaimed, staring at her. "What are you thinking? Please tell me you're kidding."

Ken's reaction had been expected, but still, Audrey felt a mix of emotions in her heart as he stared down at her with a look of outrage. She felt fear and anger. Once again, she took a deep breath in order to still her emotions and said, "I am very serious, Ken. With everything in me, I want Esther. I want us to adopt her."

Ken shook his head slowly and then gave a harsh laugh. He continued to stare down at Audrey for a long moment and began to pace the room. He finally stopped in front of Audrey again and said, "What has gotten into you, Audrey? For a while now, you have been talking almost non-stop about us having a baby, and now you've switched to wanting to adopt a child. Are you serious?"

Audrey folded her arms across her chest and said, "I still want to have a child with you... but I want to adopt Esther as well. Besides, you don't want a baby now because you say we will not have time to take care of a newborn. Esther is seven; definitely not a baby. She will not need the amount of attention that a small baby will."

"Audrey, please listen to yourself. You went to an orphanage and saw a child for the first time, and all of a sudden you want to adopt her. What's wrong with you?"

Audrey felt anger burning in her mind and threatening to spill out of her mouth, and she pushed it down. Getting mad at this time would only make things worse. "Ken, I know what I have just told you seems like it's coming out of the blue. But just come to the orphanage tomorrow and see Esther. I think after you have seen and talked to her, you will probably feel the same way I do."

"I certainly won't!"

Audrey cried, "You won't come to the orphanage tomorrow?"

"I promised Bryan I would come," Ken said. "But I will not feel the same way that you do about some little girl I meet for the first time. In fact, I am not going to meet her tomorrow. There is no way we are adopting a child. I told you we will have a baby, but not right now. But as for adoption, I have no interest in doing that. No interest at all."

Audrey frowned deeply. Why was Ken being so obstinate? "Please, Ken," she pleaded. "Please, just . . ."

Ken cut her off. "Please, Audrey! Stop it! We are not adopting a child!" He turned away from her and abruptly walked out of the bedroom.

For long time, she stood looking after Ken. She felt dread, not because she and Ken just had a fight, but because she was afraid of missing out on the opportunity to become Esther's mother. If she couldn't convince Ken about the adoption by the time they left in a month, she probably would never be able to convince him, and they would end up not adopting Esther.

The thought did not sit well with her at all, and she fell to her knees. She did the only thing she knew to do right now. She lifted up her voice and began to pray that the Lord would touch Ken's heart so he would agree to meet Esther tomorrow, and that when he did meet her, he would feel the same way she did, or at least be open to the idea of adopting her.

Since they'd started talking about having a baby, this had been her one and only prayer—that God would touch Ken's heart. Nowadays, she was constantly asking the Lord to touch his heart. Why was Ken so stubborn, anyway? Why couldn't he see things the way she did?

She stood up from her knees and sat on the bed again. All she could do now was hope and pray and believe that her hunch was right—that once Ken met and spoke to Esther tomorrow, he would fall in love with the child just as deeply as she had.

ELEVEN

Leila came out of the taxi with her suitcase and stared at the very familiar Nira market. This time, unlike the other times when she had come to Nira, it wasn't daytime. Darkness was approaching. She glanced at the watch on her wrist, a gold wristwatch that Dauda had bought for her before she left and insisted she wear. The time was almost seven p.m.

The time she'd arrived here wasn't the only thing that was different. She had taken a taxi from the airport in Bamako all the way here. It had cost an arm and a leg, but she had the money to hire the taxi solely for herself. She'd told the driver to drop her near the market, as she did not want to be driven to Malik's house so she could avoid alerting anyone of her arrival. She'd arrived at almost the time she wanted. Soon, it would be dark and the darkness would act as her protection. Then she would, by God's grace, sneak into the community and go to Malik's without Karim Keita or any of his men seeing her; at least she hoped so.

She glanced at her gold wristwatch again and then frowned at herself. She was wearing an expensive sapphire gown—a gift from Dauda, just like the wristwatch. It occurred to her that what she was wearing now, how she looked, might be startling to Malik when he saw her. She had been dressed very simply when they'd met. In cheap clothes, actually. Now, she looked totally different; like a rich man's wife. Maybe she should not have put on all these things. She removed the wristwatch, put it in her designer purse, and then sighed wearily. Maybe there was no way to hide the wealth that she had on.

She looked this way and that, and then crossed the road. Going straight to the hut where she had waited out the daytime, she stood this time, looking out the window. In just a few minutes, it would be totally dark outside. She could then go out and not be noticed until she got to Malik's house.

Fifteen minutes later, she came out of the hut, brought out her phone from her purse, and switched it on. Using the light from her phone as a flashlight, she slowly made her way through the short path she had taken to Malik's the last time she was here.

She pressed her lips tightly together as she remembered the events that happened the last time she came here. The path that she took now led to the back of Malik's house. She had been tapping on his window, trying to figure out if he was home when she'd been apprehended by Karim Keita's men. Everything had happened so quickly after that. Everything she had feared had happened to her. Malik's father had thrown her into that awful shack and had deceived her into giving Zainah up. After that, she and Zainah had been married, or rather, taken away by their husbands. Zainah had managed, through Faizan's help, to escape her husband's grasp and get her marriage dissolved. But it had taken her being shot for that to happen.

Leila sighed. She, on the other hand, had not been that lucky in terms of being reunited with the love of her life and escaping the awful marriage. She'd been bundled away by Dauda to Saudi Arabia. But

God had been faithful. Dauda had never touched her like she'd feared, and he had turned out to be kinder than she'd expected. Now, she was free to find Malik and Dauda had promised to come to Nira to have the marriage dissolved as soon as he could. God had been truly gracious to her. Now, her one prayer was that she and Malik would be reunited.

Lord, please let him be at home.

She continued to walk on the cleared path, seeing only a few people who paid her no mind. She got to the back of Malik's house minutes later, and just as she did the last time, she gently tapped on his window. Her hands were clammy with fear and anticipation. She told herself she had no need to be afraid. It wasn't like Karim Keita could force her to be married to Dauda anymore when Dauda had agreed to dissolve their marriage. However, Malik and Zainah's father was unpredictable. It would be just like him to have another friend in the wings that he wanted to marry her off to.

She told herself to stop being ridiculous. She was pretty sure Karim did not know that she wasn't married to Dauda anymore. It was unlikely that he would hurt her in any way knowing that she was Dauda's wife. She had no need to be afraid, at least for now. If he found out that she was in Nira and asked why she was here, she would tell him that she had Dauda's full permission to visit her friends here. And that would be true.

She frowned when no one came to the window. Tapping on the window again, she waited once more, her heart racing with anxiety. After another minute, when there was still no answer, she guessed that Malik was not in Nira.

And why did you expect him to be here anyway?

She had blindly come here, hoping against hope that Malik would be here. She had naively held on to the hope that God would cause him to be here when she arrived. If the Lord had miraculously made a way for her to leave Saudi Arabia and had provided everything she needed to come, she'd believed He would also keep Malik here and would give them a beautiful reunion. But, apparently, she had been wrong. She should have known that he would not be in Nira. He spent more time on that farm in God-knew-where than he did in Nira now.

Dread gripped her. Maybe Khadija would know where that farm was. Since Leila didn't know where the farm was located, she had to risk being found out by Karim and go to his house to see if she would find Khadija.

And you think Karim Keita will not see you when knock on his front door?

She shuddered at the thought. But she had no choice. She had to go to the house to find Khadija. Karim would probably see her, but she was already married to Dauda. He wouldn't dare hurt her.

With her heart racing, Leila made her way to the only house that, as usual, had light. The security lights in front of the house were on, clearly illuminating the building. The sound of the generator reverberated in the air as she approached the house. She got to the front gate, knocked on it, and then waited.

Oh Lord, please help me.

The gate swung open and a teenage boy Leila recognized as Zainah's younger brother peered at her. He blinked rapidly in obvious surprise and said, "Are you here to see Khadija?"

"Yes," Leila answered, smiling.

The boy said, "Umm, I am not sure if I should open the door for you. I don't know what my father . . ."

Someone's voice interrupted him. A male voice that Leila would know anywhere. Karim Keita's. Her heart sank to her feet.

"Who is it?" Karim Keita's voice boomed out.

Zainah's brother did not answer and Leila contemplated running away. But she chided herself for her lack of courage and stood her ground.

Remember, he can't hurt you, she thought to herself.

Karim appeared at the door and his eyes widened in shock. He quickly recovered and put on a small smile for Leila. "Well, what a surprise to see you in Nira, Leila. How come you are here? You should be in Saudi Arabia now with your husband."

Leila looked at the man who had been the cause of much of the sorrow in her life over the past months. Anger burned in her and she glowered at him, loathing him. She felt like telling him that Dauda had agreed to dissolve their marriage just to spite him and show him that his plans to imprison her for whatever reason had not worked, but she changed her mind. It would not work in her favor if she told him that. Instead, she said to him, "I am here with the full permission of Dauda. Do you think I ran away? You can call him if you want to."

Karim frowned and said, "I don't think you could run away from that man. And really, it's no business of mine anymore if you ran away or not."

Leila scowled at him, wondering where he was going with what he'd just said. She put her concerns aside and asked, "Please, where is Khadija? I would like to see her."

She scolded herself. Like he's going to tell you where Khadija is. He was probably even now wondering what he would do with her and hating the fact that he couldn't really hurt her anymore. How would she talk to Khadija now and find out where Malik was? If she couldn't speak to Khadija, she might never discover where Malik was and be reunited with him.

"Sekou, go and call your sister!" Karim ordered his son.

Leila's mouth fell open for a few seconds. She

had not expected that. All she had expected from Karim Keita was antagonism. She shut her mouth again and then waited, her eyes averted from his.

Before long, she heard footsteps again, and turned. Khadija was staring at her with an expression of shock, just as her father had earlier. "You are here, Leila!" Khadija exclaimed. She reached out and hugged Leila tightly.

Leila held the girl close for a while and then drew back again. She looked nervously at Karim and then focused on Khadija again. She whispered to Khadija, "Do you know where Malik is now?"

Khadija said, "He is at my father's farm in Dogon."

"I thought as much," Leila said to herself. She rubbed her forehead and, again in a whisper, asked, "Have you found out where Dogon is?"

Khadija shook her head and then to Leila's chagrin, she asked her father where exactly Dogon was and where in Dogon the farm was located.

"If you go to the bus station near the market," Karim said, looking at Leila, "there are buses going to Dogon. Though just one or two a day. You have to go to the bus station early in the morning or you might not find a bus until evening. Dogon is a very small village. Once you get there, just ask where Karim Keita's farm is, and you will be directed there quickly."

Leila's mouth dropped open once more and she stared at Karim. How come he had so willingly and quickly offered up all the information that she wanted? Did he want something again? From what she knew about him, he never did anything good without something bad coming after it.

She wanted to ask him why he was being so nice to her but she changed her mind. What she wanted to do now was go to the bus station and get to Karim's farm in Dogon as quickly as possible. She hugged Khadija and then hesitantly thanked Karim for his help.

Karim said, "You are welcome."

It took everything in Leila not to smirk. When he added, "Greet Malik for me when you see him," she resisted the urge to glower at him. She said to Khadija, "I will start going to the bus station now. I hope I find a bus to take me to Dogon."

Karim shook his head, and said, "No, you won't find a bus tonight. The night bus leaves at about six o'clock."

Leila's heart sank once more. What am I going to do now? The only thing she could do was to plead with Karim to let her stay in Malik's house until she could leave for the farm tomorrow morning. She tried to ask him about it, but the words refused to form in her mouth. She just couldn't bring herself to ask him anything. Instantly, she decided to go to the hut where she'd waited out the daytime and spend the night there. Surely, she would be safe in this small community. But she wasn't so sure.

Khadija said, "Please stay with us in the house tonight and then tomorrow you can leave for Dogon."

Leila shook her head and said, "No, I can't. It's okay. I'll find somewhere to spend the night."

"Don't be silly," Karim said to her. "You can stay in the house tonight and then leave for the farm tomorrow."

For the third time today, Leila's mouth fell open as she stared at Karim. He was being way too nice to her. He probably had something up his sleeve. She didn't feel comfortable at all with the idea of staying in his house. She would feel like a sheep in a den of wolves—the wolves being Karim and his men.

Khadija said, "Please, Leila. Please stay here with us."

Leila could not fathom the idea of spending the night in Karim's house. She mustered up some courage and said to Karim, "Instead, can I stay in Malik's house?" Surely, Karim still had the key to the house.

Karim shrugged. "Suit yourself," he said. He turned around and began to walk away, and then turned and said, "Khadija, get the key to your brother's house in my room and give it to Leila." He went into the main house and Khadija followed him in.

Leila stared after them in astonishment. Karim had agreed to all her requests. First, he had told her where exactly Malik was, and now he had agreed to let her stay in Malik's house. What was up with that?

Khadija came out of the house a minute later with the key to Malik's. Instead of handing it to her, she began to walk toward Malik's house with hasty steps, forcing Leila to hurry to catch up with her while she rolled her suitcase behind her.

Khadija slowed her steps and then turned to Leila. "I haven't gotten the chance to tell you how sorry I am for what happened to you the last time you were here," Khadija said. "It was all my fault that you were married off to Dauda. Please, please forgive me."

"There's nothing to forgive, Khadija," Leila said. "Karim threatened you and made you do it. You had no choice."

Khadija sighed. "I should not have given in to his threats. I'm truly sorry."

Leila said, "Really, it's okay." She put her arm around Khadija's shoulders and hugged the girl to show her she bore no grudge.

They walked together with Leila's arm around Khadija until they got to Malik's house. Khadija opened the front door and Leila walked into the house. It was dark since it wasn't connected to the generator in Karim's house, and it smelled slightly stale and musty.

"Let me go and get some candles," Khadija said and hurried away. She came back again with candles and matchsticks a minute later. She lit the candles, flooding the living room with light.

Leila turned to Khadija and asked, "When was the last time Malik came to Nira?"

"More than three weeks ago. He was actually supposed to come back yesterday, but we got a message that the farm had a serious fire and so Malik had to stay because of that. You should have seen my father this morning. He was raging and then sulking at the same time. This evening, he suddenly became himself again."

So Malik could have been in Nira if not for the fire. Maybe the fire was why Karim had been so nice to her. Maybe it had mellowed him. She couldn't hold back her curiosity anymore, and asked, "Why was your father suddenly so nice to me?"

Khadija sighed and said, "It's actually a long story. I don't know if anyone told you about it, but it concerns Zainah."

Leila lifted her brows and asked, "Was it about Zainah's shooting?"

Khadija looked surprised. "You found out about that?"

"Dauda's senior wife told me about it. She also told me Zainah was all right and that she married her Faizan later on." Suddenly, Leila felt fear grip her. Or was everything that had been told her a lie? Just so she wouldn't insist on seeing Zainah if something had happened to her friend. Was Zainah even alive? She began to freak out and chided herself again. "Is it true what was told to me?" Leila asked. "Is Zainah okay?"

Khadija nodded. "It's all true. Zainah is happily married to Faizan. Unfortunately, I didn't go to the wedding. She wouldn't even tell me where it was. I don't know where Zainah is right now." She looked up thoughtfully and said more to herself than to Leila, "He promised to come get me."

Leila frowned. "Who?"

Khadija shook her head and smiled. "No one.

Anyway, Zainah is fine."

Leila put her hand on her chest and sighed in relief. "Thank God. I tried calling Zainah's old number but it didn't ring at all. Anyway, what were you going to tell me about why your father was nice to me? You said it concerns Zainah?"

"Yes," Khadija said. She sat down on Malik's couch and Leila sat next to her. She began to recount everything that had happened; how Faizan had come to rescue Zainah from Jibril's house, how one of Jibril's bodyguards had mistakenly shot Zainah, and how she had been rushed to the hospital. "We were so scared that she would die," Khadija said. "The doctor said that her recovery was a miracle."

Khadija went on to talk about how her father had been terribly shaken by everything that happened that night, and how remorseful he became. Jibril was afraid that since Faizan had connections to the American government, the Americans would come after him somehow. He didn't waste time dissolving his marriage to Zainah and he told my father that he would not be doing any business with him anymore.

"Father regretted ever giving Zainah to Jibril when it had nearly cost her her life." She thinned her lips and then said, "Did you know that he gave you and Zainah away to Jibril and Dauda because he owed them money? After Zainah left Nira with Faizan, Jibril promised to deal with my father." She looked around the room as though there was someone else listening in on their conversation. "There are rumors that it was Jibril who sent people to burn down Father's farm." She sighed. "I think that's why my father was nice to you now. He regrets everything he did, especially since the brothers reneged on their promise not to take revenge on him after everything went south. Zainah's shooting got to him, though."

Leila shook her head in surprise. "So your father gave me and Zainah away to Dauda and Jibril simply because he owed the men money. How wicked. Zainah was lucky Faizan rescued her. Unfortunately, I had to leave with my so-called husband to another country." She nearly said the fire at the farm served Karim right, but she knew it wasn't only Karim who would be affected by the effects of the fire. Malik and even Khadija would be, too.

Khadija asked curiously, "So, how come you're here, Leila? Did you run away? And if so, how?"

"It's another long story," Leila said to her. "But in short, Dauda let me go and even agreed to dissolve our marriage."

"Oh, Leila, that's good news!" Khadija exclaimed. "Now, you and Malik can really be together!"

"Yes,' Leila said excitedly. "That's why I am here now. And I'm so glad that Zainah is totally all right. She is probably living with Faizan in America now. After I find Malik, I will go back to the women's community where I and Zainah lived for a long time and see if anyone knows how she can be contacted."

Khadija nodded. "You are right. She is most likely in America since that is where Faizan lives."

"I need to at least talk to her," Leila said.

"I wish I could go see her in America," Khadija smiled sadly.

Leila and Khadija talked well into the night, and then Khadija stood up. "It's almost midnight. I have to get home."

Leila stood up as well and hugged the girl. "Will you come and see me off tomorrow morning?" she asked.

Khadija nodded eagerly, and said, "I will."

After Khadija had left, Leila went into Malik's room and stretched out on the floor beside the bed as she had done the last time she was here. She still didn't feel comfortable sleeping in his bed. And now more so than the last time she'd stayed in his house.

She couldn't help but smile as she lay on the floor. The Lord had been so good to her these last few weeks. Everything seemed to be falling into place. Soon, she would be reunited with Malik. She couldn't wait.

"Thank you, Lord," she breathed, and then shut her eyes. Soon, she drifted off to sleep.

TWELVE

Leila woke up early the next day, brushed her teeth, and quickly showered. She changed into a light green shift dress and braided her hair. She rolled her suitcase to the living room, glanced around her, and then went out the door. She locked Malik's house and then smiled when she saw Khadija walking toward her, wearing a brown kaftan and matching trousers with a big smile on her face. She reached Leila quickly.

"You're already ready to go?" Khadija asked.

"Yes," Leila nodded and handed Khadija the key to Malik's house.

Khadija took it and put it into the pocket of her trousers. She turned to Leila and took Leila's suitcase from her before Leila could protest.

Leila walked to the bus station with Khadija in silence. She was surprised that Khadija stayed with her while she bought a bus ticket to Dogon. She sat on a bench outside the station building, waiting for the other passengers to finish buying their tickets so they could board the bus. Khadija sat next to her.

They chatted about many random things while Leila waited. Soon, Khadija began to speak to her some more about the rumors concerning the identity of the man behind the burning of her father's farm. "It's actually not really a rumor," Khadija said. "Even though Jibril hasn't said anything, everyone knows he was the one behind it. Before my father gave you and Zainah away to be married to the brothers, Jibril did threaten to burn down his farm."

"That is brutal!" Leila said, shaking her head.

"My father should have known better than to be involved with such an evil man."

"It's so weird how different his brother is," Leila said, remembering how understanding and mild mannered Dauda was. He had told her that if not for his brother, he would never have gone along with the forced marriage.

Khadija shook her head. She started to apologize again for her role in Leila's forced marriage to Dauda, but Leila stopped her. "Please, Khadija. Don't apologize to me anymore."

Khadija said nothing after that.

A man standing beside a big bus began to yell, "All those going to Dogon, get on this bus now!"

Leila stood up and Khadija stood with her. She smiled at her young friend and hugged her.

"When will you come back to Nira?" Khadija asked.

"I'm not sure," Leila answered. "If Malik is ready to come back immediately, I might come back with him . . . just to see you again. However, if he isn't, I will go back to the women's camp as I cannot live with Malik in Dogon... or here, either."

"Why not?" Khadija cried.

Leila pursed her lips and then said, "Because we are not married, Khadija."

"Oh, I understand," was all Khadija said.

Leila nodded. From the look on her face, she wasn't sure if Khadija really understood or not.

Khadija's eyes searched Leila's. "Please come

back and visit me soon," she said.

"I will try," Leila said. She hugged Khadija once more, not knowing when next she would see the girl. By the grace of God, it would be soon. Even if Malik was not ready to come to Nira right now, hopefully Dauda would come here soon to dissolve their marriage. She had to come back to Nira when he was ready to do so. She smiled at Khadija and then walked to the bus, pulling her suitcase behind her. She watched as the driver placed her suitcase in the trunk of the bus with the other passengers' bags. After that, she turned to wave at Khadija and got on the bus.

Sitting at the back, she stared out of the window while the other passengers boarded. The bus soon started to move out of the station and Leila took a deep breath. Waves of excitement went through her. She had been told that the journey to Dogon was a three-hour drive, so they would be there before noon.

Before long, I will get to see Malik, she thought. Thinking about it left her breathless with anticipation. Of course, she had to be careful with him when it came to physical contact as she was still a married woman. That dampened her anticipation slightly. She still had to wait for Dauda to keep his word.

She brought out her phone from her purse and opened her Bible app. She had learned how to download apps days after Dauda had bought her the phone and the Bible app had been her first download. She thought about how crazy it was that, just a year ago, she'd known nothing about apps or any type of technology, really. The women's camp totally isolated everyone there, which was a good thing in a way and slightly bad in another.

She read the Bible as the bus sped down the road. After a while, she started to read a novel that came with the phone. She had never bothered to read it until now. Minutes later, she stopped reading as the novel did not appeal to her. She stared out the window and watched the other cars moving down the road and watched the buildings that she had never seen before.

When the bus stopped at a traffic jam, she bought some snacks and drinks from some street hawkers who also sold their food to all the passengers in the bus. After eating the snacks and drinking the juice, which tasted more like sugar water than fruit, she leaned her back against her seat and shut her eyes briefly.

She woke up with a start and rubbed her eyes. She had dozed off unknowingly. She looked out the window again just as the bus pulled into a bus station that was far less busy than the one in Nira. When the bus stopped, she disembarked from it with the other passengers and then carried her luggage out of the trunk.

She took a few steps forward and then stopped to look around her. Karim Keita had told her to ask anyone for the location of his farm. Hopefully, the man was right and everyone knew where the farm was. She asked one of her fellow passengers, a woman who had sat in front of her on the bus if she knew where Karim Keita's farm was.

The woman shook her head and told Leila she didn't know. "I am just a visitor here," the woman said.

Leila looked around her. She saw a teenage girl of about seventeen years sitting in front of the bus station, a table with a spread of cheap candies in front of her. She went and asked the girl if she knew where Karim Keita's farm was.

"Yes, I do," the girl said. "It's not far from here." The girl peered at Leila. "You are a stranger here. I heard the farm caught fire about two days ago. I haven't been there myself but I saw the smoke all the way from my house."

Leila nodded impatiently. She just wished the girl would direct to the farm so she could be on her way. Finally, when Leila continued looking inquisitively at the girl, she gave Leila specific directions to the location of the farm.

Leila thanked her and made her way out of the bus station. She followed the directions the girl had given her, walking with determined steps until she got to the farm.

She stood staring with her mouth open at the sight before her. There was still some smoke in the air and the land in front of her, acres and acres of it, was nothing but ashes. If Jibril had truly done this, he was wicked beyond words. Her heart flooded with sympathy for the men who worked on the farm and especially for Malik. He would have been devastated when the farm started. What kind of mood would she meet him in? Hopefully, she would be able to take the edge off the pain this must cause him.

She noticed the huts that surrounded the farm. Malik lived in one of those huts. She saw a man who looked slightly lost and dressed in an off-white khaki shirt and trousers and asked him which of the huts was Malik's.

At first, he stared at her without answering, and then he said, "Malik? He lives in the brick house behind those huts there." He pointed at a row of huts, and she could make out, though barely, a zinc roof behind them.

Leila thanked him and he moved on, staggering as though he carried the whole world on his shoulders.

She reached the row of huts and walked between two of them. She found Malik's house—a tiny, unpainted building with a wooden door. It was definitely bigger than the huts, but still, it looked so small to her. As she walked to the door, she thought about how completely different from Dauda's the house was. Dauda lived in a mansion, while Malik lived here, in this tiny house. Granted, he had a better house in Nira, but compared to Dauda's, that house might as well be a hut.

She smiled as she reached the door. None of that meant anything to her, though. She would live with him in his house anytime compared with staying married to Dauda and living in his mansion. All she cared about was that they could now get married and finally be together.

However, there were two things that stood in the way of their complete happiness and their future as husband and wife. One was Dauda. He had to come to Nira and dissolve the marriage as soon as possible. The other was something more complex, but which she hoped would be resolved soon. Malik was still a Muslim, as far as she knew. She could never marry him unless he shared her faith. Hopefully, that would be resolved soon.

She took a deep breath and then knocked on the door. Tapping her feet as she waited for him to open the door, she looked around her. She was puzzled when she saw some men standing in front of one of the huts, gaping at her. When Malik did not answer the door after a while, she frowned and knocked again. She waited for some time and still no one came to the door.

He has probably gone somewhere. But where?

Three of the men who had been gaping at her began to walk toward her. They were dressed similarly like the strange man she had met earlier. She felt slightly uncomfortable at the way they were looking at her and she felt like fleeing. However, she stood her ground and stared back at them with all the boldness she could muster. They reached her, but before they could say anything, she asked, "Do you men know where Malik Keita is?"

"Wow!" One of them said with a glint in his eye. "Imagine! Such a beauty sent here just for us!"

She blinked as she looked at the men. They were actually leering at her. Their eyes clearly glittered with lust and evil intentions. She stepped back slightly, looked around her, and considered crying out for help. If they moved one step closer to her, she would. However, whether she would find help in this place was another thing. Hopefully Malik was around somewhere and would come to her rescue.

But what if he isn't around here?

Her heart raced wildly at the thought that Malik was not at the farm and that she was at the mercy of these wicked men.

The men were still looking lustfully at her. They stepped closer to her and she shut her eyes briefly. Lord Jesus, please help me. She opened her eyes again and then screamed.

That stopped them in their tracks for a few seconds as their eyes widened. And then, one of them grinned wickedly and grabbed her arm. She opened her mouth to scream again and another immediately covered her mouth.

Fear took hold of her and she prayed earnestly in her heart for deliverance. They dragged her toward a bush close by, and she started to hyperventilate and pray at the same. And then a loud voice boomed from behind, "What are you all doing? Leave her alone right now!"

Leila's heart soared as she recognized Malik's voice. And then it sank again as the men turned and laughed.

What if they also hurt him? He was alone while there were three of them.

"What are you going to do if we don't let her go?" One of the men said. "You are not our boss anymore. As you can see, this whole place has been burned to the ground." He chuckled. "We need some comforting and she will do."

Leila pressed her lips tightly together as Malik

said in a voice that was completely calm and belied the dangerous situation they were in, "Maybe you all want to never work again; because I will tell my father about this. If you don't let her go right now, you will all regret the day you were born. Maybe you would like my father's men to show you what being uncomfortable truly means. You know how brutal they can be."

The men who were holding her arms immediately stepped away and the one who had covered her mouth smiled. "We were just playing around with her. We meant no harm." He turned to the others and said to them, "Did we?"

They all chorused that they didn't mean Leila any harm and apologized profusely to Malik.

He shook his head and said, "She is the one you wicked men need to apologize to, not me."

The men turned to Leila and told her they were sorry.

She stared at them in disgust and turned away. They weren't sorry. They had meant to rape her, but the Lord had delivered her.

Malik barked, "And don't you ever come near this house again! If you so much as look at my house or this woman again, you will wish you had been born without eyes. Now go!" he ordered.

They scampered away and Leila finally turned to fully face him, her heart flooding with relief and overwhelming love for him. He still looked the same as the last time she'd seen him, though he seemed slightly world-weary. He did not look at her until the men had all gone far away.

He finally turned his gaze toward her and the look on his face made her pulse race. He walked up slowly to her, swiftly took her hand, and led her into the hut. He shut the door and immediately drew her into his arms. She trembled in anticipation as she held him tightly and lifted her head for his kiss. And then she gasped as he abruptly drew back from her.

Disappointment flooded her mind as he turned away. "What is it, Malik?" she cried.

He turned to her with an expression of deep longing on his face that made her head swim. "You shouldn't be here, Leila," he said hoarsely. "You are a married woman, remember?"

She thinned her lips. She had forgotten about that in her joy of seeing him and finally being with him. She sighed loudly and said, "I remember... now that you remind me." She looked at him in dismay and asked, "Aren't you happy to see me?" Fear gripped her. What if he had fallen out of love with her?

He shook his head slowly. "This place is dangerous for a woman like you, Leila." He turned away and moved to the end of the hut.

She drew closer to him and said incredulously, "What do you mean, a woman like me?"

"A beautiful woman like you." He looked her over. "And clearly wealthy. Does your husband know that you are here?" he asked, looking away from her again.

This wasn't the reception she had expected. She didn't understand his reticence. "He knows, Malik. That was why I came. To tell you my husband has agreed to dissolve our marriage." She said with desperation, "We can finally be together, Malik!"

He turned to look at her, his eyes wide with astonishment. "Your husband wants to dissolve the marriage?"

She nodded. "That means we can be together." She gasped when he reached her as fast as lightning and swept her into his arms. She laughed as he hugged her tightly. He drew back slightly and gently tucked a strand of her hair behind her ear. He stared into her eyes and then his gaze focused on her lips. Her heart began to race again. He was going to kiss her, and from the way he was looking at her, it would be a smoldering kiss. She wanted to kiss him with all her heart, however, she pulled back from him. Just like he said earlier, she was still married. Until she no longer was, they couldn't kiss. She looked down at his arm around her body. And she certainly shouldn't be held by him like this.

She reluctantly extricated herself from him and sighed ruefully. "Until Dauda comes to Nira and gets our marriage dissolved, we can't kiss or hold each other," she said to him in a small voice.

He looked at her for a long moment, his eyes moving over her body, causing her face to grow hot, and then he nodded. "I know that," he said. "I just wanted to forget a minute ago when I almost kissed you." He smiled sadly at her. "Are you sure it was a good idea for you to come here?"

"Maybe not, but I just had to see you."

This time he gave her a bright smile. "I am glad you came." They both sat on the single couch in the place and he looked at her again. "Talking rather than staring hungrily at each other will help us cool down," he said. "Tell me everything that happened and how come Dauda decided to dissolve your marriage."

She smiled and said, "He decided to do that at my request."

She told him everything, from the time she and Zainah were brought out to Dauda and Jibril as brides, to when she finally left Saudi Arabia and came here. She finished and fought the urge to take his hand in hers.

"I knew my father was wicked, but I didn't know the depths of his wickedness. He showed you that picture of me tied up." He told her what happened the day he was suddenly bundled away by some men and tied to a chair while his picture was taken.

"I am just glad he didn't hurt you," Leila said. This time, she couldn't resist taking his hand. "It is all in the past. Hopefully soon, we can get married and put everything bad that has happened behind us."

He squeezed her hand and smiled brightly. "I can't wait for the day I can finally call you my wife."

Her heart filled with warmth at the look of love in his eyes. Why had she doubted that he still loved her? She had no doubt about how much he loved her as she looked into his eyes now. "I love you so much," she said to him.

"I love you too, Leila. I love you with everything that is in me."

For a long moment, they stared at each other. Leila saw that he wanted to draw her close and hold her in his arms as much as she wanted him to, but they both knew they couldn't, shouldn't. As hard and annoying as it was, she was grateful that he didn't try to move close to her or she would not have been able to resist this time if he kissed her. Being alone here, what that would lead to was not difficult to guess.

Malik suddenly broke the moment with a laugh. "Well, since we can't do anything but talk, I might as well ask how your time was in Saudi Arabia." He stood, went to quickly light a kerosene lamp that was in the corner of the room, and then came back to sit next to her. He smiled ruefully again. "Don't tell me any details about you and Dauda, though. That would be hard to hear. Just tell me about the place and how your life was there. I have never visited, but I hope to one day."

She bit her lip as his words reminded her again that he was a Muslim. Of course he would love to visit Saudi Arabia. She always forgot he wasn't a Christian and that she couldn't marry him until he was. She looked at him and wondered if she should bring the topic up now. But she changed her mind immediately. It was a very serious topic and she'd just arrived. She hadn't seen him in a long time. All she wanted now was for them to enjoy each other's company. The talk about his faith would have to come soon. Probably tomorrow. She put her concerns behind and told him about her life in Dauda's home.

"I didn't go out at all, so I can't really tell you much about that country."

He frowned deeply. "Why didn't you?" He had a horrified look on his face. "You were in purdah, weren't you?"

"No, I don't think I was, though I probably wouldn't have noticed if I were."

"What do you mean?" he asked.

She chuckled and said, "I pretended to be sick the whole time I was there so that Dauda wouldn't touch me."

Malik stared at her and then shook his head. "That is kind of funny, but don't tell me anything. I don't want to know."

Leila sighed. "Nothing happened between me and Dauda, Malik. Just as I said, I pretended to be sick, although he told me later on that he knew I was pretending. Dauda was surprisingly kind to me. He wasn't angry about any of it."

Malik's mouth was open and he wore a look of surprise on his face. "He didn't touch you at all?"

Leila shook her head. "No. He didn't."

She gasped in surprise when Malik pulled her close and kissed her hair and her forehead. He stared again at her lips and then sighed. Shifting away once more, he said, "That is a huge relief, though I know it would not have been your fault if you both had…" He didn't finish his sentence.

"You are the only man I love and want to be with in that way," she said to him, gazing into his eyes.

Once again, they gazed longingly at each other for a long moment. Finally, Leila broke their gaze and looked away. "This has to stop," she said. "If we keep on like this…"

"Don't say it!" Malik stood and pulled her up.

"It's getting late. I know somewhere I can take you where you will be safe tonight."

She frowned, her stomach clenching with worry. "Will those men try to harm me again?"

He shook his head. "I'm not talking about them. I mean safe from me."

She sighed. "You would never hurt me, Malik... but I know what you mean."

She left her traveling bag on the floor and followed him out of the house. They walked past some huts and around the burned farmland. Soon, they reached a cluster of huts surrounded by mango trees. Malik stopped in front of one of the huts and knocked on the wooden door.

The door opened almost immediately and a girl peered out at them. Leila smiled when she recognized the girl from the bus station who had given her directions to the farm. "Hello again," she said to the girl.

The girl smiled back at her and grinned at Malik. She opened the door wide and let Leila and Malik into the hut. A kerosene lamp was in the corner of the room, dimly lighting the place.

"Is your grandmother home, Hauwa?" Malik asked her.

"She is," Hauwa answered. "Let me go and call her." She pulled aside a curtain made out of an old wrapper and went in. A minute later, she appeared again with an old woman who had a wrapper tied around her chest.

The old woman beamed at Malik and patted his back like he was a little boy. "You came to see me today?" She looked at Leila with curiosity.

"Yes, Mama," Malik said. "But most of all, I came because of my friend here." He smiled at Leila. "She needs somewhere to live for the duration of her stay in Dogon... and, of course, she cannot stay in my house as I am a single man. Can she stay here?"

The old woman laughed. "You don't even need to

ask, my son. Of course she can stay here." She smiled at Leila and put her hand on her arm. "What's your name, daughter?"

"Leila, Ma."

"Leila, you can stay here for as long as you want. We don't have that much space but what we have we can definitely share."

"Thank you, Ma," Leila said, smiling at the kind old woman. "I don't need much space at all."

The woman patted Leila's arm and then her smile disappeared as she looked at Malik. "I'm really sorry for what happened at the farm. Is your father aware?"

"Someone was sent to Nira days ago to tell him about it. I don't think he is coming here. I'll have to handle the fallout."

The woman nodded. She smiled again and said to Leila, "Well, come, child. You will share Hauwa's room."

"Don't worry about it, Ma. I will sleep right here."

"On the bare floor?" the old woman shook her head. "No, you will share Hauwa's sleeping rug inside."

Leila did not argue anymore. Before she followed the woman, she turned to Malik. If only I could kiss him goodbye, she thought regretfully. She couldn't even take his hand here, with this old woman and her granddaughter present. She said to him, "I'll come back to your house first thing in the morning."

"No, I will come and get you," he said to her. "It might be dangerous for you to be out by yourself."

She nodded and then sighed as he gave her a smile and left the hut.

"Do you want to bathe before you sleep?" Hauwa asked her. "I can boil water for you on the stove."

"No, don't trouble yourself. I will have my bath very early tomorrow morning."

"Then come along," the old woman said. She took Leila's hand and led her inside. The room was a very small sleeping place that wasn't really a room, more a tiny space. There were sleeping rugs on the floor which were the only pieces of furniture she could see.

"You can sleep on this one while I sleep on that," Hauwa said.

Leila smiled and thanked her. She suddenly remembered she had left her bag with her clothes at Malik's and sighed. Slightly embarrassed, she asked Hauwa if the girl could give her a wrapper. When Hauwa promptly did, she quickly shed her dress and tied the wrapper around her chest. She folded the dress carefully as she had to wear it again tomorrow to Malik's and then she put it aside. Stretching out on the sleeping rug, she took a deep breath and then said a quick prayer, thanking the Lord for bringing her to Dogon safely and for Malik. She prayed for protection tonight, asked the Lord to bless these kind women who had taken her in, and made a mental note to give them some money before she left Dogon to help them with their needs, as she could see how poor they were.

Finally, she prayed for favor as she talked to Malik about Christ tomorrow. She asked the Lord to open his heart so he would receive the gospel and come to know the Jesus she knew. Soon, she fell asleep with a huge smile on her face.

THIRTEEN

Nick entered his room at the bed and breakfast and collapsed on his bed, totally exhausted. He'd had a long day at the restaurant, checking the books to make sure that they were turning a profit. He'd already been in Rosefield for two weeks and all he'd done was work. He looked at the clock on the wall and smiled in self-mockery when he saw it was ten p.m. already.

Well, my dream to meet someone new here in Rosefield has not turned out the way I thought.

He hadn't checked his online dating profile for some time now. He brought out his phone and decided to check it. Logging on to the dating website, he opened his profile, and then began to scroll once more through the different messages he had received from various women. Suddenly he stopped at a particular profile with the username Sweet-Violet.

He blinked. The profile picture showed a very pretty girl. But that wasn't all that made him stop. There was a sparkle in her eyes that also drew him.

He began to read her profile and found that they had more than a few things in common. Best of all, she lived in Rosefield.

He looked up thoughtfully. This was the kind of girl he would like to get to know, at least for now. Of course, since he didn't live in Rosefield, there would not be talk of a relationship. Even if he did live in Rosefield, he wasn't prepared for a relationship right now. However, from her profile, he knew she would be a great companion.

He read the message she had sent him again and knew without a doubt that he wanted to message her back.

He looked at the date that she had messaged him and groaned. It was a few days ago. If he had checked his profile earlier, he would have seen the message and would have sent a reply to her. Would she still be interested in getting to know him?

He quickly typed out a message, apologizing and explaining to her that he would have replied immediately if he had only seen and checked his profile days ago. He told her she looked interesting and he was also interested in getting to know her better. He sent the message and then smiled to himself. Checking his other messages, he found he was not interested in replying to any of the other women. He logged out of the dating website, and then took a deep breath. Hopefully she would send him a message soon.

He got up to eat his dinner. He wasn't exactly hungry as he had eaten not too long ago at the restaurant, but he ate several times a day these days. It was his new food fad. He only ate healthy foods, but once in a while, he had a cheat day and treated himself to a pizza.

As he fixed himself some salad, he thought about the woman he had sent a message to. Going on a date with her would be great. He wondered where they would go on their first date, and then chided himself. You are getting ahead of yourself, man, he thought.

Who knew if she would even be interested in

messaging him back? She'd probably given up on him when he did not reply to her message after a few days. There were so many choices online. Many people, especially women who looked like her, were spoilt for choice. It was unlikely that she would accept his apology.

After fixing himself a chicken salad, he went to the bed and breakfast living room, switched the television on, and flipped through the channels mindlessly, his feet on top of the coffee table. When he finished his food, he switched the TV off, and went to his room to prepare for bed.

After brushing his teeth and changing into his pajamas, he got under the covers and then from force of habit, he reached for his phone to see if he had any messages or calls. He had deliberately left the phone in the bedroom so as not to be disturbed while he ate and relaxed in the living room to wind down from work.

Once again, he thought about the beautiful woman on the online dating site. For some reason, he was more eager than usual to find out if she had messaged him back. He began to open the dating website again, and then told himself to calm down.

What's wrong with me? Why am I so eager, anyway?

He sighed deeply. Maybe it was because he hadn't been this lonely in a long time.

He went ahead and logged into the dating site again, and then blinked in surprise when he saw a message. Hoping with all his heart that the message was from the pretty woman, he opened it and saw it was from her. When he saw that she was online, he was thrilled. Her message said that she forgave him and was still interested in getting to know him better. He quickly sent another message to her, asking about the charitable works she did, since that was something they had in common.

He was excited when, almost immediately, he

got a reply back from her. I'm at the welfare department in our church and we regularly visit the old
people's home and the soup kitchens. We also vol-
unteer at the youth center a lot. I also help counsel
some of the victims of domestic violence who take
shelter at the Gibsons'. Since you live in Rosefield,
you probably know them.

He read the message, and for a while he wanted
to tell her that he did not really live in Rosefield.
However, he didn't want her to know too much
about his life, at least for now. It wasn't important
to let her know that he was only here temporarily.
He simply wrote back; I really don't know the Gibsons. To be truthful, I only arrived in Rosefield a
few weeks ago.

That was as much as he was willing to share for
now, he thought to himself.

She asked him about his charitable works as
well, and he told her about the charities he was
involved with. From her message to him, he noted
that she went to church regularly. Which meant she
was religious.

Her being religious might not be so good considering what he wanted at this time was simply
physical intimacy. However, he was still drawn to
her and would not give up just because of that.

They chatted back and forth. They shared more
information about themselves than strangers who
had only known each other for one night and had
not even physically met should. They chatted about
their childhood and he told her about his future
plans to open a restaurant in different parts of the
country.

They kept conversing until Nick glanced at the
clock on the wall and gasped. It was already one
a.m. He had to be at work early the next day.

Reluctantly, he typed out his message to her;
Unfortunately, I have to log off now as I have to get
to work quite early tomorrow.

And then he corrected himself. Actually, it's by eight o'clock today. If I don't get enough sleep, I'll be walking around like a zombie at work.

She sent a reply telling him that she had to be at work early as well.

He finally logged out of the dating site still thinking about the pretty stranger, and then sighed as he put his phone aside. He had enjoyed their conversation tremendously. She didn't seem like a stranger anymore. And they had not even met in person. How would it be to meet her really? He couldn't wait to meet her, but he knew he had to wait. They'd only just started talking. If he told her he wanted to meet her right now, he might push her away.

He stretched out on his bed again. For the past few weeks, he had come back to the bed and breakfast and laid down on the bed, loneliness wrapping itself around him. Today, however, he felt anything but lonely. Finally, with no effort whatsoever, he drifted off to sleep with a smile on his face.

The next day, he got to work early and went straight to the kitchen. Frank was already there, setting up to start the day. None of the other chefs had arrived.

He said to Frank, "Wow! I didn't know you could leave your beautiful wife so early in the morning. Usually these days, you come in a little past the time you are supposed to."

Frank chuckled. "Nowadays? You came to Rosefield just a couple of weeks ago, and you know my routine so well."

Nick smiled and nodded. "Yeah, Frank! Yeah, I do. I don't blame you, though. If I had a wife as beautiful as Trisha, I wouldn't want to leave her in the morning, either."

Frank shook his head and laughed. "First, Trisha also has a job which she has to leave for early in the morning. Secondly, even though I would love to, it would not make sense for me to let our customers go hungry while I stayed at home with my wife. I do miss her when I come to work."

Nick smiled and then remembered his conversation with the woman he had met online yesterday. He couldn't wait to get home so he could start their conversation again.

Frank snapped his fingers in front of Nick's face, and said, "Earth to Nick. Where did your mind go to just now?"

Nick grinned and shook his head. "Nowhere."

Frank said, "No, I'm pretty sure you were lost to the world a minute ago. Tell me what's on your mind? Have you met someone?"

Nick looked away and said nothing.

Frank came and stood in front of Nick. He looked him in the eye and nodded. "You have met someone. I can tell."

Nick sighed and then decided to tell Frank the truth. "I did meet someone online yesterday." He looked up thoughtfully and then looked back at Frank. "I like her. She's actually everything I want right now. It's such a shame that I don't live in Rosefield and she does."

"There's something called a long-distance relationship, you know," Frank said.

"Frank, you know I'm not interested in a relationship right now. How many times do I have to tell you that?"

"Then why on Earth are you connecting with this girl? You say you like her, and yet you're not planning to have a relationship with her?"

Nick sighed wearily. "I told you I was just looking for a physical connection while I am in Rosefield."

Frank smirked. "And does she know you don't want a relationship? That all you want is a one-night — or is it several — Night-stands?"

Nick turned away from him and said, "Don't you have a sauce to make or something?"

Frank chuckled. "So, you're trying to evade my question. Ask yourself this; if the shoe were on the other foot, how would you feel if she treated you that way? How would you feel if a girl you liked just wanted one thing from you and one thing alone?"

"By 'one thing', you mean to sleep with me?" Nick gave Frank a tight smile. "Actually, I have heard that from several girls, but I was okay with it because I wanted the same thing."

Frank sighed loudly and said, "You are impossible, Nick! The only difference here is that I am pretty sure this woman wants much more from you than just something physical, as you said before. Just as I told you before, Rosefield is not that kind of place. She probably went on this dating site because she wanted something serious."

Nick thinned his lips and then said, "You don't know that."

Frank stared straight into his eyes and said, "And you don't know that she wants the same thing you do. Anyway, that is not the most important thing. What you need right now..."

"Don't say it!" Nick exclaimed. "You're going to tell me that what I need is a relationship with Jesus. Please, don't say it."

Frank said, "All right, then. I won't say it... at least for now. But please don't lead this woman on or any other woman on your online site for that matter. Be honest with her and let her know where you stand and what you want from her so she can decide if that's what she wants. Though I can assure you it isn't."

Nick said, "Frank, I know you haven't dated for some time now, but I can't just go and tell a girl on our first or second conversation that I want to sleep with her. That is just not done, at least by me. It's not my way."

"So your way is to keep leading a woman on and letting her think you want a serious relationship with her when in actual fact you only want her body?"

"No!" Nick retorted. "I try to guess from our conversation if she wants anything more serious than what I am willing to give. If she does, I cut it off as soon as I can. If I find out that she wants the same thing that I do, we go on from there."

Frank laughed harshly and shook his head. "I've told you before, Nick! You need to stop all this!"

Nick looked at him. He wanted to tell Frank to mind his business, but Frank was coming from a good place. An uninformed and judgmental place, but still, a good place. He finally said, "Okay good sir, I will put everything you have said into consideration. Are you happy now?"

Frank pursed his lips and then said, "All I told you is for your own good and for the good of all those women you meet. Really, I know you can be a better man."

"So, you don't think I am a better man now just because I crave intimacy."

Frank turned away. "You are totally useless, Nick," he said.

Nick laughed and then walked out of the kitchen. But when he got to the main sitting area in the restaurant, his smile melted off his face. Frank was probably right. The pretty woman online probably wanted more than he was willing to give. If she did, he would have to end it right now, before it went any further and he broke her heart.

He sighed sadly. That meant he had to continue his search. It meant his pillow would continue to be the only thing he cuddled at night until he left Rosefield. There would be no female companionship for him.

Soon, the restaurant got busy and he was lost in the hustle and bustle of it all. He stopped thinking about the online girl and about what Frank had told him and fully concentrated on work. Finally, at about ten p.m., the restaurant emptied of guests. The other chefs and the waiters and waitresses all went home. Frank walked by him, said a quick goodbye, and then walked out the door of the restaurant.

Nick called out to him and asked him to wait up. He stepped out of the restaurant, locked it, and then made his way to the parking lot, Frank walking alongside him.

"Are you angry with me?" he asked Frank.

Frank turned to look at him. "Why would I be angry with you?"

"Because you just said a quick goodbye and began to leave hastily."

"It's late, Nick. I need to get home. I haven't seen my wife and daughter all day."

Nick said, "Are you sure it's not because of the conversation we had earlier?"

"No," Frank said. "I think what you are doing is completely wrong, Nick. But you're still my friend. I'm not going to give up on you or give up praying for you."

They got to the parking lot and Frank got into his car. He stuck his head out the window and looked at Nick. "I'll see you tomorrow," he said, smiling.

Nick nodded and then waved at him. He walked to the car he had rented some days after he came to Rosefield, entered, and drove to the bed and breakfast, thinking about what Frank had said.

He began to build a wall of defense as Frank's words pricked his conscience. I'm not like Frank, he thought. I'm not going to live like a monk or something. There's nothing wrong with simply wanting physical companionship with a woman. It's not like I force anyone. It's all mutual.

As he climbed the stairs to his room, he pushed away the barrage of guilt in his mind brought on by Frank's words. But, as he got into bed and reached for his phone to log on to the dating website again, he finally admitted to himself that Frank was right. He didn't want to go on misleading the beautiful woman he'd started chatting with. If she wanted more than he was willing to give, he had to end it now.

He groaned. So much for finding companionship.

As annoying as it was to end something that had just begun, it was the right thing to do. He would tell her that he enjoyed their conversation last night but he didn't think they should go any further than that.

Finding her profile, he began to type out a message to her, but it was not the message he had decided to send her. Instead, he asked her to tell him more about her life. He sent the message and groaned again.

What are you doing, man?

He was ecstatic when she replied almost immediately.

Like the day before, they chatted back and forth. He knew from their chats that she liked him. He liked her even more now. However, this was getting to be too much. He had to end it now. He started to tell her they couldn't go any further than this, but he found himself deleting what he had typed out.

He sighed and chided himself. Tell her now.

Once again, he started to tell her that their conversation could not continue, but he noticed that she'd begun to type something out. He waited for her to send her message and then blinked in surprise when he read it.

He ran his hand through his hair and stared at the message. She wanted to meet him. This weekend. It was definitely too soon… and yet, it was not. He found that he was as eager to meet her as she seemed to meet him.

Nick, what are you doing? You're supposed to end this now.

But he just couldn't bring himself to do it. He liked this woman, and he wanted to see where things took them. He still didn't want a relationship, but he longed to see if she would be a good and willing companion, at least for now.

Guiltily knowing that he wasn't doing the right thing, he typed out his message, telling her that he wanted to meet her as well. She asked him where he would like their date to be and he smiled. Great. So he was going on a date with her. Their first date.

Pick somewhere you would like to go, he typed out and sent it.

Dinner at FRANKLY EATING was her response.

His eyes widened as he stared at her message. She wanted their date to be at his restaurant. She didn't know he was the co-owner of Frankly Eating. And he wanted to keep it that way. He ran his fingers through his hair, worried. Frank would probably see him on the date with her and know he hadn't taken his advice. The last thing he needed was a fresh sermon from Frank about not leading a woman on.

He groaned. He couldn't ask her to change the venue of their date since he was the one who had told her to pick the place she wanted to go. He took a deep breath and told her he would see her there at eight p.m. on Friday evening.

That will be great was her reply.

They chatted some more, and then once again, he told her he had to log off as he had to go to work early the next day.

After he logged off, he put his phone aside and sighed. Nick, why did you not end it?

But he knew why. He wanted to meet this woman.

He yawned and then shut his eyes and put aside his guilt and concerns. There was nothing wrong in getting to know someone. If he found out she wanted something more than he was willing to give, maybe they could just be friends.

He yawned again and tried to go to sleep. But guilt flooded his mind again, driving out every trace of sleep.

FOURTEEN

Lauren smiled as Trisha walked into the living room after putting Ruby to bed. She had come to Trisha's after the welfare meeting in church. Her date with the super cute guy she'd met online was in an hour. She felt really excited, but she had to hold it in. The last thing she wanted was for Trisha to probe until she found out about the date. Without a doubt, Trisha would object.

Sitting down beside Lauren, Trisha said, "Like I was telling you before, Audrey is really serious about her desire to adopt a little girl she met at an orphanage in Peru, but Ken doesn't want a child yet."

Lauren shook her head, surprised. She said, "I always thought Ken was the kind of person who wanted children immediately after he got married."

Trisha said, "I guess his reasoning is that he and Audrey are too busy with work right now to be the kind of parents they need to be. I'm really rooting for Audrey because she seems to be very sure about this girl, and she told me the girl is wonderful. I just want her to be happy."

Lauren sighed as her mind wandered. Ken was the one that got away. He was such a great guy, and she had let him slip through her fingers because she'd wanted a bad boy; a bad boy like her ex, Richie. It had all turned out badly for her. Trisha was right. She was usually drawn to bad boys. Hopefully, this guy she was going out with this evening would not be like the kind of man she was usually drawn to. He didn't seem like a bad boy from his profile and the messages they had exchanged. But who knew?

"Lauren?" Trisha waved a hand in front of Lauren's face.

"What?"

"You spaced out just now,"

Lauren chuckled. "No, I did not."

"Yes, you did." Trisha giggled. "What were you thinking about?"

Lauren sighed and answered, "I met someone."

Trisha squealed. "You did? Where? In church?"

Lauren didn't say anything for a short moment, wondering whether to tell Trisha the truth. Finally, she said, "I met this guy online."

Trisha stared at Lauren for a few seconds and then said, "Online. So a guy you met online has so captured your heart that you sort of phased out for some time. Just remember what I told you. Be careful."

"Yes, Mother," Lauren teased. "I told you I would be." She nearly blurted out that she was seeing the guy this evening, but she knew Trisha would probably freak out if she told her that.

They conversed for a few minutes more and then Lauren stood. "I have to go now," she said.

"So soon?" Trisha asked. She looked at the clock on the wall and said, "It's just a few minutes past seven."

Lauren shrugged. "I need to go now. I'll see you tomorrow or the next."

Trisha walked her to the door and then Lauren hugged her, told her to say hi to Frank, and left the house.

In order to get home quickly, she walked as fast as she could and got to her apartment in about fifteen minutes. She went straight to her room, quickly showered, and then went to her closet to look for something to wear; something nice enough for a first date, but that also said she wasn't trying too hard. Finally, she chose a lacy white top and dark denim jeans. She accented everything with a pair of gold heels and a gold clutch with gold chandelier earrings. She quickly applied her makeup, brushed her hair, and then looked at her reflection in the mirror. She smiled, satisfied with what she saw, and then went out of the room.

As she didn't have a car yet, she called for a taxi and waited. She glanced at her wristwatch and saw it was almost eight o'clock. She was supposed to meet her date at Frank's restaurant by eight.

Her heart suddenly began to race. Why had she decided on having the date in Frank's restaurant? Frank would probably see her with the guy and then tell Trisha about it. Trisha would give her a really hard time. She would be hurt, very hurt, that Lauren had not told her about the date.

"Well it's too late now," she said to herself.

The taxi arrived five minutes later. She got in and took a deep breath. Her hands were clammy with nervousness and her heart raced with anticipation and excitement. She looked out the window as the taxi driver pulled out of her driveway and moved into the road. Suddenly, her mind flooded with doubts. What if, as Trisha had said, this guy that seemed too good to be true was a catfish, out to scam her? Maybe he wasn't even who he said he was. Maybe his picture was false.

She took another deep breath and told herself to calm down. "It will all work out by God's grace," she whispered.

The cab driver pulled up in front of Frankly Eating, and she got out of the car. After paying the driver, she walked into the restaurant while praying that Frank would not see her. *Why didn't I think about this when I suggested this restaurant as the venue of our date?*

She smiled as a host in a black pinstripe suit led her to the back of the restaurant. The place was half-full and the ambiance was great. She'd only been here once and that was with Trisha. If not for the fact that she was so nervous, it would have been great to experience this place with a date. Thankfully, Frank was nowhere around. Probably in the kitchen.

She brought out her phone from her purse, opened the dating website, and pulled up her profile just to look at the guy's picture again and make sure she remembered him.

After putting away her phone, she looked around. He wasn't here yet. She glanced at her wristwatch and saw it was a minute to eight. Hopefully, he would be here early so she didn't have to sit here all by herself.

A waiter came and asked if she was ready to order and she told him she would wait until her date came. He left again and then her heart did a flip as she saw the guy she had been chatting with walking toward her. He'd come out of the kitchen and not from outside the restaurant. That meant he'd been here before her and had gone to the kitchen, probably to see the chef or something.

He smiled as he reached her table and her heart began to drum. He was even better looking than his profile picture. He sat and smiled at her and then she realized she didn't even know his name. All she knew was his username. That would have to change now. Beaming at him, she said, "You're here." When he reached out to her, she got up immediately. He hugged her briefly and she said, "Hi! My name is Lauren."

A strange expression crept into his face and she

frowned. It disappeared as quickly as it appeared and he said, "Hi, Lauren. My name is Nicholas."

"Nice to meet you, Nicholas."

After they had exchanged pleasantries, the waiter came to take their order. When his order was little more than a salad, she smiled curiously at him. "That's a lot of veggies for a big guy like you. What, you have something against carbs?"

He laughed. "Actually, I don't. But I used to be overweight and slightly sick. Eating healthy changed my life."

Her eyes widened in surprise and she shook her head. "I would never have guessed."

He nodded and changed the subject. He asked her about her job and then about her life in general.

She told him a lot of what she had already told him before and then some more about herself. He also told her more about himself, but she felt like he was holding back some information. However, that did not bother her. This was their first date, after all. Gradually, he would feel more comfortable about opening up to her.

By the time they stood up to leave the restaurant, Lauren felt like she had known him all her life. Thankfully, Frank did not come out of the kitchen throughout their date. That was a huge relief. She didn't want to have to deal with Trisha's concerns, no matter how well-meaning they were.

They walked out of the restaurant together and Lauren glanced at her watch. It was a few minutes past ten. She smiled at Nicholas and said, "I had a great time."

He smiled back at her and told her he'd had a great time, too.

Suddenly, an awkwardness that had not existed when they were talking in the restaurant or even chatting online came between them. Nicholas shifted his feet. She looked at him and wondered what exactly was wrong. She did not expect a kiss or anything like that as it was their first date. However, she did expect him to ask her out again. She'd had a great time and so had he. She stared expectantly at him, waiting for him to say something. But he said nothing.

Finally, he reached out and hugged her again and then backed away once more. He began to turn around and she immediately knew that he was not going to ask her out again. Instantly, panic flooded her heart. She really liked him. She couldn't let him go just like that. If she did, she might never see him again. If he wasn't going to ask her out on a second date, she would have to do the asking.

She mustered up as much courage as she could. "Nicholas?"

He turned around. "Yes?"

Before her courage could fail, she said to him, "Do you want to go out again? Maybe to see a movie or something?"

He blinked rapidly and her heart sank. He came close to her again and then gave her a small smile. He said, "Lauren, I am really sorry. I've enjoyed our conversations, but I think we should end it here."

She felt like crying. She had put herself out there and just like what had happened with Faizan, she has been rejected... again. What was wrong with her?

He smiled sadly at her and then turned around again. Suddenly, she felt angry. She knew without a doubt that he had enjoyed spending time with her. Why, then, was he turning his back on her? She couldn't keep it in anymore and called out to him again.

Once more, he turned around. "Yes, Lauren?"

This time, she walked up to him and said, "I want to know why." If she was going to be rejected again, she had to know why this guy didn't want to go on a second date with her. She had to know what exactly was wrong with her so she could change it.

Nicolas thinned his lips and then said, "You want to know why what?"

She said firmly, "I want to know why you don't want to go out again. I know for a fact you had a good time. You said so yourself. I thought there was something between us and I thought you were going to ask me out on a second date when we came out of the restaurant. Suddenly, you changed your mind. Why?"

For a long moment, he stared silently at her. Finally, he said, "Listen, Lauren, I have to be honest with you. I haven't been totally honest."

She stared straight into his eyes and asked, "What is it?"

For a few seconds, he said nothing, and then he answered, "I don't live in Rosefield."

Lauren gasped. "You don't? I thought you moved here a short time ago."

"No," he said. "I came here for work."

"Why didn't you tell me?" she asked.

He sighed loudly and then said, "To be truthful with you, when I went on the dating site, I was not looking for something serious or permanent."

She stared at him and asked, "What do you mean you were not looking for something serious?"

He said to her, "I didn't go online looking for a date, actually."

"Then what did you go on a dating website for?" she asked incredulously.

Again, he did not speak for a minute. She looked quizzically at him and asked once more what he went online to do.

"I was looking for a companion."

"A companion? What do you mean by that?"

"I mean I was looking for someone to hook up with... for the period I was in Rosefield."

Her jaw dropped and she stared at him in disbelief. So, he was that kind of guy. As usual, she had attracted a bad boy... a very bad boy, without knowing it. It was way too much for her. She shook her head slowly and then turned around. She began to march away and he called out her name.

She slowly turned and faced him. "What is it?" she barked.

"I am sorry. I really, really like you, Lauren. Actually, more than I have liked any girl in a long time. But we just met. I am leaving Rosefield in about a week. There's no point going on a second date."

She nodded and said, "Of course. I guess now you're free to go look for someone to hook up with." She felt disgusted and turned around quickly. She marched away. He called out to her again, but this time, she did not respond.

She did not bother calling for a taxi. She walked to her apartment building in her heels and got there panting. Unlocking her door, she entered the living room and then sank onto the couch, feeling exhausted, angry, and terribly sad.

Suddenly, she couldn't keep it in anymore and said, "Lord, why does this keep happening to me?" Why had she invested so much hope in someone she had never met before? Why did she feel so heartbroken when she hardly knew the guy?

Shake it off, she scolded herself. She couldn't sit here mourning for a guy she'd just met. It was insanity. She had to move on so she could meet other people.

She held her head in her hands. She wasn't up to going online again to meet anyone. She wasn't even sure she wanted to do that anymore. Who knew what kind of guy she would meet next? Perhaps he would be like this one. She would have a deep connection to him and then find out he was married or something like that. It would not surprise her if that happened. She shook her head. Tomorrow morning, when she had the peace of mind to go on that dating site again, she would delete her profile. Maybe she was never meant to find love. If that was so, she would have to deal with it.

She stood up and went into her room again. Shedding her clothes and kicking off her shoes, she sat on the bed for a minute, thinking about what had happened on the date. Everything had gone so well. She had put way too much hope on this date and on the guy. If only she had not done so, her heart would not feel as heavy as it did right now.

Nicholas' face appeared in her mind, taunting her. He was so handsome and so attentive when they spoke. And they had so many things in common. How could he not want a real relationship with her?

That isn't all, she thought. He also doesn't live in Rosefield.

But surely, long-distance relationships worked sometimes?

But do you want a long-distance relationship?

She certainly didn't want one. It was bound to fail. She sighed heavily and then stood up again. She went into the bathroom, quickly showered, and then changed into her nightgown. Laying on her bed, she thanked God she had not told Trisha, or anyone for that matter, about this date. She would have had a lot of explaining to do. Trisha would have said, 'I told you so.' That would have made her feel even worse than she did right now.

She sighed heavily and looked up at the ceiling. "Lord, I am through with all this," she said. "If I am meant to be single, then I accept it as your will."

Her heart felt heavy. Even with the disappointment she'd faced tonight, she didn't want to be single any longer. Yet, she knew there was a huge possibility that she would not meet the right person.

The thought was very unsettling.

*****

Nick got home and collapsed onto his couch. He felt terrible. He had just told the woman who he liked more than he'd liked any woman in a long time that he wasn't interested in pursuing a relationship with her. Worse, he'd told her he had only wanted someone to hook up with when he went online. Of course he had not gone on their date thinking that, but still, from the expression on her face, she had been grossed out.

He sighed. Was it really true he didn't want a relationship with her? And was it true he was not interested or ready for a relationship right now? Because lying down here, he felt ready to pursue a relationship with Lauren. He really liked her. She seemed pure, too good for him. She was warm and funny and witty. Where would he meet someone else like her?

He told himself to let it go. It was for the best. There was no way he was going to have a relationship now, not to talk of a long-distance relationship. It was totally impossible.

But his mind refused to let her go. Still, he had to. Even if he changed his mind now and decided he wanted a relationship, he'd messed everything up. He had told her the truth. He had told her he was only looking for someone to sleep with. He knew she was religious. There was no way she would give him a chance after that.

But you do want a chance, don't you?

He didn't know the answer to that question anymore. He'd thought he didn't want that kind of chance until he met Lauren. Now he just wasn't sure. A girl like Lauren didn't come along every day. But there was no point trying to pursue a relationship with her or get her to forgive him and take him back. He was leaving Rosefield in a week and he would never see her again.

It's all for the best anyway, he told himself. Relationships complicated things. They muddled a man's life.

His mind went to Frank and then to Trisha. If there was any relationship that made him question his decision to say stay single, it was theirs. They were so in love. And not only did they love each other very much, they liked each other. They had a great relationship. They seemed slightly co-dependent, but maybe that was part of their charm. And they could never keep their hands off each other no matter who was there. That was the kind of relationship he wanted if he ever had one someday. But that day was definitely not today.

He sighed loudly. You have to forget about her.

He stood up to go to bed and her face appeared once more in his mind. He groaned. Forgetting about her would probably be one of the most difficult things he'd ever done.

FIFTEEN

Audrey woke up feeling both excited and scared. Today, Ken was coming to the orphanage with her and Sienna. Hopefully, she would get him to see that Esther was a lovely girl and agree to adopt her.

She turned briefly to look at Ken. The bedroom was still dark and she couldn't see his face. Slipping out of bed, she went into the bathroom and showered. She came out and then switched the lights on. Ken opened his eyes and she smiled at him. "It's time to get up," she said cheerfully.

He groaned and covered his face with his pillow.

She laughed and came to remove the pillow from his face. He groaned again and she said, "We are supposed to go to the orphanage early this morning, Ken. Remember?"

Ken opened an eye and looked at her. "We are supposed to be on vacation, Audrey. Remember?"

She chuckled and then went into the closet to change into a knee-length yellow dress. She smiled to herself. The dress matched the color of the children's hostel. She zipped up the dress and then turned to look at Ken, who was still lying in bed. She said, "Wake up, sleepyhead."

Ken moaned and then climbed out of bed.

She went out of the room after she had brushed her hair and found Sienna in the living room with a cup of coffee in her hand. She smiled at Sienna, who was already dressed in a pair of jeans and a white blouse.

"Mary will be leaving tomorrow," Sienna said. "Are you ready to run the orphanage?"

Audrey shook her head and then came to sit down beside Sienna. "About that. You never mentioned anything about me running the orphanage until I came here."

Sienna laughed and said, "You should see the look on your face. You're only going to be running the orphanage for about a month, Audrey. It's not like it's a permanent thing. Besides, going there every day will give you the chance to see Esther regularly."

Audrey stared at her and said, "I don't have to run the orphanage to see Esther regularly."

Sienna shrugged. "Well, that's what you're going to do now."

"But I don't know anything about running an orphanage."

Sienna chuckled. "You'll be running it with me, silly. Don't worry about it. Everything will be fine."

Audrey looked at her for long moment and then said, "Okay. I love the kids anyway, and as long as you're with me, I guess I can do it."

Sienna said, "I won't be at the orphanage every day. That's the point of having you help me out, Audrey."

"What? How am I supposed to manage if you're not there with me?"

Sienna's brows lifted. "Remember, I'm a new mom. That's why I need your help. Don't worry, Audrey. You'll be fine. It's not rocket science anyway." She took a sip of her coffee and said, "So, Ken is still not open to the idea of adopting Esther?"

"Not that I know of," Audrey said. "Anyway, he'll

see Esther today and hopefully change his mind."

"Well, I hope so. But Ken can be stubborn some-times."

"You're telling me! I am married to the guy. I know."

"He is just as stubborn as you are," Sienna smiled.

"I'm not stubborn!"

"Yes, you are."

Bryan came into the living room and smiled at Audrey. She smiled back at him and he kissed the top of Sienna's head. "You girls are already ready?"

"Yes," Sienna and Audrey chorused.

Sienna looked at Audrey and asked, "Aren't you going to have breakfast?"

"No. I'm too nervous to eat now. I will have something to eat when we get back."

Bryan went in again and Audrey chatted with Sienna about the baby, about Trisha's pregnancy, about the orphanage. Twenty minutes later, Ken strode into the living room in jeans and a plaid shirt. His sleeves were rolled up, and he looked very handsome. Audrey smiled at him in apprecia-tion. She stood, walked up to him, and kissed him on the lips.

He smiled at her. "What's that for?"

"For being the most handsome husband in the world."

He chuckled and then kissed her cheek. He said, "Where is Bryan? I am ready to go."

Veronica, the nanny, came out carrying Ethan.

Audrey smiled at the baby. He was still asleep and looked so cute. She went up to the nanny and lightly kissed Ethan on his fat cheeks. When Bryan came out to the living room, Sienna quickly gave instructions to Veronica about Ethan and told her they would be back in a few hours.

They all left the house ten minutes later. All the way to the orphanage, Audrey kept praying that Ken would at least consider the adoption once he saw and spoke to Esther. She still wanted a baby, but right now the adoption took precedence. Because they had less than a month in Peru, she had to get Ken to agree to it so they could start the process as soon as possible. If he did not agree and they left Peru, it would probably be the end of her desire and plans to adopt Esther. She could not let that happen.

They got to the orphanage and Audrey got out of the car with Sienna. It was a Saturday and Sienna had told her the kids slept in on Saturdays.

Sienna said, "Since they wake up on weekdays at about six o'clock because of school, they usually wake up around ten o'clock on Saturdays."

"That's good," Audrey said.

They all went to the administrative building and into the office where Audrey had met Mary yesterday.

Mary was at her desk and she looked up when they walked in. She got up and hugged each of them and greeted them warmly.

The men soon excused themselves and went out of the office, talking. Sienna and Audrey sat facing Mary.

"So, you leave tomorrow," Sienna smiled at Mary.

"Yes, I do," Mary said. "I'm really excited about starting a new life with my husband soon, but I will miss this place."

"We are going to miss you," Sienna said. "We need to briefly show my sister what exactly it takes to run this orphanage. At least let her know that it's not as difficult as she thinks."

Audrey smiled and said, "I'm sure it's more difficult than I think."

For almost an hour, they talked about the orphanage. After Mary finished explaining what she did daily at the orphanage, Audrey said, "Well, I guess I could manage, at least until a new person is found. I hope someone will be found very soon."

Sienna said, "I hope so, too."

Audrey looked out as a bell began to ring. She turned to Sienna. "What's that bell ringing for?"

Before Sienna could answer, the kids began to pour out of the yellow building and Audrey said, "Never mind."

Sienna chuckled. "They are awake now."

Audrey's heart raced excitedly. She would get to see Esther. And Ken would also get to meet her; the little girl hopefully would become their daughter one day. Audrey stood up and said to Sienna, "I am going to find Esther now."

Sienna laughed. "Esther is not running away, Audrey. You'll get to see her soon enough."

"No, I want to see her now."

"Okay, then," Sienna said. "You can go. I have some things to discuss with Mary now. I'll catch up with you later."

Audrey put her hand on Sienna's shoulder, smiled at Mary, and then left the office. A few of the bigger kids came out of the other building some distance away from where the administrative building was and she glanced at them. They were teenagers and she wondered how they felt still living in an orphanage after all this time. It was a good orphanage, but she couldn't imagine how they would feel not having families of their own. Her heart went out to them and then she forcefully turned her gaze away. She had to go find Esther.

She walked toward the yellow building, excitement flooding her. Some of the kids turned to look at her and one of them, a little boy who looked around five, ran up to her and stared up at her. She stooped down to look at him and smiled. "How are you, darling?" she asked him.

His smiled but did not answer, and then she realized she had spoken to him in English. She asked the question in Spanish and he told her he was fine.

She straightened, ruffled his hair, and then looked around her. Esther was not outside yet. She considered walking into the hostel, but thought better of it. She wanted to speak to Esther alone. She would probably be crowded by the other children if she went in.

If only I could adopt them all. But she definitely couldn't. All the children were precious. However, Esther held a special place in her heart. No matter how resistant Ken was, she couldn't let the girl go.

Speaking of Ken, where was he? She looked around her but didn't see him or Bryan. She sighed. They were probably around somewhere. She hoped she would find Ken once she saw Esther so he could meet her.

She turned to the orphanage again and smiled. Esther was coming out of the building with another little girl. Audrey watched her. She was talking with the other girl while skipping. Audrey's smile widened. From the little she had seen, Esther was always skipping, and she always looked happy, except for yesterday when Audrey left the orphanage. Remembering that moment tore at Audrey's heart. Esther had looked so sad.

Audrey waited for Esther to turn in her direction. When the little girl did, Audrey beamed.

Esther's eyes widened and her entire face lit up. She let go of her little friend's hand and ran to Audrey.

Audrey caught her as she jumped up and lifted her up in her arms.

Esther hugged Audrey tightly, and Audrey put her down. "I told you I would be back," she said, touching Esther's cheek and smiling down at her.

Esther took Audrey's hand and said, "Do you want to see my doll and teddy bear?"

Audrey nodded. "I would love to."

Esther led the way to the hostel and led Audrey to her bunk. She let go of Audrey's hand and opened the locker beside the bunk.

Audrey looked around her. There were kids everywhere, talking and laughing. Some played and ran around the room, while others sat on the bed, chatting.

Audrey faced Esther again as the little girl brought out an old doll with half her hair gone, and a ratty teddy bear. Audrey smiled as she looked at the doll and the teddy bear. For some reason, she had envisioned dolls and teddy bears like the ones Ruby owned; new and neat. But these ones looked really old. She made a mental note to buy Esther a new doll and teddy bear and then sat down with the girl on her bed.

Esther brought out a tiny feeding bottle and pretended to feed the doll. After a while, she handed the bottle to Audrey and gently placed the doll in her lap.

Audrey smiled and thanked Esther for trusting her enough to let her feed the baby doll. She put the feeding bottle on the doll's mouth and then made a sucking sound with her tongue and teeth.

"Why are you making that sound?" Esther asked, giggling.

"Well, it's the sound a baby makes when they're sucking on a feeding bottle," Audrey said, smiling.

For some reason, Esther found it hilarious and laughed out loud. Audrey continued to make the sound, prompting more laughter from Esther. After that, Audrey played with Esther's teddy bear.

Soon they began to play a mini game of hide-and-seek, which involved not just her and Esther, but the doll and teddy bear as well. Even though she was an adult, Audrey enjoyed the game. Esther went to hide behind the door of the next room and Audrey pretended not to see her. She loudly asked some of the children if they had seen Esther and they stared amusingly at her. One of them, a girl dressed in a white floral gown, pointed at the door and said, "There she is."

Audrey smiled as Esther giggled, but she looked away and said, "Where? I don't see her."

The child laughed and pointed again. "There! She is right there."

Audrey looked up at the ceiling and the children watching her roared with laughter. The child in the floral dress pointed again at the door and said, "Esther is there. She's behind the door."

Audrey hid a smile and looked down at the floor. "I can't see her," she said. "Is she hiding under the carpet?"

The kids shook their heads and laughed again.

Finally, Audrey went to the door and grabbed Esther's hand.

Esther laughed and said, "Okay, it's your turn to hide."

They played for about ten minutes more, and then Audrey took Esther's hand and led her out of the room.

Clutching her doll tightly in one hand and holding Audrey's in the other, Esther skipped beside Audrey.

Audrey searched around the orphanage grounds looking for Ken and Bryan. Soon, she found them near the gate of the orphanage, talking. Bryan was pointing at a building some distance away and Audrey approached them, wondering what they were talking about.

Ken turned to her as she approached and then raised his brows when he looked at Esther.

Audrey and Esther reached him and Ken's brows rose even higher.

"I've been looking for you," Audrey said. She smiled and said, "This is Esther."

Bryan smiled, gently patted Esther's head, and then excused himself.

Audrey briefly watched him go and then turned to Ken. Esther was looking up at Ken with an inquisitive expression on her face. Ken was also smiling at her. Joy flooded Audrey's heart. Ken looked like he already liked Esther. This could go well. This could go really well.

Audrey said, "Ken, well, do you…?"

He cut her off. "I'll speak to you later." He hurried away before she could say anything more.

Audrey's eyes widened in surprise and then her heart sank. Ken just walked away without even speaking to Esther. Audrey had thought everything was going to work out. Clearly, he didn't want to get attached to Esther in any way.

Suddenly, she felt physically ill. It was clear he had no interest in adopting Esther. He wouldn't even speak to her. Thankfully, Esther had no idea of his rejection. At least he'd smiled at her.

Audrey looked down at Esther, who was looking up at her, her eyes glowing. She took a deep breath and tried to let go of her growing anger. For Esther's sake, she couldn't let her anger show. But once they got home, she would have it out with Ken.

You will do no such thing, a still, small voice said in her heart.

Her mouth fell open. Without a doubt, she knew it was the Lord speaking to her. She wanted to cry out and ask why not. Ken was so stubborn. He didn't even speak to Esther at all. Why would she not confront him about that?

She walked on with Esther while silently asking the Lord why she couldn't talk to Ken about it. However, she heard nothing more. She had a choice to either obey the voice or ignore it. Right now, she didn't know which she would choose.

She had never felt as much sorrow as she did now, except perhaps when she had lost her parents. What would she do if the opportunity to adopt this precious little girl passed her by? Plus, Ken still wasn't interested in having a baby yet. It was all she wanted.

Once again, she cried out to God in her heart, but she still heard nothing. She had to speak to Ken about it once they got home. She had to let him know how this was affecting her. And she had to talk some sense into him.

She pushed away her anger and sadness and focused her total attention on Esther. Throughout her stay at the orphanage, she focused on Esther, talking to the little girl and trying to find out more about her life; the things that made her happy or sad. She knew she was investing more and more of her heart into the little girl, which would make the hurt even worse if Ken completely refused to consider the adoption. But she could not help it.

She walked around the orphanage grounds talking to Esther. Sometime later, Sienna joined them. They chatted and laughed and then at last, Esther let go of her hand. She looked up at Audrey with a smile and said, "Can I go and play with my friends?"

Audrey wanted to say yes immediately, but looking at the little girl, she knew what Esther was asking. She wanted to know if Audrey would still be here when she finished playing with her friends.

Audrey bent down and looked into Esther's eyes. "You can go, Esther. I promise I will not leave without saying goodbye to you. And I will come back tomorrow."

Esther nodded and then skipped away.

Audrey watched her with her heart aching. She felt Sienna's hand on her shoulder and turned. "Ken refused to even speak to her," she said.

Sienna rubbed her back comfortingly and said, "I am so sorry. Are you sure you don't want me to ask Bryan to talk to him?"

Audrey remembered the voice she had heard; the voice she was sure was the Lord's. She took a deep breath and then nodded. "Okay," she said. "I think it will be a good idea to ask Bryan to speak to Ken.

I doubt I'll be able to get through to him anyway."

"Once we get home, I'll let Bryan know," Sienna said.

Audrey nodded again.

Half an hour later, they were all ready to leave. Audrey left Sienna, Ken, and Bryan, and went in search of Esther. She found her near a small building at the back of the administrative building with some other girls. Esther spotted Audrey and ran to her.

Audrey hugged Esther tightly. She drew back slightly and put her hands on Esther's cheeks. Smoothing down the little girl's hair, she said, "I have to go now, Esther. But just as I said to you before, I'll be back tomorrow."

Esther did not look as sad as she had the day before when Audrey wanted to leave. Audrey knew it was because Esther trusted that she would keep her word. Unfortunately, Audrey did not have the same excitement as she had the day before when she'd started thinking about adopting Esther. This time, she had anger, sadness, and dread. The adoption might never happen. Sienna had promised to ask Bryan to talk to Ken about it, but Audrey doubted it would do any good.

Esther hugged Audrey again, and Audrey kissed the girl's cheek. Straightening, Audrey said once more, "I'll see you tomorrow." She turned around and began to walk away and then turned back again. Esther waved at her and she waved back before turning around once more.

All the way to Sienna and Bryan's, it took everything in Audrey not to bring up the matter about Esther with Ken. She held her peace, but she knew it would even take more self-control to keep from confronting him once they got to the house.

Audrey looked out of the car window as they

sped down the road. Sienna took her hand but said nothing, and Audrey knew that her sister was giving her space to think.

They got to Sienna and Bryan's house, and Audrey immediately went into the room she shared with Ken and sat on the bed. She covered her face with her hand and then took a deep breath to stop herself from breaking down. Ken walked into the room and she felt anger burn in her heart. He smiled at her, but she did not smile back. She looked away and then stood up when he came and put his hand on her shoulder.

She was burning on the inside, wanting to give him a piece of her mind, but knowing it would do no good. Maybe Bryan would be able to get through to him, though she doubted it.

"So, you won't speak to me?" Ken asked. He came to stand in front of her, invading her space.

She glared at him for a full minute, wanting to let him know how she felt and then turned away. She went to sit down on the bed again.

"I thought you would want to talk about what happened at the orphanage today."

She said not a word to him.

She felt his eyes boring into her, but she refused to turn to look at him. Once again, he put his hand on her shoulder, and she shrugged it off. He sat beside her and put his arm around her.

She turned to glower at him, and then stood and stared him down. She had to leave this room. If she stayed here a minute longer, she would say something she would regret later.

"Audrey... baby, please let's talk," Ken said.

She shook her head slowly, laughed harshly, and said, "Let's talk? For what?" She pressed her lips tightly together and glared at him. And then marched out of the room. She went into the living room, which was now empty, and sat on the sofa. Lifting her eyes to the ceiling, she said, "Lord, I don't know what you are doing, but whatever it is, please do it quickly. Please let Ken change his mind about this. I don't know what I will do if we leave Peru without knowing for certain that we're adopting Esther."

She sighed sadly and picked up the remote control from the coffee table. She switched the TV on and flipped through the channels to distract herself from her pain. She would wait for Sienna to speak to Bryan and see if anything would come of it. She doubted it, however. Ken was as stubborn as a mule. Once he set his mind on something, he never changed it. He had set his mind on the fact that he wanted no children right now, and nothing would change that.

SIXTEEN

Leila smiled at Hauwa and told her she was leaving the house. "Please, tell your grandmother that I will be back a little later today," she said.

Hauwa waved to her as she left.

Leila began to walk to Malik's house. She looked around at the surrounding huts and the farm just a short distance away. A few men were on the farm, working at the part that had not been burned. She thinned her lips and thought about her stay in Dogon. She had been here for a couple of days already and apart from the first day she arrived, she had yet to sit down and have a full conversation with Malik.

She'd thought she could share the gospel with him on the day after she arrived, but everything had gone too fast. Malik was consumed with work on the farm, helping the farmers who had lost everything with their basic needs and trying to make up for the crops that had been burned. Leila, on the other hand, had been fully welcomed by Hauwa and her grandmother and had been busy helping the women with the cooking and the housework. Sometimes, she helped Hauwa sell her candies at the bus station.

It was such a different life from the one she had lived for the past few months in Saudi Arabia. However, it wasn't that different from her life at the women's camp. She found she was perfectly at home in this place. Apart from the incident with those farmers who'd tried to take advantage of her, she actually found that she liked this place. The only thing she didn't like was the fact that she and Malik hardly had time for each other. She hoped that would change today, but she was not holding her breath. The need on the farm was still great and Malik was too occupied there. She had thought they would be able to leave for Nira by now, but it had not been possible.

She got to the front of his house and knocked. For the last two mornings, she'd come here without finding him at home. Yesterday afternoon, she had found him near the farm talking to some of the farmers. He'd told her he would speak to her in the evening. Even though he had kept his word and come to Hauwa's grandmother's house in the evening to see her, the caretaker had come there looking for him with news that he was needed urgently at a farmer's house.

On her journey to Dogon, she had been so worried that they would not be able to keep their hands off each other when they were together. But they'd hardly spent any time alone.

She began to turn around when Malik did not come to the door, and then turned back again when the door opened.

Malik beamed at her. "Leila, my love! I didn't know it was you. I thought it was a caretaker."

She entered the house and, without thinking, hugged him tightly. She began to lean in to kiss him and then remembered she shouldn't. She sighed and drew back.

He groaned and shut his eyes. "This is just torture," he said.

She laughed at the look on his face and then took his hands. "It won't be long before we can kiss each other the way we want to." She started to say that they would be able to get married once her marriage to Dauda was dissolved, and then remembered he was still a Muslim. She could not marry him yet. She had to speak to him right now.

Her heart raced as she opened her mouth to talk to him about Christ, but he looked out the window and said to her, "I am so sorry, Leila. It's time for prayers. Will you wait for me here while I go and pray in my room, or will you go back to Hauwa's house? I will come and get you once I finish."

She shut her eyes briefly, disappointment and guilt flooding her heart. This was exactly why she had to speak to him soon. She said to him, "Don't worry about it, Malik. I'll go to Hauwa's now."

He smiled at her and in his eyes she saw his love for her shining. She smiled back, her heart flooding with love for him. If only he was a Christian and she was not married, they would get married now and she could stay here with him.

She left his house and made her way back to Hauwa's grandmother's house. Guilt and fear dogged her steps. She couldn't marry him until he became a Christian, but what if he never did? What if marrying him was not even part of God's plan for her life?

The questions tore at her heart and fear gripped her. She couldn't imagine going on living without him. But what if the Lord made it clear to her that she was not supposed to marry him?

Do not be unequally yoked with unbelievers, a soft voice in her heart said. She bit her bottom lip and tried to push her worries aside.

You know it's not right, Leila. How are you sure he will come to Christ? You should break it off with him now.

She wanted to cry out at the persistent voice in

her heart that would not let her be. Malik just had to accept Christ. He had to. They were destined to be together.

Then you should be sure that he will come to Christ when you share the gospel with him.

But she wasn't sure. She came from a strict Muslim community back in her hometown in Morocco. She knew how difficult it was for a Muslim to come to Christ. Unless the Lord moved miraculously, it might never happen for Malik.

But he will because he loves me very much, she thought.

How are you sure that will happen? And even if he does convert, will it be a true conversion, or will it just be because of you?

The troubling thoughts followed her all the way to Hauwa's house. She entered the hut and sighed wearily.

Hauwa came out from the inner room and shook her head. "You didn't see Malik?"

Leila said, "I saw him."

"How come you're back already, then?"

"He wants to pray right now." Leila looked around the hut and said, "Where is your grandmother?"

"She's still sleeping," Hauwa said. "You know she came back late yesterday. She was exhausted after visiting all those farmers who lost their property."

Leila nodded. She said to Hauwa, "Is there anything around you want me to help you with?"

Hauwa shook her head and then said, "You could keep me company again while I sell the candies. They're almost finished and my grandmother will have to go to the next town to get some at the confectionery again."

Leila nodded. "Okay. Are you ready to go now?"

"Let me just change and then we will go."

Ten minutes later, they left the hut, with Hauwa carrying a tray of candies on her head. They reached the bus station where Hauwa sold her candies, and Hauwa carefully brought down the tray of candies and placed it on the floor beside a wooden table. Quickly, with the cloth she'd used to carry them, she wiped the wooden table down and placed the tray of candies on it. She arranged the candies carefully on the table and Leila helped her out. After they finished, they sat on the bench next to the table.

There were already people roaming around the bus station. Some were entering the buses on their way to various destinations, while others went into the bus station to buy tickets. Leila thought about her plan to go back to the women's camp. She wished she could speak to Zainah about Malik now. But at the same time, maybe not. She knew exactly what Zainah would tell her. Her best friend would advise her to leave Malik alone since he wasn't a Christian. At least, that was what Zainah had told her to do when she'd first found out about her and Malik in Nira.

Leila felt Hauwa's hand on her shoulder and turned to the girl.

Hauwa smiled at her, watching her with an inquisitive expression. "What's wrong, Leila? You looked really down after you came back from Malik's house. Did you have a fight?"

"No." Leila smiled at her. "No, we didn't."

"Then what's wrong?"

Leila sighed and then studied Hauwa's face. The girl reminded her of Khadija. She was thoughtful and caring, and had a great attitude and intelligence for her age. Leila said to her, "I just have some things running through my mind."

"Is it about your relationship with Malik? You know, he's like a brother to me."

Leila chuckled. "What do you know about relationships, Hauwa?"

"I know that you and Malik love each other. I

think you are going to get married soon."

Leila shut her eyes and sighed again. She wondered how much she could tell the girl and then decided to bare her heart. Hauwa was only eighteen, but she seemed to be wise beyond her years. Besides, Leila needed someone to unburden her heart to.

"There's nothing more I want than to marry Malik now, but there are complications."

"What kind of complications?" Hauwa asked.

"Big complications," Leila said. "For one, I am still married to someone else."

Hauwa's jaw dropped and she stared at Leila for a long moment. Finally, she said, "How come? I thought you were single."

Leila said, "It's a long story, but the short version is that I was forced to marry someone. That was after I met Malik and fell in love with him. Thankfully, my husband has agreed to dissolve the marriage."

Leila chuckled in spite of herself when Hauwa rubbed her palms together in clear glee. Hauwa said, "That means you can get married now, so what's the problem?"

"The problem is that I don't know when my husband will actually dissolve the marriage and I'm growing impatient," Leila said. She looked into Hauwa's eyes and wondered whether to tell her the second reason why she was so troubled. Hauwa and her grandmother, like most people around here, were Muslims. They both knew she was a Christian because she'd told them, but Hauwa might not understand if she told her that she could not marry Malik because he wasn't a Christian, and that she wanted to share the gospel with him so he could become one.

Hauwa said, "There's something else you're not telling me."

Leila smiled. "You are pretty perceptive for your age."

Hauwa smiled and looked at her expectantly.

Leila didn't say anything for a few seconds and then she said, "You know that I am a Christian, Hauwa."

Hauwa nodded.

"As a Christian and someone whose faith means everything to me, I cannot marry Malik unless he shares my faith."

Hauwa said, "I understand that. There are some Muslims who won't marry someone who isn't Muslim. But from what I know, Malik doesn't care about that. He loves you. I know from the way his eyes sparkle whenever he sees you that he wants nothing more than to marry you."

"Yes, I know. But I cannot marry him unless he becomes a Christian. A true Christian."

"But why?" Hauwa asked.

"Because Jesus is the most important person to me and as much as I love Malik, I love Jesus more. I cannot be Malik's wife unless he loves Jesus the same way I do."

Hauwa stared at Leila, her eyes shining with many questions. She said, "Just now, when you talked about your love for Jesus, your entire face lit up and you had a glow about you. It was so strange . . . and yet one of the most beautiful things I have ever seen."

Leila blinked. This wasn't what she had expected when she started talking to Hauwa about Malik. An opportunity to bring this special girl to Christ or at least plant seeds of the gospel was right before her. However, she knew that if Hauwa converted, the people in this village, including her grandmother, would make her life miserable. It was one thing for them to entertain a Christian in their home, but it was another for one of them to become a Christian. They would not be able to abide that.

But what about Malik? a small voice in her heart asked her. You're planning to get him converted as well. And you have not cared about what his community will say or do to him if he converts.

She sighed. That was different. Malik was an adult who did not depend on anyone for his livelihood and upkeep. He could take care of himself. Most of all, they could move to the women's camp together. He didn't have to live amongst people who were hostile.

She turned to look at Hauwa, who was still looking at her with an inquisitive expression, and knew without a doubt that she had to share the gospel with her. This was an opportunity the Lord had placed before her, and there was no way she was going to pass it up.

Leila said, "Hauwa, who is Jesus to you?"

Hauwa shrugged and said, "He's a great prophet. We all know that." Hauwa sighed. "I know Christians think he is the son of God, but we know better."

Leila had expected Hauwa to say words like that, but what she did not expect was the hesitancy and uncertainty in Hauwa's voice and face as she said the words. She seemed ripe and ready to receive the gospel. Leila wondered about that. There were no Christians around except for her. Her eyes widened. Could it be that Hauwa had been watching her for some time?

She put her hand on Hauwa's shoulder and said, "You are right. I believe that Jesus is the son of God." Leila began to share the gospel with her — everything she knew about the Lord. She countered all objections before Hauwa gave them and placed the evidence of the gospel before her. Finally, when she finished, she said, "You need to make a decision, Hauwa. What do you want? Would you like to be a follower of Jesus?"

She held her breath as she searched Hauwa's eyes

and waited. Was she right about the girl? Was Hauwa ripe for the harvest, and would she come to the Lord now or reject Him?

Leila blinked when, without warning, tears began to pour down Hauwa's face. "I have been watching you for some time now, Leila," Hauwa said. "I have been watching the way you carry yourself, the way you sing in the morning when you wake up. The words of the songs that you sing are so touching. One time, I heard you praying. You were talking to God as though you knew Him personally; as though He was truly your father. I want that." She nodded. "I want to receive Jesus."

Even though Leila believed in the power of the gospel to save, her mouth still dropped open for a second. The girl was ready to receive Christ now. Finally, she said, "Do you believe that Jesus is the son of God, Hauwa?"

Hauwa looked at her for a few seconds and then nodded. "I do."

Leila said to Hauwa, "And you do know that it might be risky for you to accept Him into your life?"

Fresh tears poured down Hauwa's face and she nodded.

Leila smiled and then took her hand. She looked around, knowing that she had to make the prayer brief since they were in public, and not in a very Christian-friendly place. She prayed in a very low voice, asking Hauwa to repeat the words after her. She told her to confess that Jesus was a Lord and that he died to rescue her from her sins.

"I ask you to come into my life right now," Leila said, and Hauwa repeated the words after her.

After they finished praying, Leila hugged her and said, "Hauwa, you are now a child of God and you belong to Jesus. Welcome to the family!"

Hauwa's face lit up with a huge smile. Suddenly, a beam of light briefly shone on the girl's face and then disappeared. Leila's eyes widened in surprise and then she smiled. That was clearly supernatural. Hauwa was now a new creature in Christ.

Hauwa laughed with pure joy, and Leila laughed along with her.

"I feel like a brand-new baby," Hauwa said. "How come?"

Laila answered, "It's because you have just been born into the family of God. It's a spiritual birth."

"I am so happy," Hauwa said. "I can't contain this joy. I have to tell my grandmother."

Leila sobered immediately. She knew the kind of trouble Hauwa would be in once she began to share her faith. However, she couldn't stop the girl, no matter what persecutions she would face in the future. Hopefully, she would not be treated the way Leila had been treated in her own community when she'd given her life to Jesus. Like Zainah, she had first been ostracized and then chased out. Thankfully, she had met Miriam, who had taken her to the women's camp. Leila looked at Hauwa with her new-birth glow and the huge smile on her face and knew she might have to be Hauwa's Miriam one day. However, for now, she would let things be.

Someone walked up to the table and asked to buy some candies. Hauwa sold the candies to the man with a huge smile on her face. Other people began to come and Leila marveled at that. It was as though the Lord had kept the customers away until Hauwa had come into the family.

They stayed at the table, intermittently selling candies to people, while Hauwa peppered Leila with questions about the kingdom of God and about Jesus. Leila answered her questions with great joy in her heart, but with a sliver of dread. Would the same thing that had happened to her happen to Hauwa, too? She could not predict the future, but whatever happened, God would take care of Hauwa.

From time to time, Leila's mind went to Malik.

Maybe he had already gone to Hauwa's grand-mother's house. He would be disappointed that she wasn't there. He was probably at the farm now or helping one of the farmers with something.

If only Malik could come to Christ as easily as Hauwa had done. She would have to speak to him before the end of today. Hauwa's salvation had increased her faith. There was nothing impossible with the Lord. If He'd saved Hauwa, then He would definitely save Malik.

Leila kept talking with Hauwa and then she turned and looked around her. She was surprised when she noticed that it was already getting dark. How long had they been sitting here talking? Where had the time gone?

She opened her purse and brought out her wrist-watch. She looked at it. The time was almost seven o'clock. She gasped. "Hauwa, I have to go."

Hauwa held her hand. "Where are you going?" she cried.

"I have to go find Malik. I need to share the gos-pel with him like I have shared it with you."

Hauwa let go of her hand. "Then you must go now," Hauwa said, smiling.

Leila smiled back at her and then hurried away. It was getting late. She had to speak to Malik this evening in his house and then hurry back to Hau-wa's grandmother's. She didn't want to spend too much time in Malik's house alone with him.

She got to Malik's and found that the door was locked. She knocked and waited, but he did not come to open the door. She groaned. She had guessed right. He was still somewhere on the farm. She turned and scanned the farm, but because it was getting dark, she could not see so well.

She considered waiting for him, but she also did not want to be outside when it was dark. After what had happened to her on the day she arrived, she knew she had to be careful. She was never out this late unless she was with Malik. She had to go back to Hauwa's grandmother's now and hope that Malik would come to see her tonight. If he didn't, she would have to wait to speak to him tomorrow. No matter what, before the end of tomorrow, she would share the gospel with him. She would know one way or the other what his decision was and if they had a future together.

Fear, hope, and doubt raged in her heart as she walked back to Hauwa's grandmother's house. She reached the house and saw that Hauwa's grandmother was not yet back from the next town, where she had gone to buy more candies to sell.

Leila went into the inner room and changed into a simple kaftan. She came out to the small living room again and sat on one of the benches that was placed there. She brought out her phone from her purse to read her Bible while she waited for Malik, but she found that the battery was dead. She groaned, dropped the phone back in her purse, and folded her hands to wait.

After a while, she grew bored, and went into the bedroom. Malik would call for her when he came.

Soon, she fell asleep and then some time later, she heard voices — that of Hauwa and then her grandmother's. In her subconscious, she willed the voices to include Malik's. But they did not. She fell into a deep sleep after that, but not before drowsily praying that God would give her the right words to say to Malik; words that would show him how much the Lord loved him.

SEVENTEEN

Lauren came back from church and went straight to her bedroom, feeling exhausted. She had gone straight to church from work for the welfare meeting. Today, they had gone to the Youth Centre and then to The Fruitful Vines. She glanced at her wristwatch and saw it was already a few minutes to ten o'clock.

She sighed and changed out of her work clothes into her nightgown. Today, she felt too tired mentally and physically to get something to eat. As usual, stifling loneliness surrounded her as she climbed into bed. It was always the same thing. Once she came home after work every day, the reality of her life and her situation crashed down on her. She was a single woman in her mid-thirties without children or any hope of having any soon.

She picked up her Bible from the bedside table and opened it to read, and her mind travelled to Nicholas as usual. Since their date at the restaurant, when he told her that he couldn't see her again, she hadn't heard from him or seen him. As much as she was angry with him, she also missed him. She missed the conversations they had on the internet.

She also missed seeing his handsome face.

It's for the best, she thought.

She began to read her Bible, but when she could not concentrate, she groaned. If only she had never met Nicholas. In just the short time she'd known him, she had fallen for him. It was definitely too fast to fall for a guy, but she could not control the way she felt.

You have to forget about him, Lauren. But it was easier said than done. She groaned again and put her Bible aside. She briefly said a prayer and shut her eyes to go to sleep. Usually, she caught up on one of her TV shows, but today she was not in the mood to watch television. In fact, she had not been in the mood for any of her regular routine since the day that Nicholas told her he didn't want to see her again.

It was strange how she felt now. Before she met him, she had been lonely and had prayed and asked the Lord to send someone. However, she did not have this heart-wrenching, empty feeling that she had now. Once again, she wished she had never met him. Not even when Faizan told her he couldn't date her did she feel this sad and empty. And she thought she liked Faizan. In spite of what Nicholas told her on their date, she still had feelings for him. There was something different about him. Something that drew her to him.

"Lord, please help me to forget him," she prayed. She switched the light off and prayed she would fall asleep soon.

Thankfully, she soon began to drift away. And then, she suddenly jerked up when her phone rang. She blinked, wondering who would call her at this time of night. Maybe it was Trisha, or her other friend, Sally.

She stretched out her hand and took her phone from the bedside table. She glanced at it and her eyes widened in shock as she saw it was Nicholas calling her. They had exchanged numbers before their date the last time. She didn't even remember she still had his number on her phone. She had planned to delete it but had not. She stared at it, her heart thudding.

Should I answer this? She shook her head and dropped her phone on the bed.

It finally stopped ringing and she shut her eyes. Why was Nicholas calling her? What did he want? What if he wanted to apologize and tell her he wanted to see her again?

Well, it was too late for that. He'd made it very clear that he didn't want to have a relationship with her. What he wanted right now, she was unwilling to give. So why exactly was he calling? Had he changed his mind and now wanted a relationship with her? But he had told her that he didn't live in Rosefield. Surely that had not changed. Just as he said after their date, there was no point. Like him, she did not want a long-distance relationship.

Are you sure about that?

She pressed away the uncertain thought and then switched the light off, shut her eyes, and tried to go to sleep once again. But sleep would not come. She groaned and tossed and turned on her bed. And then her eyes flew open as her phone rang again. For a few seconds, she stared at it. And then she switched the light on, reached for the phone, and, without thinking too much about it, answered.

"Yes?" She didn't want Nicholas to know she had kept his number, so she kept her voice neutral.

"Hi, Lauren," Nicholas said. His voice sounded hesitant and uncertain. "It's me… Nicholas."

She pretended to be unsure of who he was. "Nicholas? Oh, Nicholas." She injected a bit of non-chalance into her voice and asked, "How are you doing?"

Immediately the words left her lips, she chided herself. How are you doing? What did that even mean?

Nicholas answered, "Umm…. not so great, Lauren. Since the day we had that date and I told you I didn't want to see you again, I haven't been able to get you out of my mind."

Lauren's eyes widened and she sat up. She hated herself right now for seeming too eager to hear what he wanted to say. But she was eager. She wanted to know whether he wanted them to be together.

Nicholas continued, "Even though I've only seen you once and we have only spoken briefly online, I loved our date. I enjoyed talking to you and felt like I'd known you all my life."

He paused, probably waiting for Lauren to say something. But she said nothing.

He went on again. "I'm so sorry for the way things ended. I wish I'd never said what I did."

Lauren finally said, "Nicholas, you were right for saying what you did say. I mean, just as you said, you don't live in Rosefield. You don't believe in long-distance relationships. I don't like long-distance relationships, either. How is it going to work out if we get together and then you leave Rosefield? Besides, you're only looking for something casual. I want something more."

Oh, no! What did I just say? She groaned as embarrassment flooded her. She had just insinuated that he wanted to see her when he had said nothing of the sort. He had only apologized for what he said at their date, but he did not tell her he wanted them to be together. She had just gotten ahead of herself.

She held her breath, her heart beating with shame. He had rejected her then; he probably would do it again.

"Lauren, I know I said I can't do a long-distance relationship, and you were right. I was definitely not looking for something serious. But when I met you, I knew you were different. I have tried to forget about you but I just can't. Will you forgive me and give me one more chance?"

Lauren's heart beat wildly. She had been dreaming of this since their date. However, every time she thought about this kind of scenario, she had always scolded herself for doing so, knowing it would never happen. But now, it actually had. She couldn't believe it. He'd said he was just looking for someone to hook up with; now he was saying he wanted something deeper. But was that really true? She didn't know what to say to him.

"Lauren, are you still there?"

Lauren took a deep breath and said, "I am here. I just don't know what to say to you, Nicholas."

He said, "Say you will go on another date with me and give me another chance. I want to get to know you better. I own a restaurant, and though I am not a chef, I can whip up something great for both of us. Will you have a private dinner with me at my restaurant on Sunday evening? It will just be the both of us as the restaurant is usually closed on that day."

Her heart drummed as she considered his request. Should she accept his apology and go on this date with him? With all her heart, there was nothing she wanted more, but had things really changed? Did he really want to have a relationship with her? He had said he couldn't be in a long-distance relationship. Had that truly changed now? And could she handle a long-distance relationship herself?

She sighed. She did not know the answers to all these questions, but one thing she knew was that she wanted to see him again and she wanted to give him another chance. She finally said, "Okay, Nicholas. I'll go on another date with you."

He hollered and she couldn't help laughing out loud. "Thank you," he said. "When exactly can I pick you up on Sunday evening?"

"Umm . . . probably at about seven or eight."

He said, "It's a date, then!"

After the call ended, Lauren sat on her bed and leaned back against her pillow. She couldn't believe the conversation she'd just had. Just when she was thinking about Nicholas and longing to see him again, he'd called, apologized, and asked her on another date.

She felt excited as she thought about seeing him again and getting a chance to be in a relationship with him. And then all the concerns she'd had earlier crashed down on her again. Once more, she couldn't answer the questions that crowded her mind. But none of the questions took away the exhilaration she felt right now. She felt nothing but hope for the future despite the many concerns in her mind.

"Lord," she prayed, "please let this work out." She wanted things with Nicholas to work out with all her heart. "Please, let him be the one."

You don't even know if he's a Christian or not, a tiny voice in her head said. In fact, you can be sure that he's not, especially with what he told you the last time about just wanting someone to sleep with.

She pressed her lips together tightly and then pushed the thoughts from her mind. People could change. Just because he wasn't a believer now didn't mean he wouldn't become one soon. For now, she would take one day at a time. They had very limited time to be together before he left Rosefield. She wouldn't waste it on worrying about his faith or the future. She intended to enjoy the time she spent with him and cement their relationship so that by the time he left, he would not forget her. That was her plan for now.

*****

Leila rose from the mat on the floor and rubbed her eyes. She looked down at Hauwa, who was still asleep, and then at Hauwa's grandmother sleeping at the other end of the room. She yawned and stretched and then went out of the room and opened the front door of the hut. Going outside, she grabbed a metal bucket from the side of the hut and took it to the well not far away to draw water to have her bath. It was still quite dark outside, but she wanted to hurry up and get to Malik's house before he left again. Today, not only did she want to share the gospel with him, she wanted to spend time with him as well. After all, that was why she had come to Dogon. She missed him. They needed to spend time together, though they had to be careful as they would be alone.

She finished fetching water from the well and reentered the hut. Quickly, she shed her nightgown and wrapped a towel around herself. She carried the water to the small bathing room outside the hut. After bathing, she went back to the house and hurriedly changed into a long, striped dress.

She stepped out of the sleeping room and re-membered the last time she had worn this dress. It was when she and Zainah lived with Fatima and her children. She was going out to meet the man she'd been dating at the time. Zainah had been shocked by the dress, telling her it was too tight. But the funny thing was that the last time she saw Zainah, which was in Nira, Zainah had been wearing a similar dress. However, she understood Zainah's line of thought at the time. They had lived mostly in long boubous and kaftans with their hair wrapped in scarves at the women's camp. Maybe she needed to take Zainah's advice today, as she was going to spend time alone with Malik.

She went back into the room, opened her suitcase once again, and brought out a long scarf. Hauwa stirred and she looked down at the girl, thinking she was about to wake up. But she didn't. However, in an hour's time, Hauwa would be up and ready to go sell her candies. It would be a brand-new day for her as a follower of Christ. Leila quickly whispered a prayer for Hauwa, asking the Lord to be with her and keep her in Him no matter what she faced.

Leila wrapped the scarf around her body and left the house. As it was still dark, she ran to Malik's house and arrived at his front door, panting.

Knocking on the door, she waited for Malik to open up for her and whispered a prayer, asking the Lord to give her the right words to say to Malik.

Seconds later, the door opened, and Malik stared wide-eyed at her in his pajamas. He reached out to take her hand and gently pulled her into the house. He wrapped his arms around her, hugging her, and then drew back quickly. "How come you are here so early?" he asked.

"I wanted to make sure I caught you at home," Leila answered.

Malik threaded his fingers through hers and smiled. "I went to Hauwa's grandmother's house yesterday to get you, but you weren't there. I figured you had gone to the bus station with Hauwa and began to head there. But Abu stopped me on the way and told me my attention was urgently needed at the farm. I'm really sorry, Leila. I know I should have come after I finished at the farm, but it was late. I knew you would probably be preparing for bed by then. I didn't want to disturb you or Hauwa and her grandmother."

"That's okay, Malik," she smiled at him, touched by how considerate he was. His eyes looked bleary with sleep, and as he rubbed them, her heart did a flip. He looked so adorable that it took everything in her not to lean in to kiss him. She took a deep breath and said, "I have something really important I need to speak to you about."

He gave her a nervous smile and said, "I also have something very important to ask you. But you can go first."

Leila lifted her brows as she looked at him. He looked anxious and she wondered why. What she had to talk to him about was really important, but she was itching to know what he wanted to ask her.

"What do you want to ask me, Malik?"

"No, tell me what you want to speak to me about."

"No, you go first."

"Are you sure?" he asked.

She nodded.

He looked back and then led her to the couch. They both sat down and he said, "Wait here. I'll be back in a second." He stood up before she could say anything and left the living room. Less than a minute later, he came back again and sat down next to her. He took her hands and wove his fingers through hers. His eyes searched hers and he said, "Leila, I haven't known you for too long, but I fell in love with you the very first time I laid my eyes on you and knew I wanted to be with you forever."

She smiled sweetly at him, her heart filling with affection for him.

He continued. "The more I know you, the more I love you," he said. "I love everything about you. I've fallen deeply and totally in love with you. You're beautiful, kind, selfless, and the best woman I've ever known."

She beamed at him. "I love you too, Malik. With everything in me."

He smiled. "Leila, you have become my world. You and my daughter, Fanta. I never want to let you go." He knelt on the floor, put his hand in his pajama pocket, and then brought out a box.

Leila's mouth dropped open as he opened the box and showed her a small engagement ring inside. "I've known that I wanted to marry you for a long time and immediately when you came here and told me your husband had agreed to dissolve your marriage, I sent someone to Bamako to buy an engagement ring for you. The man came back two days ago and I have been waiting for the right moment."

He squeezed her hand and went on. "I know the ring is not as expensive as the one you have on, but it was all I could get now. I promise to get a better one soon, but I just want to ask — will you be my wife, Leila, and the mother of my daughter?"

Leila covered her mouth and swallowed the sob rising within her. They had talked about marriage a lot, almost from the first day they met, and she knew without a doubt that they would get married one day. However, this gesture of Malik's, buying her a ring when he didn't have much and proposing to her now, was such a surprise. It was very romantic. She felt overwhelmed with joy and love for him. Tears fell down her face as she gazed at him.

Malik grinned. "Leila, you haven't answered my question. Will you marry me, my love?"

Leila laughed and said, "Of course I will marry you, Malik. You know that."

He slipped the ring on her finger and stood up again.

She wrapped her arms around him and began to weep. "I love you so much, Malik," she said.

He ran his fingers through her hair and said, "I love you too, Leila. I can't wait for the day when we can finally get married."

She pulled back from him and looked into his eyes. If only she could kiss him now, she thought. From the way he was looking at her, she knew he was thinking the same thing. But it couldn't happen now. They had to wait until her marriage was dissolved. Still, that did not dilute the joy she felt now. This made everything so real.

But you know you can't marry him. Not until he becomes a Christian.

She shut her eyes in alarm. She still hadn't shared the gospel with him. She had to speak to him now.

"What is it, my love?" Malik searched her face.

She shook her head and said, "Nothing. I am so happy!"

She sighed and brushed away her concerns. She didn't need to talk to him right now. This was such a happy and emotional moment. She didn't want to spoil it. She would speak to him soon, but right now, she wanted both of them to enjoy the moment.

Malik reached out and hugged her tight. He kissed her forehead and then quickly drew back.

"I'm sorry," he said.

She smiled sadly. "It's okay," she said. She wanted to kiss him the way she had been dreaming of ever since they were separated at Nira, but she couldn't. When would Dauda come to Nira so their marriage could be dissolved? The earlier he did, the sooner she could marry Malik.

You still have to share the gospel with him. He might not even accept the Lord.

She shuddered at the thoughts in her mind and, once again, brushed them aside. This was not the time to worry about that. For now, they needed to celebrate their engagement.

"Let's go out and celebrate," she said.

He lifted his brows and asked her where they should go. "We really have nowhere to celebrate in this place," he said to her.

"Well, let's go to Hauwa's. We can tell her and her grandmother that we are officially engaged. I'm sure Hauwa's grandmother will cook something delicious for us."

He grinned. "Well, that sounds like a great idea."

They left the house holding hands and walked leisurely to Hauwa's grandmother's house. Leila's heart was full of joy; more joy than she had ever felt, except for the day she came to Christ. This was everything she had dreamed of for years — getting married and starting a family. Actually, it was much more than she had ever dreamt of, because not only was she getting married, she was marrying someone she loved with all her heart. There was nothing better than that.

EIGHTEEN

Nick finished preparing the food in the restaurant kitchen and smiled at Leon, Frank's sous chef. Leon had assisted him in preparing the food. Nick had told Lauren he would cook for her, but he did not realize how much pressure that would place on him. He liked her much more than he thought and that was why he had called her even after he'd decided it was best to go their separate ways. After he invited her on another date and promised to cook, he had panicked as he wanted to impress her.

Why did I tell her I was going to cook for her? he had scolded himself. He owned a restaurant. He could have told one or two of the chefs to prepare something nice for both of them. Instead, he had bragged about his culinary skills. Since he told her he would cook for her and didn't want to lie to her, he had come to the restaurant today after buying the ingredients needed for the dishes he planned to make. However, knowing that he would need help, he had invited Leon to assist him. He had still not told Frank he was seeing Lauren again and therefore couldn't ask for his help.

He thanked Leon and then covered the dishes he

had prepared. He had also enlisted the help of one of the waiters for the private dinner. He glanced at his watch. It was a few minutes after six. He was supposed to pick up Lauren in less than an hour. He had to go and change quickly so he could go pick her up at her house.

He went into the room where some of the staff changed before and after work and shed his jeans and T-shirt. He put on the white dress shirt and pants he had hung in front of the closet and pulled on his black dress shoes. He glanced at the full-length mirror near the door, buttoned his shirt, and quickly brushed his hair.

He found he was a little nervous as he got into the car he'd rented when he first arrived in Rose-field and began to drive to Lauren's. She had given him her address after he invited her to go on this date with him. His heart beat with excitement and nervous anticipation.

He whispered harshly to himself, "Why are you so nervous? It's just a date. You've been on tons of dates."

But this felt slightly different. For the first time in a very long time, he felt like he could be in a full-fledged relationship. Actually, he ached to be in a relationship with her. However, he still wasn't sure it was the best thing to do. But it was what he wanted.

The drive to her house was a short one. He pulled up to a small bungalow and walked up to it. Ringing the bell, he waited for her to open the door. He took a deep breath, looked down at himself, and once more, scolded himself for being so nervous.

You are acting like this is your first date. Get yourself together, man.

The door opened and Lauren beamed at him. His heart did a flip as he gazed at her. She looked so beautiful. She was dressed in a knee-length black dress which showed off her slim but curvy figure.

Her blonde hair was down almost to her waist, and her eyes sparkled as she looked at him with the most enchanting smile he'd ever seen on a woman.

"You look absolutely amazing," he said to her.

"Thank you," she said, still smiling at him. "You look great yourself."

He was surprised when she took his hand and pulled him into her house. She pointed at the sofa near the door and asked him to sit down. "I'll be out in a minute," she said.

He nodded and smiled as she quickly left the living room. He looked around the place. It was small but cozy. He loved the center rug on the floor the most. The other furniture was plain, but the center rug seemed expensive and lifted up the entire room. He leaned back on the cream sofa as he waited for her to come out.

He asked himself if he was sure about this. He was committing himself now to a new relationship and yet he still had to leave this small town in about a week. Lauren was worth giving up his single life for, but would the distance affect the relationship? Could he be faithful to her with the distance between them? He was used to having a string of one-night or several night-stands, as Frank called it. He had not been in a committed relationship in a long time. But he wanted to be exclusive with Lauren. He would do everything in his power to stay faithful and committed to her. He had to explore this relationship.

She walked out of the living room and once again he was taken with her beauty. He could truly say that she was the most beautiful woman he had ever dated, and he'd dated quite a few beautiful women.

"I'm ready," she said to him with a smile.

He stood up and went to open the door.

They both stepped out of the house. After she'd locked the door, he took her hand and they walked to the car together. Once they were in, he buckled his seatbelt and turned to look at her, his heart racing wildly. He resisted the urge to lean in and kiss her. She definitely would not welcome that as she wasn't like most of the girls he had dated in the past.

He looked away quickly and started the car. As he drove to the restaurant, he intermittently inhaled the enticing scent of her perfume. She smelled like roses and something else that made his head spin.

He got to the restaurant and parked right in front of it. Quickly, he opened his door and went to open hers. She looked at the restaurant with wide eyes and an uneasy look crept into her face.

A knot formed in the pit of his stomach. "What is it, Lauren?" he asked, trying to hide the worry he felt.

"Umm . . . nothing," she answered. "I just didn't expect you to bring me to such a nice restaurant. I thought it would be a more informal place."

He looked her over. "But you are dressed for a nice restaurant, Lauren. And yes, I run this nice place with my partner."

The uneasy look returned.

He smiled to put her at ease and breathed a sigh of relief when she smiled back at him and the worry disappeared from her face.

He took her hand as she came out of the car and held on to it as they walked into the restaurant together.

He led her to the table he had reserved. Not that anyone was in the restaurant, but he liked this part of the restaurant because of how secluded it was. The lights were low but not low enough that they could not see each other. He'd asked one of the waiters to light candles and everything had been set on the table for both of them.

Unlike the other tables in the restaurant, this one was more like a booth. It was specifically for couples who wanted a measure of privacy on their date. It had a single chair so a couple could sit side by side rather than facing each other. That was another reason why he had chosen this particular booth. He wanted her right beside him. That way, he could take her hand whenever he wanted to and maybe, just maybe, she would want to kiss him some time into their date. But if not, he still wanted her right beside him.

They sat down and he was happy when she slid close to him. When he took her hand, she smiled sweetly at him, causing his pulse to race.

Mike, the waiter he had asked to help out with their dinner today, came and began to list the dishes on the special menu that Nick had given him. Lauren turned to him with a smile and asked, "Did you cook everything on that menu?"

"Most of it," he said. "Obviously, I did not make the desserts."

The waiter went away and then Lauren said, "I am glad you asked me out again, Nicholas."

"I am glad I did, too," he said.

During the starter, they talked about random things, light topics. They talked about her job as an elementary school teacher and his work at the restaurant. By the time the main course arrived, the conversation had moved to more serious things like what their future plans were and what they wanted in the relationship. Nick told her that when he pictured his future, he had always pictured himself single, until the day he met her. "I told myself that I would remain single unless I met the kind of woman that would make me want otherwise. When I met you, I knew you were that kind of woman."

She beamed and took his other hand on the table. She wove her fingers through his and his heart began to drum. He liked that she was just as touchy-feely as he was. He had not known her for long, but he could see that she felt the same way about him that he did her.

They talked late into the night, and after each course, she complimented his cooking, causing him to smile broadly with pride. He always reminded her that he'd had help from one of the chefs but she still insisted he was a great cook.

At about midnight, they finally stood up to leave. His hand found hers easily and once again, she threaded her fingers through his. Her hand felt so natural in his. To him, it was a sign that they belonged together and could make this work even though they lived in different cities.

On the drive home, they continued their conversation about the future of their budding relationship. When he finally pulled up in front of her house, he felt an aching sadness. He didn't want this date to end.

They both got out of the car and he walked her to the front of the house.

"I had a great time," she said.

"I did, too," he told her, looking deep into her eyes.

She made no move to open the door as they both stared at each other. Finally, she said, "Do you want to come in?"

Her question took him by surprise and he blinked. He couldn't speak for a long moment as he fought with himself.

She said, "Just for a night cap."

Again, he stared into her eyes and knew it would not be a great idea for him to come in. He would feel no remorse if one thing led to another and they became intimate. However, she was religious. He knew she would feel terrible afterward. It was not the right thing to do, at least right for now.

He squeezed her hand and smiled at her. "I should get going, Lauren. It's really late. I have to be at work early in the morning."

She looked disappointed, but there was a slight look of relief on her face also. She said, "You are right. I have to be at work early in the morning as well."

For a few seconds more, they stared at each other, neither of them wanting to move away. Finally, he let go of her hands and said, "I will call you tomorrow, Lauren." He leaned in, kissed her cheek, and walked back to his car.

He got in the car and stuck his head out the window. She was still standing in front of her house, looking at him. He waved at her, started the car, and drove away.

At his room in the bed and breakfast, he sat on the bed. He couldn't stop the huge smile that took over his face. He'd had a great time with her. Without a doubt, he knew he wanted to see her again... as soon as possible. He would call her tomorrow and set up another date, probably for the coming weekend.

Suddenly, his heart sank as he remembered he was leaving Rosefield on Friday. The reality of the situation crashed down on him. Their relationship was going to be a long-distance one. He couldn't imagine how hard it would be, especially for him. He loved physical contact and being able to touch and hold the person he was with.

How will this work?

He sighed. It had to work. You didn't meet women like Lauren every day.

He couldn't resist reaching for his phone and sending her a text message, telling her how much of a good time he'd had on their date. After that, he lay on the bed and then worry filled his mind again as he thought about leaving Rosefield on Friday.

He had to find a way to see her before then. He could call her after work tomorrow and try to set up another date before Friday. Of course they would have to talk about how the relationship would be handled once he left Rosefield. But somehow he knew they would make it work, because he really liked her. And from the way she had looked at him throughout the evening, he was sure she really liked him, too.

It will all work out, he thought to himself as he stretched out on the bed. It had to.

*****

Lauren walked to Trisha and Frank's feeling exhilarated and nervous at the same time. She'd just left work, but rather than go straight home, she was going to see Trisha. Frank would still be at the restaurant. And so would Nicholas. He had called her just as she closed from work and asked her on another date, this time on Wednesday after work. He had said it was just a casual date and that he would pick her up. She couldn't wait to see him again, but she could not forget what had happened on their last date when they had first arrived at the restaurant.

It has been a lovely date. She had gotten to know him better and knew for sure she wanted a relationship with him. She could see both of them together. However, there was one thing she wanted to clear up; one thing that had been bothering her for a while. She now knew that he was the guy Trisha and Frank had talked about some time ago. The friend who was a player. When Nicholas had pulled up at the restaurant yesterday, she had almost smacked herself on her forehead. Why had she not known all along that he was Nick, Frank's friend and work partner? The one Frank had gone to pick up at the airport weeks ago?

She had managed to hide her surprise from him. Because he had told her his name was Nicholas, she had not made the connection immediately, even though she should have, especially since he'd told her he co-owned a restaurant. She had probably made an unconscious effort not to connect the dots because she didn't want him to be the player Trisha had told her about. That was why she was going to Trisha's house today. If she was going to be in a relationship with Nicholas, she had to know the whole truth about him. She needed to find out if Nicholas was really as promiscuous as Trisha had made him out to be. Because if he was, she could not handle that.

She arrived at Trisha's and rang the doorbell.

Trisha appeared at the door seconds later with Ruby in her arms. "Hey, Lauren! I wasn't expecting you today."

Lauren shrugged. "I came straight from work."

"I just left the bookstore not too long ago," Trisha said.

"I know," Lauren said. "You usually get home from the store around this time." Lauren smiled at Ruby and touched the little girl's cheeks.

Ruby giggled and Lauren chucked her under the chin. She came into the house and sat on the couch. Trisha sat beside her and Ruby immediately slid down from her lap.

Trisha turned to watch Ruby toddle to the other end of the living room. When the little girl started to play with her toys on the floor, Trisha turned back to Lauren.

"I have something to tell you," Lauren said. "But please, promise you won't judge me and that you will be honest with me."

Trisha stared at her for a minute and then said, "What do you want to tell me? You're making me nervous."

"Please make me a promise that you won't judge me, Trisha," Lauren repeated.

Trisha sighed. "It depends on what you are about to tell me."

In spite of herself, Lauren chuckled. She said, "Please, Trisha, be serious. Promise me."

"Okay," Trisha said. "I won't judge you."

"And promise you will be completely honest with me."

"I'm always honest with you, Lauren."

Lauren nodded, took a deep breath, and said, "I met up with that guy I met on the online dating site."

Trisha's jaw dropped and she exclaimed, "Lauren, it's too soon!"

"Actually, I have gone on two dates with him already."

Trisha shook her head slowly and said, "Wow! Don't you think you're moving too fast?"

"You haven't even asked how the dates went or what kind of guy he is."

Trisha shrugged. "Alright, Lauren. What kind of guy is he? Is he a good guy?"

"I think he is a great guy, but that is why I came here to talk to you." She pressed her lips tightly together, her heart racing with worry. What Trisha told her now would determine how her relationship with Nicholas would go from today or if they would even have a relationship. She added, "Both dates were at Frank's restaurant, Trisha."

Trisha raised her brows, a surprised expression on her face. "And Frank did not see you guys? Of course he didn't. He would have told me if he had."

"He didn't see us," Lauren said.

Trisha gave her a small smile. "He took you to a nice restaurant. I guess that is a good sign. Unless he wasn't the one who suggested the date at Frankly Eating. Please tell me he was."

Lauren said, "He was the one. The second time he asked me to go on a date with him, he told me it would be a private dinner at his restaurant."

Trisha frowned and a confused look appeared on her face. "What did he mean by that?" And then her mouth fell open. She shook her head slowly. "No, it can't be! Is Nick, Frank's friend, the guy you're talking about?"

"He is," Lauren said softly. "I call him Nicholas, though."

"Lauren!" Trisha shook her head. "Why didn't you tell me before?"

"Obviously, Trisha, I didn't know it was the same Nick. I didn't make the connection until he took me to the restaurant on Sunday."

Trisha stared at her for a long moment, worry and concern written clearly on her face. "Do you remember what I told you about him?" Trisha asked.

"I do. That's why I came to talk to you," Lauren said. "I really, really like him. I think I want to be with him, but I can't forget what you told me." Lauren looked into Trisha's eyes. "I want to ask, Trish, were you really serious about everything you said about him? Is he really that bad?"

Trisha said, "Lauren, I am going to be honest with you. I like Nick as a person, but he has made it clear that he's only interested in one thing when it comes to women. He doesn't do it spitefully, but from what Frank has told me about him, he doesn't have a faithful soul. And he isn't ashamed to talk about his one-night stands." She took Lauren's hand and said, "Besides, he's not a believer, Lauren. You know better than to date someone who doesn't share your faith and values."

An overwhelming sadness settled in Lauren's heart as she listened to Trisha's words. She knew they were all true. Nicholas had told her he was only interested in hooking up with her the first time they met. She was sure he was serious about wanting a relationship with her now, but that didn't mean that he would be faithful to her. And with the long-distance relationship, the likelihood of him remaining faithful was nil. Most importantly, he wasn't a believer. She knew she shouldn't be involved with a non-believer in the first place.

Trisha squeezed her hand and smiled sadly at her. "You look so dejected, Lauren. I'm so sorry. I didn't know you had fallen this hard for him. But you told me to be honest with you and I have been honest. You will have to make your decision. I can only tell you what I think. And I hope you do make the right decision."

Tears formed in Lauren's eyes, but she blinked them back. Just when she thought she had met the one she'd been waiting for, this had come to light. As much as she wanted to believe that people changed and Nicholas could, she knew it might never happen. She didn't want to be in another similar relationship to her marriage. She had sworn not to be involved with someone who did not share her faith ever again. Getting involved with Nicholas would be just that. She was certain he wasn't an abuser like Richie, but if the relationship was riddled with infidelity, she would feel just as brutalized as she had with Richie. Only emotionally, rather than physically.

She felt a sob rising up in her and pushed it down. She said in a voice choked with emotion, "Oh Trisha, I really like Nicholas. But you're right. I need to end things with him." Her heart hurt just thinking about ending the blossoming relationship. "He wants us to go on another date on Wednesday."

Trisha said, "He is leaving Rosefield on Friday. I hope he told you that."

Lauren nodded. "He did. He wanted us to go on one more date before he left." She couldn't hold back the tears anymore and they fell down her cheeks. She brought out a tissue from her purse and quickly dabbed at them.

Trisha shifted closer to her and hugged her. "I'm really sorry, Lauren."

"He seemed so perfect, Trish," Lauren said. "Why oh why isn't he a Christian with the kind of morals that would make a good relationship? Why, Trisha?

Why can't I find someone to spend the rest of my life with? And you were right. I tend to be attracted to bad boys. Clearly, I am doing something wrong or there's something in me that attracts them."

Trisha did not say anything. She just continued to rub Lauren's back soothingly.

After a long while, Lauren drew back from Trisha. "I think I have to go home now. I have to call Nicholas as soon as possible and tell him it's over so it wouldn't seem like I've been leading him on."

Trisha smiled sadly. "I wish I knew a guy who would be great for you, but I don't."

Lauren felt her heart breaking, but she shrugged. "It's not your responsibility to find me a guy, Trish." She felt herself wanting to break down again and then bit her lip to keep from crying. "I guess I have to keep waiting on the Lord until He brings someone to me. But I am so tired of waiting." She looked into Trisha's eyes and sighed. "What if I never meet anyone?"

"Stop it, Lauren!" Trisha put her hand on Lauren's shoulder. "You will meet someone soon."

"But what if it's too late for me to start a family by the time I meet that person? And will the person be someone I really connect with the way I connected with . . . ?"

She couldn't bring herself to complete the sentence or she would break down. She stood up and went to the door.

Trisha followed her and touched Lauren's arm. "If you need anything, don't hesitate to call me."

Lauren nodded and left the house.

All the way to her house, Lauren resisted the urge to fall apart. She felt an overwhelming sadness. It wasn't just because she was devastated by the fact that she had to end things with Nicholas when she liked him so much, but also because she had thought she had finally met a man she could spend the rest of her life and start a family with.

She got to her house and tossed her purse onto

the couch. Tears fell down her face. She had to make the call now. If she postponed it, she might never tell Nicholas that this relationship wouldn't work. She could imagine how he would feel. It was the way she had felt when he told her they couldn't be together. He would probably feel even worse because this last date, they had both felt a deep connection with each other. Her words would take him by surprise, she was sure.

Before she could change her mind, she reached for her purse and brought out her cell phone. Quickly, she dialed his number, and then her heart drummed as his phone began to ring.

Lord, please help me, she cried out in her heart.

"Hello, Lauren!" his voice came on the line. "I'm so glad you called."

She bit her lip until she felt as though she would bite through it. Suddenly, she couldn't keep in her emotions anymore and broke down. She said through a voice choked with emotion, "Nicholas, I am so sorry, but I can't see you anymore."

"What?" he exclaimed.

"You were right the first time, Nicholas. The relationship is not going to work. I'm sorry." She ended the call and tossed her phone aside.

Her phone immediately began to ring and she ignored it. It stopped ringing and she covered her face with her hands. It began to ring again and this time she turned it off so he would not be able to call her again. She tossed her phone aside and folded herself on the bed in her work clothes. She didn't have the strength to change into her night-gown. This would be her life for a long time. A life of loneliness. Of coming home to an empty house. She had thought after she met Nicholas that things would be different, but now, with the relationship over before it had begun, loneliness would be her only companion.

"Lord, why?" she cried out. She listened, but heard nothing.

NINETEEN

Leila hugged Hauwa's grandmother and said, "Thank you so much, Ma. Thank you for letting me stay in your home and for treating me so well. I will never forget you."

The old woman placed her hands on Leila's cheeks and said, "Be well, my dear. Take good care of yourself," she looked at Malik, who was standing near the door. "And take good care of him, too."

Leila smiled and said, "I will. Take care of yourself, too."

Hauwa walked up to her with tears in her eyes. She said to Leila, "I am going to miss you so much."

Leila reached out and gathered her in her arms. She whispered in Hauwa's ear, "Remember to draw closer and closer to Jesus every day. He'll always be with you."

Leila drew back and saw that tears were streaming down Hauwa's face. She wiped away the tears with her thumb and beamed at Hauwa. "You have been so kind to me. You and your grandmother." She looked at Malik and then looked back at Hauwa. "I hope you will be able to come to me and Malik's wedding when we finally get married."

Hauwa smiled through her tears and said, "I

would love that." She lowered her voice and whispered, "Thank you for sharing the gospel with me. You changed my life."

Leila nodded and hugged the girl again. She finally let her go and then grabbed the handle of her suitcase. Malik came and took the suitcase from her and began to pull it behind him. Leila turned again. She waved at Hauwa and her grandmother and then followed Malik out the door.

Malik's small duffel bag was slung over his shoulder. He took her hand while he pulled her suitcase with his other hand. He smiled at her and said in a voice filled with excitement, "I can't wait for you to meet Fanta."

Leila raised her eyebrows and chuckled. "I've met her before, remember?"

"Yes, but you only met her once and at that time we didn't know where our relationship was going. Now we know that you will soon be her new mother."

Leila's stomach lurched at his words. She still hadn't shared the gospel with him. She took a deep breath and told herself to calm down. The Lord had touched and saved Hauwa when she'd shared the gospel with the girl. He would also do the same for Malik. They were going to Nira now that Malik had finished everything he was doing in Dogon. He would not be too busy to spend as much time with her as she wanted. She would be able to now share the gospel with him.

They walked side by side until they reached the bus station. They both entered the bus station and stood at the back of the line to buy their tickets to Nira. Malik put his hand around her, drew her close, and beamed at her. She smiled back at him and whispered, "There are people watching us, Malik. You know how conservative this place is. We're still not married, remember?"

He groaned and let her go. Discreetly, without

looking at her, he took her hand. She chuckled at the look on his face.

Their turn finally came and Leila opened her purse to buy their tickets. Malik stared at her. "What are you doing, Leila?" he asked.

"Buying our tickets," she said, chuckling. "What does it look like I'm doing?"

He shook his head and said, "I mean, why do you want to buy our tickets?" He didn't let her answer but said, "I will buy them."

She wanted to argue and tell him she had more than enough money for both of them. She knew he wasn't paid that much on the farm and she had money that she had saved in Saudi Arabia, and the money Dauda had generously given to her. At this time, she knew she had more than him. However, from the way he looked, insisting on paying for both of them would not be the right thing to do. She shrugged and let him pay.

After he collected their tickets from the woman behind the counter, they both went out of the bus station together. All around them, people were boarding buses heading for different destinations, or roaming around the bus station grounds. A few traders were selling their wares, which they carried on their heads. Leila's mind went to Hauwa. She usually came out to sell her candies here at around eight o'clock in the morning. It was still a few minutes past seven. Leila smiled. She would miss that girl. Hauwa reminded her of Khadija. She turned to Malik as they found empty benches and said, "I can't wait to see Khadija again. I really like that girl."

He smiled at her. "It seems you and my sisters are kindred spirits. Talking about my sister, have you heard from Zainah? We still don't really know where she is."

Leila said, "She's probably in America now with Faizan. She was trying to get me to go to their wedding before your father deceived her and made her come back to Nira. They are probably married now and living happily together."

Malik stared into her eyes and took her hands. She raised an eyebrow and he said, "I know, I know. People are looking at us. But I just can't resist. I can't wait until we get married so we can hold hands wherever we are without raising eyebrows."

Again, guilt invaded her mind and she sighed. I will tell him about Christ soon. This is not the place nor the time.

They talked about the farm and the harvest. Malik told her they had tried their best to plant the remaining seeds in the parts of the farm not affected by the fire. "It's left to be seen how much produce we will harvest by this time next year," Malik said. "It will be really small. I feel so sorry for the farmers who have toiled continuously on that farm. I wonder what my father will say about it all when I get home?"

Leila absentmindedly caressed the back of his hand with her thumb. "When I went to Nira, your father didn't seem particularly troubled, even though Khadija told me he had heard about it. But I remember Khadija also saying he had been mad at everyone when he received the news and had raged and cursed everyone out. She told me he later calmed down for some reason."

Leila pressed her lips together, wondering whether to tell him what Khadija had said about her suspicions concerning the fire. Finally, she decided to tell him about it. "Khadija told me that everyone thinks Jibril, your father's so-called friend and Zainah's ex-husband. had sent people to burn down the farm. He had threatened to do so at one point."

Malik nodded. "We've also heard the rumors

here. I wouldn't be surprised. Every time I see that man, he has a wicked gleam in his eyes. I think he and his brother were behind the fire."

Leila pursed her lips and, without thinking, she said, "I doubt that Dauda had anything to do with it."

Malik raised his brows and stared at her in surprise. He said, "How come you're defending him, Leila? It wasn't just Jibril who threatened to burn my father's farm down. Even if he did not say the words, he was there when his brother told my father that. Surely, he's just as guilty as his brother."

Leila said, "Dauda did not strike me as someone who would just burn down another's farm. He seemed like a very kind person when I lived in his house."

"How kind can someone who forced a woman to marry him be?" Malik said in an incredulous voice.

"He told me if it wasn't for his brother, he would not have even thought about marrying me without my consent."

"But he did marry you without your consent. He's just as guilty as Jibril."

She wanted to say she did not believe that he was, but she changed her mind. The more she defended Dauda, the more Malik would wonder why she was defending him. She smiled brightly at him and said, "Well, it doesn't matter who is guilty. All that matters is that soon, Dauda will come to Nira and dissolve our marriage, and then you and I will be free to wed."

Malik smiled tenderly at her. "I can't wait for that to happen," he said. "And I am sorry for doubting you. If you say Dauda is a good person, then I believe you. At least he agreed to dissolve the marriage."

Leila wanted to caress his cheeks, but she settled for his hand. "Thank you," she said to him.

They changed the topic and talked about his

daughter, Fanta. He told her about the little quirks and funny things Fanta did. "She's growing so fast," he said. "I know it's selfish to wish she would remain a child forever, but I just can't help it. Sometimes, I feel like I will wake up one day and she'll already be an adult, ready to get married and leave me."

Leila laughed.

"It's not funny," he said, shaking his head at her.

"I'm sorry," Leila said, still laughing. "It's just the way you said that you'll wake up one day and she would be an adult, ready to get married." Leila smiled at him and said, "Don't worry about it, Malik. You still have many more years to spend with your daughter."

He said to Leila, "Talking about fathers and daughters, you've never told me about your parents. Is your father still alive? What about your mother?"

Leila shut her eyes briefly as pain stabbed her heart. She opened her eyes and sighed.

Malik said softly, "I am sorry, Leila. If it's too painful for you to talk about, then you don't have to."

She replied, "It's okay. My mother died when I was only four. Growing up, I always wished I had a mother. It was kind of painful not to have one. My father did the best he could for me and my elder sister. At least, I thought he did. I thought he loved me until I came to Christ and he turned his back on me. So did my sister. I was devastated by that. I never looked back after I left my hometown to the women's camp. I haven't seen or heard from them since."

Malik threaded his fingers through hers and his eyes searched hers. He said, "Don't you ever wonder about them, Leila? Don't you want to see them again?"

"I used to think about them a lot a few years after I went to the women's camp. But the women there gradually became my family. Zainah helped mend my heart. It's not like I have totally forgotten about them, but I hardly regard them as my family now."

Malik nodded. "I understand. I think you will relate well with Fanta. You both have the same experience of losing your mothers at an early age. I'm so thrilled that I have you, Leila. Fanta will not grow up without a mother because you will be her mom." He rubbed Leila's back and said, "You will make such a great mother for Fanta. And maybe, even though you did not grow up with a mother, getting to be a mother yourself might help to heal some of the wounds you have from being mother-less."

"I hope so," Leila said. She felt tears stinging her eyes as she said, "Do you really think I will be a great mother?"

"The best," Malik said. "I have no doubt about it."

"Thank you," she said to him. Hope and guilt warred in her heart as she talked about being a mother to Malik's daughter. She wanted that very much. But what if Malik did not accept the gospel? Right now, he was beyond excited that he would have her as his wife, and also a mother for his child. But if she shared the gospel with him and he refused to accept the Lord, he would be devastated, just as she would be.

Worry and fear threatened to strangle her. She looked down to the floor and exhaled. Please Lord, please let him accept you. She knew it was wrong for her to want him to come to the Lord mostly so they could get married, but it was how she felt.

He lifted her chin with his finger and stared into her eyes. "What's wrong?"

"Nothing," she lied.

He shook his head. "Something is wrong, Leila. Tell me what it is."

She sighed and said nothing for a long moment. Finally, she opened her mouth to tell him why she looked sad and then started when a man beside a bus near them began to yell, "Everyone going to Nira, get onto this bus right now!"

She forced a smile and stood up. "Let's get onto the bus," she said to Malik.

He stood up, pulled her suitcase in one hand, and carried his small duffle bag in the other.

They both watched as the driver put her suitcase and his small bag into the trunk. After that, they got on the bus and sat in the second row. Leila sat near the window, while Malik took the seat next to her. The bus soon filled up and the driver shut the doors.

The driver, a short man with a goatee, got into the driver's seat and soon they moved out of the bus station. Malik said, "Nira, here we come!" He looked at Leila and added, "I feel so different this time going to Nira with you. It feels . . . what can I say? It feels nice, and I am definitely more at peace with you beside me." Once again, he took her hand and squeezed it.

On the journey, Leila and Malik chatted and laughed. She buried her worries in her heart. There was no point worrying right now. She would share the gospel with him when they got to Nira and pray with all her heart that he would be receptive to it.

The driver soon stopped at a canteen located in a small village. Leila and Malik came out of the bus with some of the other passengers and went in. They chose an empty table and sat facing each other. They ordered their meal and once it came, they dug in.

Leila laughed. "This feels like a date," she said.

"A date?"

"You know, a date. It's when two people who like each other or want to explore a relationship go out somewhere and spend time together getting to know each other better."

He smiled. "I know what a date is, Leila. I was just surprised because I didn't think about it like that until you said it."

She said, "Well, I didn't know what a date was until I learned about it when I was in a small town in North Africa with Zainah. I went out on a few dates with a guy I met there." After she had spoken the words, she wished she had not told him about going on a date with another guy, even though it was before she'd met him.

He didn't seem put out or jealous. He said, "After Fanta's mother died, I considered remarrying several times, but I never found any woman who I wanted to settle down with." He looked away from her and she frowned. He turned back to her again and said, "This sounds a little strange, but before you came to Dogon, I was thinking about getting married again. Not to someone I know, but just getting married so my daughter would have a mother. I figured that since you were already married to Dauda, there was no hope for either of us. I didn't want my daughter growing up without a mother and staying in my father's house continuously."

Leila was surprised by what he had said, but she totally understood. She said to him, "I see why you would do that. If I were in your shoes, I would probably do the same thing."

He took a sip of water and then said to her, "I am so glad you came back to me, Leila. Thank God I don't have to marry a random woman and try to see if she will be a good mother for my daughter. I love you, and I know you love me and would love Fanta because of that. You have so much love in you and will be a great mother."

She smiled widely. "Thank you for saying that, Malik," she said. For the umpteenth time that day, she looked at the ring he had given her. It was a beautiful engagement ring, but it filled her heart with guilt as she stared at it. She would never totally be comfortable with him and the idea of marrying him until she and Dauda had dissolved their marriage and until he had come to share her faith.

They finished their food and then went back into the bus again. For the rest of the journey, they continued to chat, enjoying each other's company. Finally, the bus approached the Nira bus station and Leila said to Malik, "It's so strange. For years I stayed in one place and never saw the rest of the world. Now, for the past year, I have been traveling from one place to another. Nira especially seems like my second home now. Granted, a home where a lot of bad things have happened, but one of the most beautiful things that has ever happened to me happened here."

He said with a tease in his voice, "Really? And what is that beautiful thing that happened to you here?"

She laughed. "As if you don't know. You happened to me."

He grinned at her. "And you, my love, like my daughter's birth, are the most beautiful thing that has ever happened to me."

She melted at his words. Once again, it took everything in her not to lean in and kiss him.

They left the bus station together after they had taken their luggage and crossed the road. They followed the path that Khadija had pointed out to her months ago and got to the back of his house in no time. Going around to the front, Malik asked her if she would come with him to his father's house so he could get his keys, or if she wanted to wait.

"I'll come with you," she said.

They left their luggage near Malik's front door and walked the short distance to his father's house. Malik knocked on the gate and then waited. Leila looked at him and sighed happily. She couldn't believe she was standing next to him now. After all she'd gone through and how long she had searched for him, they were finally together. If not for all her worries about her marriage and his faith, she would be the happiest woman in the entire world. Once he accepted the Lord and her marriage to Dauda was dissolved, nothing would be able to mar her joy. They would be so happy together.

The gates opened and Khadija stared at both of them. She let out a shout and threw her hands around Leila and Malik at the same time. She drew back with a huge smile on her face and said excitedly, "You're both here!" She looked at Leila and grinned. "You're finally with Malik! I'm so happy you found each other again."

Malik beamed at his sister and then asked, "Is my mother home?"

Khadija answered, "She went to the market. And so did my mother."

He said, "That means Fanta is not in the house?"

Khadija nodded. "She went to the market with your mother. I think they will soon be back."

"Can I have the keys to my house?"

"Won't you come in?" Khadija asked. She looked at Leila and then turned back to her brother.

Malik said, "I am really tired now. And I don't want to see Father just yet. I suppose he is at home?"

Khadija nodded. "He is."

"Do I have to come in before I get the keys to my house?"

Khadija chuckled. "Of course not. I'll go get them for you." She turned to smile at Leila and then left to get the keys.

Leila said, "I am glad you didn't decide to go in. I'm not up to seeing your father either."

Malik shrugged. "I will see him soon enough, but I am in no mood to see his face right now. I just wish Fanta was at home. I can't wait to hold her in my arms. It's been weeks."

"I understand," Leila said.

Khadija came back, dangling the keys to Malik's house on her finger. She handed them to him and said, "Papa is complaining. He told me to ask why you won't come in."

Malik's mouth turned up. "He knows exactly why." He turned around and said to Leila, "Let's go, my love." He took her hand.

They began to walk toward his house and Khadija came alongside Leila.

She peppered them with questions, asking them about the farm and what state it was in. Malik told her in as few words as possible how much the fire had affected the farm and the crops. They got to the house and Malik unlocked the door. They all entered the house and sat on the couch, talking.

Khadija stayed for another thirty minutes and then she said, "Let me leave you lovebirds alone."

Malik scowled at her as she stood up. "What do you know about love, Khadija?"

She giggled and said, "I know a lot about love."

He said with a voice filled with humor and a slight warning, "You had better not know anything about it."

"Why not?" she asked. "Soon, Father will probably want to get a husband for me."

Leila frowned and Malik shook his head. "I hope that doesn't happen," Leila said.

Khadija shrugged. "It might not be so bad." She smiled at both Leila and Malik and said, "Let me go now. I will come back in the evening." She left the house and Leila turned to Malik, her heart racing. Without a doubt, it was time to tell him what she had been postponing for some time now. It was time to share the gospel with him. But first, they had to talk about the sleeping arrangements. She said to him, "Where am I going to sleep for the duration of my stay in Nira?"

He lifted his brows and said, "I had not thought about that."

She said, "Maybe I should take your father up on his offer. He told me I could stay at his house when I came to Nira some days ago. Maybe I should swallow my pride and fear and stay there."

For some time, Malik said nothing and then he nodded. "That might be the best thing for you to do. As much as I don't want you staying in the same house as my father, we have no choice." He gave her an encouraging smile. "Since Fanta has been staying there without any problems, I will have to believe that you can stay there safely, especially when you told me he was nice to you the last time you went there. Though we can't always trust that he doesn't have something up his sleeve."

She said to him, "You are right. We have no choice right now."

Leila stared at Malik for a full minute while her emotions roiled. Finally, she took his hands and said, "I have something really important to talk to you about."

"What is it?" he asked.

She took a deep breath and tried to let go of her nervousness. She said, "Malik, you know I love you very much."

He nodded.

She said, "The thing is, I love you so much that I want you to know the kind of joy and peace I have in Christ. I want you to come to know Jesus."

For a long moment, he stared at her with an incredulous expression on his face. Just when she thought he wasn't going to say anything and was about to continue, he said, "I love you very much, Leila. But I don't expect you to become a Muslim. Why would you expect me to be a Christian?"

Laila took another deep breath and went on. She told him about her life in Christ, how she had come to the Lord and what He meant to her. She shared the gospel with him more passionately than she had ever shared it with anyone. As she talked, she prayed in her heart that the Lord would touch him and that He would use the words she was speaking to save him. After she finished her passionate ser-monette, she said to him, "Malik, would you like to accept Jesus as your lord and savior?"

While she shared the gospel with him, the ex-pression on his face had been mostly unreadable. Now, he was scowling. He said, "Leila, I can't be-lieve that you would ask this of me. I was born a Muslim and this is my faith. If you cannot accept me and everything about me, that means you don't really love me. I'm not going to convert to Christi-anity. As much as I love you, I have my own faith and you have yours."

Her heart could not have ached more if he had stabbed her with a knife. He was actually rejecting the gospel. She should not have been surprised, but she was. With all her heart, she had hoped that after she had shared with him, he would accept Christ into his heart like Hauwa had, or at the very least, consider it. She sighed heavily and said, "Please, Malik. Please. At least say you will think about it."

"I am not going to think about it. I'm a Muslim and always will be. I love you and I want to mar-ry you. It shouldn't matter what religion we both practice. The only thing that should matter is that we love each other."

Panic rose in her heart at his words. She couldn't marry him if he wasn't a follower of Christ. Why, oh why had she not listened to Zainah when she'd warned her about this? Now, she was head over heels in love with Malik and the idea of spending the rest of her life without him seemed incompre-hensible. And yet, she would have to if he refused to accept Christ. She had to obey the Lord. If she mar-ried him, not only would she be disobedient, there was a likelihood that he might pull her away from her faith in Christ. That was why the Bible warned against being unequally yoked with unbelievers.

The panic in her heart increased and she put her palms together in a pleading gesture. She pleaded with him to turn to Christ, but he obstinately refused.

She said to him, "Malik, I can't marry you if you don't share my faith." The words were painful to say, but she said them because at this point, she was desperate.

He said to her, "I can't believe you would say that to me. True love is accepting everything about a person. It's either you accept me for who I am or you don't accept me at all." He removed his hands from hers and stood up. "I want to marry you, Leila, but you have to decide. Are you going to love me and marry me just the way I am or not?"

She stood up and stared at him for a long moment. Her emotions were a mess and with everything in her, she wanted to say, "I will marry you the way you are, Malik." But she knew she couldn't. She would be disobeying the Lord. She loved Malik, but she loved the Lord more.

With tears in her eyes, she said, "I am so sorry, Malik. I can't do it."

He said in a cold voice, "Then that means you don't love me and we can't be together."

"But I do love you," she said, trying not to break down.

"No, you don't," he said in a tortured voice. "Listen, Leila. I would rather not see you right now. And if you insist on holding on to this view of yours — that I need to convert in order for us to be together, then it means that we can't go on seeing each other."

Leila wanted to scream, to fall on the floor and weep, but she held herself together. She said, "Please, Malik. Please consider..."

"There is nothing to consider," he said once more in a cold voice. "Maybe it's better you leave now."

Her mouth fell open and for a few minutes, she gazed at him. Finally, she knew he was right and she nodded. She took her suitcase from the corner of the living room and, with her heart breaking into tiny pieces, left the house without looking back.

She reached Malik's father's house and knocked on the gate.

Khadija came out and stared at her. She looked down at Leila's suitcase and then up at her face again. "What happened, Leila?" she asked, her voice ringing with alarm.

"It's a long story, Khadija. For now, I would rather not talk about it. Can I stay here, just for tonight? I'll leave tomorrow."

Khadija nodded. "But promise you will tell me what happened."

Leila did not say anything. She entered the compound when Khadija opened the gate wide. She followed Khadija into the house and to a room decorated in white and red furnishings. "This is my room," Khadija said. "You can stay with me as long as you like."

"Thank you." Leila sighed. She would leave Nira very early tomorrow morning and go back to the women's camp. Leila said to Khadija, "Can I have some time alone?"

Khadija gave her a concerned smile. "Of course." She backed away and quickly left the room.

Suddenly, Leila's feet couldn't hold her anymore and she sank to the floor and finally broke down. As she wept, she knew without a doubt that the pain in her heart now would always be there. She had lost Malik and nothing would ever heal the wound in her heart caused by her loss. Nothing would ever be the same again.

TWENTY

Audrey looked at the clock on the wall and saw it was nine p.m. already. The time had flown by so fast today. She had to head home. But first, she had one last thing to do at the orphanage.

She stood up from her chair behind the desk. Today was her last day as the interim director of the orphanage. Tomorrow, she would go back to America with Ken.

She sighed wearily as she walked to the door and then looked back at the office she had occupied for about a month one more time. This vacation had not gone as she had expected. It was one of the most difficult times of her life and also one of the best. She had enjoyed running the orphanage temporarily, mostly because of the children. She'd also enjoyed spending time with Sienna and baby Ethan. But best of all, she had enjoyed spending time with Esther, the girl that had captured her heart.

And yet, spending time with Esther when she knew she would not get to adopt the little girl had also been extremely difficult for her. In addition to that, she and Ken had fought more on this vacation than they ever had before. She knew they still loved each other, but she carried a lot of hurt in her heart against him. He'd totally refused to talk to Esther. Now, they were leaving tomorrow and she would not get to adopt the little girl. She sighed sadly. That thought left an ache in her heart.

She left the office and slowly strode out of the administrative building. The grounds of the orphanage were brightly lit, but there were no staff or children around. She had to go and say her final goodbye to Esther. She was not looking forward to that at all.

She felt like weeping. If only Ken weren't so stubborn. She had tried to see things from his point of view, but it was impossible. First, he didn't want them to have a baby. Now, he was totally against adopting a seven-year-old child. It just didn't make any sense to her, all his explanations notwithstanding.

She walked into the children's hospital and went straight to Esther's bunk. It was already bedtime for the children and most of them were in bed. Esther would probably be in bed as well. Audrey wished she had taken note of the time earlier. She had been wrapping up her work at the orphanage since she was leaving tomorrow. Time had gotten away from her. Now, Esther would be asleep. As much as she didn't want to wake Esther up, she had to tell her she was leaving tomorrow. She had not been able to yet because she could not bring herself to tell Esther she was not going to be her mommy. They had become so close during this past month; she knew Esther would be devastated when she told her she was leaving tomorrow.

Audrey sighed again as she walked up to Esther's bunk. Esther was on the top bunk and as Audrey had already guessed, fast asleep. For a long moment, Audrey gazed at her, her heart aching. Finally, she touched Esther's hair and kissed her forehead. Esther opened her eyes and Audrey smiled at her.

Esther smiled back and sat up on her bed. She

reached out and gave Audrey a hug.

Audrey pushed down the sob that was rising up in her. How would she muster the courage and strength to tell Esther that after today, Esther would not see her again? She pressed her lips tightly together and forced herself to smile. She took Esther's hand, and said, "Esther, honey, I came to say goodbye."

Esther beamed at her. "Goodbye. I'll see you tomorrow," the little girl said. She started to lie back down on her bed, but Audrey held her hands and whispered, "We won't see each other tomorrow, Esther." She paused for second as Esther's eyes widened in surprise. In a voice choked with emotion, Audrey said, "I am leaving for America tomorrow."

Tears swam in Esther's eyes and she said, "When will you be back?"

Audrey blinked back the tears in her eyes and said, "I am not coming back, honey. I am so sorry."

Esther shook her head slowly and then she let out a yelp that startled Audrey. "No, no! You can't go!"

Audrey glanced around the room to make sure Esther had not woken up any of the other children. She looked at Esther again and said, "Esther. I know. I feel really sad as well. But I'll call you regularly. And we can video chat as well."

Esther shook her head and said cried, "You can't go! I thought you would be my mommy. Why would you leave me here?"

Audrey felt her heart breaking. Tears flowed down her cheeks. She reached out and hugged Esther fiercely and said, "I am truly sorry, Esther. I wanted to be your mommy as well. Things didn't work out, that's all. But I'll never forget you and, just as I said, I will call you regularly. I promise."

Esther said, "But I don't want to talk to you on the phone. I want to come with you. Please take me with you." She began to cry.

Audrey tried as best as she could to soothe the girl. She said, "At this time, Esther, it won't be possible to take you with me." She hugged the little girl again and rubbed her back, trying to comfort her. She let Esther cry on her shoulder until she was cried out. Finally, Audrey laid Esther back on the bed and brushed back her hair. She kissed Esther's cheeks and smiled down at her.

Esther said, "I love you."

Fresh tears fell down Audrey's cheeks and she whispered, "I love you too, Esther. Never forget that. Remember, we will talk regularly on the phone and do video chats. It will be just as though I'm still here with you."

Audrey knew it was not going to be the same, but she didn't know what else to say. She kept gazing at Esther, watching her sniffling. And then her eyes gradually closed and she soon fell asleep again. She began to snore lightly and Audrey slowly backed away.

She walked out of the children's hostel, sad and angry. Sad because she had to leave Esther, and angry at Ken. However, she knew her anger at him had to go. They were husband and wife and she had to find a way to live peacefully with him or their marriage would not last. And, in spite of everything, she still loved him dearly.

As she'd done for the last few weeks since she'd started running the orphanage, she walked out of the orphanage gate and went to the next building where Bryan's office was located. It was a three-story building and Bryan had an office on the second floor. He worked there when he was not holding a church outreach or revival. Usually, she came to his office around seven o'clock and then they left for the house together.

He looked up as she walked in and smiled. "I have been waiting for you for about an hour now. I was wondering where you were."

She said, "I had to put my affairs in order."

He nodded.

She said, "I also had to say goodbye to Esther."

Bryan thinned his lips. He had a grim expression on his face as he asked, "How did she take it?"

"She was sad, as I expected she would be. She cried and asked me to take her along. I told her it was not possible to do that, but that we would talk on the phone regularly." Audrey sighed loudly and sat on the chair across from Bryan. "My heart feels really sore." The tears came again and she angrily dashed at them. "I wish Ken had agreed for us to adopt her, Bryan. I wish he weren't so stubborn."

Bryan shrugged. "I tried to talk to him about it, but he told me neither of you are ready to have a child right now."

Audrey shook her head. "That is one thing that annoys me about it all. Ken speaks for me as though I don't have a mind of my own. I've told him time and time again that I am ready to be a mother, but he insists that I am not."

Bryan said, "I am sorry, Audrey. The only thing I can do is to pray for both of you. I hope you work things out. I know you love each other very much and I pray that this doesn't cause a rift in your marriage."

Audrey said nothing. It had already caused some rift in their relationship. She was all talked out about this issue. It was so tiring, heartbreaking, and annoying. There was nothing left to say.

Bryan began to gather his things and five minutes later, they left his office and walked to his car. The ride home took about half an hour and immediately after Audrey walked into the house, she went straight to the bedroom.

Ken was standing in front of the closet. Behind him on the floor was his suitcase. She looked at him and without a word, began to shed her clothes. She had already finished packing and all she wanted to do now was go to bed. They had an early flight tomorrow.

Ken said to her, "You are back, Audrey. I'm just packing now. You've finished packing, haven't you?"

She refused to speak to him. Only God knew what she would say if she did. She was angry at him and utterly upset. Nothing good would come out of her mouth right now.

Changing into her nightgown, she went into the bathroom to wash her face and brush her teeth in preparation for bed. When Ken followed her into the bathroom, she groaned. She stared at his face through the mirror and said harshly, "What is it?"

"We can't go on like this, Audrey."

"Go on like how?"

"Like this, Audrey. Not talking to each other."

"And why do you think we are not speaking to each other?" she asked bitingly.

He sighed loudly and answered, "It's because of that adoption thing, isn't it?"

Audrey laughed harshly and said, "That adoption thing? Is the thing you're referring to the child that I asked you to consider adopting? And also, what about the fact that you've flatly refused for us to have a baby?"

Suddenly, she remembered the voice that had spoken to her some time ago, telling her not to fight with him about this, and pursed her lips. Knowing it was God's voice, she would be in disobedience if she kept talking with Ken.

Ken said, "I've tried to explain why we can't have kids now."

She wanted to bark at him and give him a piece of her mind, but she said nothing. Instead, she ignored him and began to brush her teeth. After that, she washed her face and left the bathroom again, leaving him standing there. She applied moisturizer on her face and climbed into bed.

Ken climbed in beside her and reached out for her.

She smacked his hand away and moved away from him. "Please, just leave me alone!" she said.

He touched her shoulder lightly and then shifted away.

Turning her face to the wall, she sighed sadly, and then forced herself to go to sleep.

*****

Audrey woke up the next morning with a heavy heart. She got out of bed and glanced at the clock on the wall. It was already seven o'clock. The flight was at nine. They had to get to the airport as soon as possible.

She quickly went into the bathroom. And then she blinked and came into the room again. Ken was not in bed. She usually woke up before him and had to wake him up. Maybe he's in the living room with Bryan, she thought. She got into the bathroom again and showered quickly.

After that, she put on a light green shift dress and ballet flats. She brushed her short hair, glanced at the mirror, and frowned. Where on Earth is Ken?

She looked at the clock on the wall again. It was now seven thirty-five. They would be late if they didn't get going. She walked out of the room to look for Ken and bumped into Sienna holding baby Ethan. "Oh, I'm so sorry, Sienna," Audrey said.

Sienna smiled. "Ethan and I came to say goodbye to Auntie Audrey."

Audrey reached out and took Ethan from Sienna. She kissed his cheeks and said, "I'm going to miss you, little boy."

Ethan looked up at her and smiled.

She kissed his nose and beamed at him, and then she hugged Sienna fiercely.

Sienna wiped away the tears from her eyes. "I wish you could stay here forever."

Audrey laughed in spite of the tears falling down her cheeks. "Unfortunately, I have to go, but I will miss you terribly. And I'll also miss this precious little boy." She hugged Sienna again and then drew back. She said, "By the way, have you seen Ken anywhere?"

Sienna shook her head. "I haven't seen him."

Audrey frowned. "I thought he might be with Bryan in the living room."

"Bryan is still in our bedroom," Sienna said.

"That's strange." Audrey put one hand around Sienna's shoulders while holding Ethan in the other and they went to the living room together. She looked around. Ken wasn't here, either. They went around the whole house searching for him, but they did not find him. Sienna went into her bedroom to tell Bryan they were searching for Ken, while Audrey stood at the door.

Bryan came out of the room almost immediately and said to Audrey, "Have you searched the whole house?"

"Yes," Audrey answered. "Everywhere. I guess I'll have to call him," she said. She sighed loudly. "Where can he be? We will be late for our flight for sure." She went back to the bedroom and took out her phone from her purse. Dialing Ken's number, she listened as his phone rang. He didn't pick up and she groaned. Ken, where on Earth are you?

Once more, anger rose in her heart against him. And then it turned to worry. It was unlike him. He was a very disciplined person. Since they had a flight early this morning, he usually would be the first person to hurry up so they could leave for the airport. "Lord, where is he?" she muttered.

Bryan and Sienna walked into the room and Sienna asked, "Have you called him?"

Audrey answered, "I have, but he didn't answer

his phone."

Her phone suddenly rang and she blinked. She picked it up, stared at it, and saw it was Ken. Letting out a huge sigh of relief, she answered. "Ken, where on Earth are you?"

He said, "I'm at the orphanage, Audrey.."

Audrey's jaw dropped and she said, "What in the world are you doing at the orphanage?"

"It's a long story, Audrey and I'll tell you about it later. But the short version is that after we spoke last night, for the first time I realized how hurt you were. How much I hurt you, especially because I did not speak to that little girl at the orphanage that you wanted me to meet. I decided to at least meet her before we left Peru. And I have, Audrey. And now I see why you want us to adopt her. I love her, Audrey. She is a lovely little girl. But more than that, I feel like it's the Lord's will for us to become her parents. There is more to tell you about why I changed my mind, but that will have to be in person."

Audrey's mouth fell open and joy flooded her. For a long moment she could not speak, and then she screamed with excitement, and said, "Really Ken, you're serious? We can adopt Esther?"

He said, "I'll put my phone on speaker now. Say hello to Esther."

"Hi, Mom," Esther said.

Audrey's heart soared. It was the first time Esther had actually called her mom. That meant Ken had told her they would become her parents soon. "Hi, Esther!" Audrey said with exhilaration.

"Is it true you will come and take me to America soon and be my mommy?"

Audrey could not contain her joy. Tears fell down her cheeks; tears of joy.

"Yes, Esther. It is true."

"Yay!" Esther said happily.

She spoke with Esther for a short while and then

she said to Ken, "All right, honey, you have to come back now or we will miss our flight."

"I am so glad you are speaking to me again," Ken said. "I just want to make you happy."

Audrey smiled. "You have made me very happy."

"I'm on my way back now, sweetie." He added in a naughty voice, "And maybe when we get back to America and have the house to ourselves, we can start making babies. What do you say about that?"

Her eyebrows lifted in surprise and for a few seconds, she was speechless. And then she screeched. "Ken, please tell me you are not pulling my leg!"

"Why would I pass up on that kind of opportunity?"

She screamed again and said, "Oh, Ken! That would be great! I can't wait!"

"I need to apologize for being so selfish, Audrey. Anyway, I'll see you soon."

The call ended. Audrey turned around and then fell into Sienna's arms, overwhelmed with happiness. She wept for joy and then hugged Bryan. "Ken finally agreed for us to adopt Esther and he wants us to start trying to get pregnant."

"I am so happy for you," Sienna told her.

Bryan grinned. "Ken finally came to his senses. I told you to leave it to God." Bryan looked at Audrey and added, "Maybe that was why Ken refused to have a baby yet, no matter what you told him. I think it was the Lord's doing. He used that to make you open to adopting Esther. Now that you are going to adopt her, Ken has finally agreed to have a baby."

Audrey smiled and said, "I think you are right, Bryan. We will be back here in a few months to start the adoption process. I'm beyond excited."

Sienna held Audrey's hands and they began to jump up and down, just like they did when they were little girls.

Bryan shook his head as he watched them, and

then he said to Audrey, "Congratulations. Soon you will have a house full of kids."

Sienna said, "I'm so happy that you will be Queen Esther's mom. That girl is very special."

Audrey nodded. "She is. I love her very much." She added, "And I love Ken so much! I can't wait to give him a big hug."

"Let me go and prepare the car to take you guys to the airport," Bryan said, and left the room. Sienna hugged her again and then left as well.

Audrey lifted her eyes up and said, "Thank you for everything, Lord!" She picked up her purse from the bed, and then, like Esther, skipped out of the room.

A LOOK AT:
BLESSED WITH LOVE

Trisha is no longer a lonely single mother struggling to make ends meet. But just as she thinks she's found her happy ending, the past rears its ugly head. And this time, the threat is far greater than any she's faced before.

A devoted mother to her adopted daughter Esther, Audrey struggles with a secret desire to conceive. Is this part of God's plan, or should she be satisfied with the blessings she's already received?

Life in a women's camp in Mali, Africa, is not what Faizan envisioned when he asked Zainah to be his wife. The days are quiet and uneventful, until an afternoon walk leads them to stumble upon a shocking surprise. Faizan swears Zainah to secrecy, but in a moment of weakness she confides in best friend Leila, leading to life-changing consequences for them all.

COMING MAY 2020

ABOUT THE AUTHOR

Like the characters in her stories, Emma Easter juggles a range of identities.

In the low-income community where she works, Easter is known as a family medicine physician who treats patients of all ages and backgrounds.

College friends see her as an accomplished musician, having studied and mastered five classical instruments—but behind closed doors, she's just as comfortable rocking an air guitar to Creed. And when she isn't giving her heart, soul, and sanity to her three young children she's indulging in her most secret identity of all: meeting new characters, crafting fresh plots, and exploring every corner of her imagination.

Across all these different roles, one cohesive thread has tied everything together: her faith and love of Jesus Christ.

Find more great titles by Emma Easter and Christian Kindle News at https://christiankindle-news.com/our-authors/emma-easter/

ABOUT THE AUTHOR

www.ingramcontent.com/pod-product-compliance
Lightning Source LLC
Chambersburg PA
CBHW030534270626
47155CB00024B/3035